Swift
Run

——⁓⁓⁓⁓——

Also by Laura DiSilverio

Swift Edge
Swift Justice

Swift Run

LAURA DiSILVERIO

Minotaur Books

A THOMAS DUNNE BOOK

New York

A THOMAS DUNNE BOOK FOR MINOTAUR BOOKS.
An imprint of St. Martin's Publishing Group.

www.thomasdunnebooks.com
www.minotaurbooks.com

LIBRARY OF CONGRESS CATALOGING-IN-PUBLICATION DATA

DiSilverio, Laura A. H.
    Swift run : a mystery / Laura DiSilverio.—1st ed.
    p. cm.
    ISBN 978-0-312-62381-4 (hardcover)
    ISBN 978-1-250-01732-1 (e-book)
    1. Women private investigators—Fiction. 2. Mystery fiction. I. Title.
PS3604.I85S97 2012
813'.6—dc23

2012033907

First Edition: December 2012

10 9 8 7 6 5 4 3 2 1

For Sam Furiness, cousin and reader,
who makes my life richer with his thoughtfulness,
intellect, and friendship

Acknowledgments

Thank you to my family—my husband, girls, and mother—for understanding my passion for writing and encouraging me, always, to write. Thanks to my agent, Paige Wheeler, and my editor, Toni Plummer. A big thank-you to lawyer Bob DiSilverio for explaining the laws related to harboring fugitives. Finally, thanks to my unfailingly helpful and honest critique group—Lin Poyer, Amy Tracy, and Marie Layton—for pushing me to make my books better.

Swift Run

1

Oprah said, or maybe I heard it on Ellen, that public speaking scares more people than spiders and snakes and heights put together (and they all give me the heebie-jeebies, too). Having lots of company didn't make me feel any better as I struggled into the Spanx hose that made it possible to zip my skirt and slipped on the new Louboutin pumps I shouldn't have bought even on sale. They were an investment, I told myself guiltily. I needed to look professional for my presentation to the managing partner of a law firm in hopes he'd retain Swift Investigations. Hm, which earrings said competent and trustworthy, but fashionable? My gaze lighted on the clock: 7:30. It only took twenty minutes to get from my Broadmoor house to downtown Colorado Springs, and my appointment wasn't until nine, but I wanted to make sure I was there in plenty of time. Things have a way of happening to me, even when I plan ahead.

My bedroom door flew open. "Mom, I need more lunch money."

My forehead puckered as I stared at my beautiful fourteen-year-old Kendall. She's slim and blond, the image of me, Les always said, when he first met me. Thirty-five years and thirty—well, forty—pounds ago. "Honey, I gave you a check just last week. What happened to it?"

She shrugged. I hate that shrug. She started doing it when she turned eleven, and it's the only answer I get from her half the time. "Dunno. Must have lost it."

"Baby, didn't we talk about how you need to be more responsible?" I pulled a twenty from my purse, which left me with only seven dollars. "We all lose things from time to time. Why, I can't find the new diet book I bought last week, the one that says you can lose five pounds a week if you eat Greek yogurt at every meal, but—"

"I'm late." With a flip of blond hair, she turned to go.

"Wait. Which do you like better—the black earrings or the topaz?" I held one of each up to either ear.

"Whichever."

"Kendall, get your ass down here or I'm leaving without you."

She whisked herself out the door as her brother, my son, Dexter, bellowed up the stairs. I started to tell him we didn't use that kind of language in this house; "tush" or "fanny" was preferable. The door slammed shut behind them before I made it to the landing. Les had given Dexter a red BMW for his sixteenth birthday, and while it was nice that I didn't have to drive the kids to school, I never knew where Dexter was anymore. My friend Albertine said that was a good thing. "Trust me," she'd said last time we discussed it, "no mother really wants to know what her teenage son is up to."

Unfortunately, the principal, the police, and the truant officer insisted on keeping me updated on some of Dexter's activities, so I couldn't exist in blissful ignorance. Sighing, I slipped the earrings in, picked up my purse, made sure the CD with the PowerPoint presentation was in it, and left.

The conference room Danner and Lansky's snooty receptionist showed me into was intimidating. An oblong table of dark, shiny wood took up most of the room. Matchy-matchy chairs with maroon upholstery lined either side. Nubby gray carpet and heavy drapes muffled any sounds and made the room feel like a funeral parlor. What the place needed was a few accent pillows or framed posters with yellows and pinks to brighten it up. Some plants would help, too. A laptop computer, a projection screen, and some sound equipment gleamed darkly from a cabinet near the podium, and I was glad I'd gotten here early enough to figure out how to work it all. If that was possible. Saying Mr. Danner would be in in five minutes, the receptionist slipped out. I fumbled the CD case from my Coach bag and opened it. Oh, no. I stared at the empty case in dismay. I must have left the CD in my computer.

My breaths came fast and shallow, and I dropped the CD case. I couldn't call Charlie for help because she was still recovering from a bullet wound in her fanny, which was why I was here in the first place. Maybe Albertine—. Reschedule. I needed to reschedule the meeting.

I was about to scurry after the receptionist when a door at the far end of the conference room opened and a man stepped in, trailed by a woman in her midforties and a younger man. Too late! I was trapped. I forced a smile.

"You must be Ms. Goldman." The older man, about my age, stepped forward with a friendly smile and his hand outstretched. He was short and slim, with an expensive suit and watch and thick gray-brown hair. "I'm Rich Danner."

"Georgia Goldman," I said, flustered. I shook his hand. "But I go by Gigi. G. G. for Georgia Goldman, get it?"

"I get it," he said with a hint of a smile. "I'll bet you're from Georgia, too."

My accent gave me away every time. "Atlanta, originally." He seemed nice, not the ferocious legal shark I was expecting, and I relaxed an itty bit.

Danner's two associates took seats halfway down the long table. Danner sat at the front and gave me an expectant look. "Let's get started."

Blinking nervously, I explained about not having my slideshow. "S-so I'm just going to wing it," I said, twisting my bangle round and round my wrist.

"Wing away," Danner said.

Stuttering a bit to start, I told him about Swift Investigations, emphasizing Charlie's credentials as a former Air Force Office of Special Investigations agent and her many years in the private investigator business.

"And you?" Danner asked, giving me a penetrating look.

"I'm kind of new to being a PI," I admitted. He didn't need to know about Les dumping me and running off to Costa Rica with his personal trainer, leaving me with only the house, the Hummer, and half interest in Swift Investigations. "I do a lot of the computer searches," I said, hurrying on to tell him about how we could help his firm with employee background checks, process serving, surveillance, and other investigation needs. "We're really good and we work hard," I concluded fifteen minutes later, rubbing my sweaty palms down the sides of my skirt. The skin on my neck prickled, and I hoped it wasn't a hot flash coming on.

"I don't know why we can't give Swift Investigations a try," Danner said, rising. "As long as there's no padding of the expense account. That's why we're looking for a new PI firm."

I nodded vigorously. "Yes, sir. I mean, no, sir. You won't catch us falsifying expenses."

"I won't catch you or you won't pad them?"

My mouth fell open, but he laughed, signaled to his staff, shook my hand, and headed toward the door he came in. "By the way, I like your earrings. Shows you march to the beat of a different drummer. That can be useful in an investigator." He disappeared.

It wasn't until I got to the garage where I'd left the Hummer and peered in the rearview mirror that I realized I'd put on one black and one topaz earring.

I called Charlie on my way to the office to give her the good news. "They gave us a couple of background investigations to get started on," I said, glancing happily at the short stack of folders on the passenger seat. I asked how she was feeling, although I knew she'd say "Fine," like she always did.

"Fine." She congratulated me on landing Danner and Lansky's business. "If it weren't for this stupid infection, I'd be back in the saddle. The doc says I can come back to work next week."

Her wound had gotten infected because she had ignored the doctor's advice about taking it easy. Charlie's not too good with being told what to do. The surgeon had chewed her out but good for trying wind sprints less than ten days after getting shot. "I'll hold the fort," I promised, turning into the strip mall parking lot where Swift Investigations was located.

You'd think a PI firm would be up a flight of dingy stairs in some seedy building—at least, that's where they always seemed to be in the old movies I watched—but no. Swift Investigations sat in a perfectly ordinary strip mall on Academy Boulevard, a couple of miles south of the United States Air Force Academy. We shared a parking lot with a Mexican café called Guapo Bandito that made yummy sopaipillas; a bridal shop where I was hoping to get a discount on Kendall's prom dress; Domenica's, a sex toys store run by a lovely woman named Carol; and Albertine's, the Cajun restaurant and bar owned by my new friend. Everyone's so neighborly that I enjoy coming to work every day.

Chilly wind and traffic noise chased me into the office. It's a small place, and kind of bare bones, but Charlie put the kibosh on my plans to make it more homey; she insisted that our clients preferred a sparse, businesslike atmosphere. I added a couple of plants, though, and photos of my kids on my desk, and a coffeepot, so it wasn't quite as plain as when I'd started working here six months ago. I patted the bison head hanging behind my desk—Bernie was part of my costume on my first ever undercover job as a PI—and started the coffeepot. Decaf. My body didn't seem to process coffee the same way now that I was in the midst of the Change, and too much caffeine revved up my bladder, which made things difficult, to say the least, when I did surveillance. Not that I did much surveillance since the meth lab fiasco. I poured myself a cup and was taking my first sip when the door opened. I turned, expecting to see Carol from next door, or maybe Albertine.

A slender twentysomething woman with honey-colored hair stood in the doorway. She had flawless tan skin, amazing cheekbones, and boobs like cantaloupes stretching her thin white sweater to its limits. Long legs in stretch jeans and high-heeled, midcalf leather boots completed the look of model-like perfection. A surge of hatred rose in me, so intense it made my hands shake so my coffee spilled.

"Same old Gigi," the beauty said, stepping in and closing the door with a snap. "Still klutzy as ever."

I opened and closed my mouth, but no sound came out.

"You look like a goldfish," she observed, sauntering forward to perch on the edge of Charlie's desk.

How dare she? "I don't—. What do you—? Get out, you . . . you bitch!" I don't think I'd ever called anyone that, and I only wished I'd had the nerve to use the C-word.

My words didn't faze Heather-Anne Pawlusik, the personal trainer and home-wrecking tramp who ran off to Costa Rica with my Les.

"Tut-tut," Heather-Anne said, arching one perfectly shaped eyebrow. "Is that any way to talk to a paying customer?"

"What?" I goggled at her.

. "You're a private investigator now, right?" She looked

7

around the office, eyes skimming Charlie's pristine desk, glancing off the lavender in-box and ceramic figures painted years ago by Dexter and Kendall on my desk, and lingering on Bernie, who gazed at her with—I was sure—disapproval. "Well, I need to hire a private investigator."

My brain unfroze sufficiently for me to ask, "Where's Les?" I looked past her to the door, but it remained closed.

"Now, that," she said, "is the sixty-four-thousand-dollar question."

It took me a minute. "You want me—us—to find Les?"

"Exactly."

2

~~~~~

"Would you like some coffee?" I asked, my raised-in-the-South politeness taking over. "I mean—" I couldn't make myself take back the offer.

Heather-Anne curled her lip. "No, thanks. I gave up caffeine three years ago—it's bad for the complexion." She ran a hand over her revoltingly smooth, unwrinkled, twentysomething face.

About to tell her it was decaf, I bit the inside of my cheek. I didn't owe her anything, not even a cup of Decaffeinated Mocha Hazelnut Supremo. "You can leave now," I said, concentrating on sucking in my stomach as I returned to my desk. No amount of sucking—unless it involved a liposuction tube—was going to make it as flat as Heather-Anne's.

She looked taken aback. "What?"

"Go away. Get out."

"Now, Gigi, I know you were probably a little pissed at me and Les—"

A little? I blinked at her. I was horribly hurt and depressed. Les leaving was the worst thing that ever happened to me.

"—but these things happen. It's nothing to hold a grudge over." She looked at me like I was being unreasonable.

I was about to tell her again to get lost, but she withdrew a roll of cash from her purse, and I heard Charlie's voice in my ear telling me a paying customer was a paying customer and we didn't have to like everyone we worked for. Sensing my hesitation, she peeled off ten bills. "Here's a thousand dollars to get you started."

She held the money out to me, and I noticed her French-manicured nails were as perfect as the rest of her, although kind of boring compared to my garnet-painted ones. "I don't know . . ."

"Oh, come off it, Gigi. Les always said this place was the worst investment he ever made, that he'd be amazed if it was showing a profit by 2020. So don't pretend you don't need this." She dropped the bills to my desk and one fluttered to the floor. Ben Franklin stared up at me, offering me no help with this decision.

I turned away, brushing against an acrylic box on my desk and knocking it over. Paper clips rained to the floor. I ignored them. "No."

"No?"

Heather-Anne acted like she'd never heard the word before. "No." I said it louder. "I'm not going to find Les for you." I drew myself up, glad to be taller than Heather-Anne.

"But . . . but you have to!" She looked to be on the verge of tears.

Something in her voice—fear, maybe—made me ask, "Why?"

"Because he's in danger."

I bit my lip. Part of me wanted to say "Good!" and throw Heather-Anne out. I didn't want anything *really* bad to happen to Les, though, even though he'd dumped me. If he was in danger . . .

"What kind of danger?"

"I'm not sure exactly, but I know it's serious. I think someone's after him. He wouldn't have run off if he didn't fear for his life. He wouldn't!"

I eyed her uncertainly, not completely believing her but hearing real fear in her voice. Come to think of it, there'd been people after Les when he deserted me, too: the victims of his embezzling. Some of them would still be happy to rip his head from his shoulders. Reluctantly, I reached for the bills and tucked them into my desk drawer, pretending I didn't notice Heather-Anne's triumphant smirk. Trying to act professional, even though I wanted to scratch her perfectly beautiful face and rip out clumps of her perfectly highlighted hair, I pulled out my notepad. I tried to remember the sorts of questions Charlie asked when a client came in with a missing person case. "Um, okay, Heather-Anne. I need some information from you. What makes you think Les is missing?"

"Because he hasn't come home."

"In how long?"

"Four days."

"And where is home? I mean, I know from his lawyer that Les went to Costa Rica, but where exactly?"

"A little town on the coast. Tamarindo. It's paradise. We've got a place on the beach—"

"Address?" I choked on the word, trying to block out the images her words brought up: my Les and Perfect Miss Skinny sunbathing, splashing in the surf, drinking mai tais on the lanai or whatever they called a veranda in Costa Rica.

She gave it to me, and I wrote it down carefully. "We'll need copies of his last several credit card bills, his ATM and bank records, his phone bill—" I noticed she was looking a little uncomfortable, twirling a strand of honey hair around her finger. "What?"

"Les and I kept our finances separate," she said airily. "I don't have access to that stuff."

"The bills didn't come to your house?" I widened my eyes at this evidence of . . . what? Les might have set up housekeeping with Heather-Anne, but he hadn't trusted her. Hah! At least we'd shared a joint checking account. Which enabled him to clean out every penny when he took off.

"He has a postal box. So do I. I do have this." She pulled out a cell phone bill and handed it to me. "He left it on his desk after he paid it. Usually he shredded things." She slid off the desk and wandered the office, twiddling with the blinds wand, brushing her fingers across the ficus leaves, clinking the letter opener and markers in my Hello Kitty pencil holder.

I clicked the pen against my teeth, trying to figure out

what else Charlie would ask if she were here. The heck with it. This was a golden opportunity to snoop into Les's personal life post-me, and I didn't even try to resist temptation.

"I apologize, Heather-Anne," I said, not one bit sorry, "but I've got to ask you some personal questions. Were you and Les . . . having difficulties?" They must be—right?—if Les had run off. "Financial issues? Was he seeing, that is, was there another woman?" *What goes around comes around*, I told her in my head, almost hoping Les had taken up with some Costa Rican sexpot.

Heather-Anne's eyes narrowed. "You're enjoying this, aren't you? I came to you because I figured of all the PIs in this town, you were the one most likely to have insight into Les, to be able to track him down, because, well, because you were married to him for longer than I've been alive. I didn't think you were the kind of person to taunt me, to try and make me feel bad—"

"I'm not! I didn't mean—"

"It's okay," she said, wiping at her eyes, even though I hadn't noticed any tears. "I understand."

"It's just that if you want us to find Les, I've got to know some things."

Heather-Anne raised her chin, shaking her hair back. "No, there weren't any other women, and no, we weren't having problems. We were blissfully happy, insanely in love with one another. In bed—"

I definitely did not want to hear about their sex life, so I jumped up and went to pour myself a cup of coffee. The carafe chattered against the mug. "What about money?" I asked loudly. Returning to my desk, I set the mug down carefully.

"Financially, well—"

I looked a question at her when she hesitated.

"Les seemed . . . worried the past few weeks."

"Worried? About what?"

"Well, you know that when we went to Costa Rica there were some . . . questions about his financial dealings on this end."

"He embezzled from several of his companies and there's a warrant out for his arrest, if that's what you mean." The people he'd cheated had been harassing me, making my life miserable, since he left. The angry calls had petered out the last couple of months, maybe because they'd realized you couldn't get blood out of a turnip.

She nodded. "Right. Well, I got the feeling that maybe some of his former business partners were taking matters into their own hands, that they were tired of waiting for the justice system to catch up with Les."

"Oh, no." My hand flew to my mouth. "Did someone threaten him? Is that what you meant about him being in danger?"

"I don't know about that, exactly," Heather-Anne hedged, "but he was edgy recently, seemed to be looking over his shoulder, got more secretive, and made a point of going outside to take phone calls."

"You have no idea what was going on?"

"None." Heather-Anne widened her eyes at me. Her expression reminded me of something . . . Kendall! She looked just like my daughter did when she told me she'd "lost" the report card I was supposed to sign.

I wrinkled my brow. "What makes you think he's in this

area? I mean, why come to Colorado to hire an investigator, rather than L.A. or Chicago? Do you think he wanted to see the kids?" I held my breath. Maybe he was regretting the divorce . . . maybe he really wanted to see me.

Heather-Anne snorted, and my hopes crumpled like a balloon stuck with a pin. "Not hardly. I . . . I knew his card number and password, and I got the credit card company to send me this." The piece of paper she handed me had a highlighted entry for an airline charge for a flight from San José, Costa Rica, to Denver.

"One way," I said. The paper trembled in my shaking hand. Had he bought a one-way ticket because he wasn't going back, because he was returning to me and the kids? If so, why hadn't he called?

"Just find him. Please." Real worry showed on Heather-Anne's face. "And it's got to be soon."

"Why?"

"Because . . . because I miss him so much. Here." Heather-Anne thrust a card at me. On the front was her name and the words PERSONAL TRAINER. On the back she had scribbled *Embassy Suites, Rm 115,* and a phone number. "Call me there when you have news."

Before I could think of anything else to ask her, she was striding through the door, bumping into Albertine on her way out so Albertine had to juggle the beignets she was carrying. A gust of chilly wind blasted in. The last few days had been in the fifties, but typical February weather had returned today.

Albertine set the napkin of beignets on my desk and helped herself to one. She's a tall woman with shiny black skin, even fatter than me. I've never asked her age, but I think she's in her late fifties or early sixties. She's got a Louisiana accent thicker than molasses-drenched grits, and the best smile this side of the Mississippi. She moved to Colorado after Hurricane Katrina and has opened three restaurants. Even though we only met last August when I became a PI, she's one of my best friends.

"Was that an actual client, Gigi?"

"Yes," I said glumly. I reached for a beignet and bit into the soft, doughy goodness. Albertine could cook like nobody's business.

Albertine shot me a look, dusting powdered sugar off her turquoise tunic-length sweater. "That is not the reaction I'd've expected," she said, "from a businesswoman with a rent check to write."

"That was Heather-Anne Pawlusik," I said. At Albertine's questioning look, I added, "Les's Heather-Anne."

"Say what, girlfriend?" Albertine's brows snapped together. "That skinny white woman is the skank who ran off with your lawfully wedded husband?"

Skank. I liked the sound of it. "Uh-huh." Putting my elbows on the desk, I let my chin fall into my cupped hands.

"And she sashayed in here like sugar wouldn't melt in her mouth and had the nerve to try and hire you for something?"

"Yes."

"You gave her what-for, I hope?" Albertine eyed me doubtfully, knowing I wasn't the "what-for" type.

"She gave us a thousand-dollar retainer."

"Money isn't everything, girlfriend." When I didn't answer, she asked, "What'd the skinny bitch want?"

"To find Les."

Albertine burst out laughing, a sound as rich as pecan pie that made me smile despite myself. "At least you had more pride than to try and hunt him down when he ran out on you."

It wasn't pride. I'd had no money to hire a PI, and by the time I got the idea of being one myself, well, it seemed like too much water had gushed under that bridge. Besides, I basically knew where he was . . . and with who.

"I guess there's something to be said for finding Les," Albertine mused. "If you catch up with his criminal white ass you might pry some of the child support he owes you out of him."

"Unlikely." Les had so far not paid one cent of the court-ordered support.

"I know where I can get a cattle prod. Or you can sic the cops on him."

"Ooh, I couldn't do that!"

Albertine glared at me. "Why the hell not? Aren't you angry at that scum-sucking lowlife?"

"It doesn't do any good to get mad." That's what my mama always said when my daddy'd been drinking down at the stripper club.

Albertine's eyes about popped out of her head. "Say what? That's the dumbest thing I ever heard," she said without waiting for me to answer. "Gettin' angry's healthy. Let me help you get your mad on, girlfriend."

I had to smile at her enthusiasm. "Maybe later."

Albertine changed tacks. "What's Charlie think of this?"

"I haven't told her yet, but you know she'll be in favor of

it. Charlie doesn't believe in discriminating against clients based on anything other than their ability and willingness to pay."

Shaking her head slowly, Albertine said, "She might surprise you."

For a few minutes, we speculated about why Les might've left Heather-Anne, with Albertine suggesting it was because Heather-Anne wanted them to join a nudist colony so she could show off her hot bod. I choked on my third beignet, and she pounded my back, grinning.

"How's your diet going?" Albertine asked.

I stuck my feet farther under the desk, feeling guilty about my new shoes. Albertine was helping me with my finances and had put me on a spending diet. The Louboutin pumps were not supposed to be on the menu.

"Gigi . . ."

"It's hard," I confessed. "I'm not used to having to watch every dime. I'm no good at it." I'd been good at it, as a girl, when there'd been six of us kids and Daddy hadn't held on to jobs very long, what with his drinking and all, but then I'd met Les not long after I got out of beauty school. When we got married, well, it was a relief not to have to pinch pennies so they squealed like a stuck pig anymore.

"You won't get good at it if you don't try," Albertine said. She wagged a finger at me. "How're you gonna send Dexter to college if you don't quit buying every pair of designer shoes that calls your name?"

I jumped. Albertine guessing about the shoes spooked me, but the thought of Dexter and college bothered me more. If Dexter didn't get his grades up I wasn't going to have to pay for college because he wasn't going to get into one. I tried to consider that a silver lining but hated to think of my son eking out a living as a Walmart greeter.

"Girlfriend." Albertine shook her head. "You're supposed to call me when you get the spending urge, right? Like an AA sponsor."

"I will. Really." I truly wanted to change my spending habits.

She let it drop and mentioned that her sister was sending her youngest daughter to Colorado Springs to work for Albertine. "I just hope she's got more brains than Sissy," Albertine said, heading for the door. "Otherwise, I'll be losing customers faster than Tony Stewart drives a quarter mile."

As soon as she'd left, I picked up the phone to call Charlie. Then I put it down again. It'd be better to give her this news in person, especially since I needed her advice on how to go about finding Les. Locking the office, I took my notes and the two documents Heather-Anne had provided and drove to Charlie's house. She lived a couple of miles west of the office, in a small house located behind St. Paul's Episcopal Church. When I knocked on the door, she called, "Come in," and I entered hesitantly. I'd only been here a couple of times.

"Charlie?"

"In the kitchen."

I followed her voice and found her on her knees grouting a section of slate tile in the breakfast nook. Glancing over her shoulder, she said, "I thought you'd be the tile delivery guy."

"Should you be doing this?" I asked.

She slicked her mink-dark bangs aside and pushed to her feet, lurching a bit to her weak side. She's only five foot three, five inches shorter than me, but she seems taller. Maybe because she works out and is so athletic. Unlike me. I thought guiltily of the expensive treadmill in my living room that I hadn't used since Christmas.

"I'd go stir-crazy if I stuck to the doc's list of approved activities," she said. "Pepsi?"

"No, thanks." I knew better than to ask for an iced tea or a Coke; Charlie only kept Pepsi and beer on hand. I guessed that came from being raised in parts of the country that didn't understand hospitality the way we Southerners did. She got a Pepsi from the fridge, popped the top, and took a long drink.

"What brings you out this way?"

Putting on a bright voice, I told her we had a new client. When I gave her the name, she was silent for a moment. "Heather-Anne the home wrecker?" she asked finally.

"Yes," I admitted in a small voice.

"Are you insane?"

I stared at her. "A paying client is—"

"She stole your husband, deprived your children of their father—and God knows they need a disciplinarian around—and made it necessary for you to work for a living. In *my* PI firm. You can't tell me you want to work for her."

"She gave us a thousand dollars to start with. Cash."

Charlie paused only the briefest moment before saying, "Tell her to put it where the sun don't shine."

Her support surprised me, and I smiled. I suddenly felt better about tracking down Les for Heather-Anne. "It's okay, really."

"No, it's not." She stomped to the recycle bin and slammed the Pepsi can into it. The movement caused her to wince, but I knew she'd snap my head off if I suggested she sit down.

"She said Les is in danger, that one of his former partners might be out to get him. I can do this without getting all emotional. I already—"

"Gigi, you can't visit a Hallmark store without getting all emotional."

"Some of those cards are so *moving*. The people who write them must—"

"What story did our new client feed you?"

I sat at the maple-topped table Charlie had shoved to one side while she tiled and told her everything Heather-Anne had said. When I finished, I watched her think, waiting for her to tell me where to start.

"If one of Les's partners is looking for revenge, why would Les run to Colorado?"

Good question. I wished I'd thought to ask Heather-Anne.

Charlie let it go. "Here's what we'll do. We know he flew into Denver two days ago. I'll get on to the rental car companies and see if he rented a car. I can do that from here. You make a list of places he might go, people he might call here in Colorado. We don't know he's still here—he might've boarded another flight after landing at DIA—but we've got to start somewhere."

"He always used Avis."

"Good to know. This is why Heather-Anne hired you. Us. She's definitely not a dummy. You wouldn't happen to have his Avis loyalty card number?"

I hefted my purse onto my lap and dug through it for my wallet. Piling the can opener, mini curling iron, pepper spray, six lipsticks, and other stuff on Charlie's table, I found my old Avis card behind the two pieces of a Nordstrom's card the clerk had scissored the last time I tried to use it. Charlie copied down the Avis number.

"What about the cell phone bill?" I asked.

Charlie nodded. "Use a reverse directory and track down names and addresses." She scanned the pages. "A lot of these numbers are international—Costa Rica, most likely—and a lot are cell phones. If we don't get a lead on him some other way, we can start calling these numbers and see who answers and what they know about Les. I hate to do that up front because someone might warn him we're looking for him."

I sighed with relief. Even though I'd watched Charlie hunt several missing persons, and I'd helped her with a couple of them, I didn't really know how to go about it on my own. I was better at process serving and doing background investigations. "Thanks, Charlie. I'll get started on that list right away."

"We'll find him," Charlie promised. "I just hope you're not sorry when we catch up with him."

3

After Gigi left, Charlie wiped the grout haze off the section of floor she'd tiled and cleaned up for the day. The prospect of digging her teeth into a new investigation was more enticing than another few hours on her knees forcing grout into the gaps between tiles. Absently massaging her butt cheek, she swallowed the horse-pill-sized antibiotics the doc had prescribed and reached for the phone.

The Avis clerk who answered was perfect for Charlie's purposes: young and gullible. Deciding that her best bet was to impersonate Gigi, Charlie introduced herself as Georgia Goldman and gave the clerk Les's loyalty card number.

"I've done the stupidest thing, and I hope you can help me," she said, not attempting Gigi's heavy southern accent. "My husband and I rented a car in Denver two days ago, and I left my sunglasses in it when he dropped me off. They're prescription and they cost a fortune. He was going to make a few sales calls around the state and then fly to Costa Rica, and I can't catch up with him. You wouldn't happen to know when he's bringing the car back, would you? I can drive up to Denver to get my glasses back."

Keyboard clickings told Charlie the clerk was buying her story. "I'm sorry, Mrs. Goldman," the young woman said, "but I don't see anything about your glasses. Your husband turned the car in yesterday, and there's no note about sunglasses. I can call our office in Aspen to make sure, if you'd like?"

Aspen. Bingo! "Oh, silly me," Charlie said. "Here they are in my *green* purse. I was looking in the pink one." Gigi's purses were large enough and heavy enough to contain supplies for a monthlong Himalayan trek, and Charlie figured she could misplace a Subaru in one of them, never mind a pair of glasses. "I'm so sorry to have bothered you."

"No problem," the clerk said sunnily.

Hanging up, Charlie drummed her fingers on the table. No way could she drive to Aspen: Her ass wasn't up to the trip, and the doc would kill her for trying. However, the Embassy Suites where Heather-Anne Pawlusik was staying was less than half a mile from Charlie's house. Charlie itched to suss out Swift Investigations' newest client for herself; Gigi saw people through rose-colored glasses and was apt to give someone the benefit of the doubt—even the woman who'd run off with her husband. She slipped on her Nikes. The doc was encouraging gentle exercise now that they'd zapped the infection, and it struck Charlie that a walk to the Embassy Suites would let her kill two birds with one stone.

The Embassy Suites sat perpendicular to I-25. A small perimeter of grass and trees—shades of midwinter brown, tan, and gray—surrounded three sides. It backed onto a ravine where a creek roared after thunderstorms but sludged gently along the rest of the time. Three or four other hotels and a spattering of chain restaurants were its nearest neighbors. Slipping into the building through its restaurant at the I-25 end, Charlie strode confidently into the lobby and angled toward the ground-floor guest rooms.

She turned into the corridor and passed the elevators as a door midway down the hall banged open. Heather-Anne's room? Charlie wondered. A man barreled out, and she got an impression of height and a gray cowboy hat as he strode away from her, disappearing into the atrium. Too young, dark, and skinny to be Les Goldman, she thought, looking over a planter of greenery to see the back of the man's hat bobbing toward the front entrance. She continued down the hall to 115, and it was, indeed, the room the man had slammed out of. It seemed Miss Heather-Anne Pawlusik had brought a boyfriend with her to look for the missing Les. Interesting. Of course, it could be a brother or cousin, Charlie thought, trying to give their client the benefit of the doubt, or even a hotel employee checking on a malfunctioning television or counting bottles in the minibar, but the man hadn't worn a uniform or the kind of friendly expression that hospitality workers had surgically applied when they first started the job.

Drawing even with the door, Charlie noticed that the man had slammed it open so hard that it had failed to latch on the rebound. Tempting. Too tempting. A glance up and down the hall showed no one in sight, although a maid's cart sat outside a room four doors down. "Heather-Anne?" she called, in case the woman was inside. When there was no answer, Charlie nudged the door wider with her shoulder so she didn't leave fingerprints and slipped inside, letting the door clunk closed behind her.

A scan showed the standard Embassy Suites sitting room:

couch, TV, coffee table, chair. A laptop case, open, sat to the right of the couch, and Charlie eyed it longingly . . . but no. Powering up Heather-Anne's laptop was too big a risk for potentially no reward; in all probability, her files were password protected. Charlie made for the bedroom, elbowing the closet door open on her way. A pair of women's jeans, two blouses, and a slinky dress hung on the rod, and strappy sandals and athletic shoes were tossed on the floor. No men's clothes. Hm. Maybe Mr. Cowboy Hat really was a hotel employee . . . or maybe he had no more business in Heather-Anne's room than Charlie did.

The unmade bed told Charlie she needed to hurry; the maid could come in at any time. Starting with the nightstand, she stooped to read the data on a prescription bottle and discovered Heather-Anne was taking Zoloft, which Charlie thought was an antianxiety med. A half-read copy of a historical romance lay facedown on the table, and a hotel notepad lay next to the phone. Ripping off the top sheet, Charlie stowed it in her jeans pocket. She might be able to raise impressions and read what had been written on the page above.

Conscious of time flitting by—she'd been in the room four minutes already—Charlie ducked into the bathroom. Without touching any surface, she noted the litter of toiletries and high-end cosmetics on the counter and a wet towel crumpled on the floor. A faint smell of sandalwood hung in the air. The room told her nothing about Heather-Anne except she had enough money to afford expensive lipstick and wasn't a neatnik.

Passing the closet again on the way out, Charlie halted. Lots of hotels had safes these days . . . she spied the safe, its door closed, on a shelf beside a stack of extra pillows and blankets. She reached for the ridged dial set in the middle of the door, knowing fingerprints wouldn't show on the corrugated surface. As she gave it a twist, she heard the snick of a key card going into the door lock. Damn! She didn't know whether to hope the maid or Heather-Anne came into the room.

Quickly grabbing the linens off the shelf, she held them chest high so the pile hid her face and started toward the door.

"Who are—?" The voice was young, half irate.

"Gotta wash the linens," Charlie said, hurrying past with her face shoved into the musty-smelling pillows. They really could use a spin through the Maytag.

"I haven't used those. Why—?"

"Bedbugs."

Before Heather-Anne could do more than squeak indignantly, Charlie scooted out the door. She turned away from the maid's cart and found a door leading to a stairwell. Dumping the pillows and blankets on the first step, she ran up to the second floor, feeling the pull in her injured glute. At the top, she rubbed her ass, peeked into the empty hall, and strolled toward the elevator, trying to slow her pulse rate, which had skyrocketed when she heard the key in the door. By the time she rode the elevator to the ground floor, her breathing was back to normal, and she walked toward the main doors as if she were a guest headed out for a touristy day at Garden of the Gods.

As Charlie passed the reception desk, she heard a clerk say into the phone, "Absolutely not! We've never had bed-bugs in our hotel, ma'am. Let me connect you to house-keeping."

4

~~~

When Charlie called to tell me that Les had dropped off the rental in Aspen, I knew immediately where he was—with our friends Cherry and Moss Fitzwater. Excited, I found their number and dialed it. After four rings, it went to voice mail.

"This is Cherry. And this is Moss," went the message. "We're visiting Singapore this month, so don't expect to hear from us anytime soon. If you're a burglar, keep in mind that we've got a sophisticated alarm system, a mean dog, and a caretaker in residence."

I knew their "mean dog" was a bichon frise even smaller than my shih tzu, Nolan. Cherry's giggles followed Moss's stern announcement. "Oh, and check our Facebook page for photos of the trip."

Listening to their voices made me sad. I wished I'd been able to keep them as friends when Les left me.

I called Charlie back to tell her I knew where Les was.

"You'll need to go up there," she said.

"Me? To Aspen?"

"Yes. It's good he didn't answer the phone, and it was smart of you not to leave a message. We don't want to warn Les that we're on his tail."

Not leaving a message was more because I hadn't thought about what I wanted to say than about not warning Les, but I said, "Right," like I'd had the same thought. "But I can't go to Aspen, Charlie. The kids—"

Charlie wasn't listening to excuses, though, and I was on my way to Aspen well before lunch. I'd arranged for Kendall to stay at a friend's house and let Dexter talk me into letting him stay home alone, packed, and traded vehicles with Charlie since she'd pointed out that Les would recognize the Hummer. Charlie had bought a new-to-her Subaru Outback a couple of weeks ago to replace the one that got smashed in Estes Park, and I liked feeling closer to the road than I felt in Les's Hummer. I still didn't think of it as mine. I bounced in the seat, excited about heading off on my own for the first time in . . . why, I didn't think I'd taken a trip alone since before the kids were born. I marveled at that as I made the turn-off to 470 outside Denver, sure I didn't need a map since Les and I had stayed with Moss and Cherry several times before we split. Besides, with any luck, I'd catch Les on the slopes. I knew exactly where he liked to ski, and I was confident that on a beautiful day like this he wouldn't be able to resist the runs, no matter what brought him to Colorado.

By midafternoon I had parked at the Intercept Lot off 82, where Les always parked, taken the shuttle to Snowmass, where I knew Les liked to ski, and bought a lift ticket for a sum that would have paid for four manicures. Charlie'd suggested I stake out Moss and Cherry's house, but if I could catch Les on the slopes, I could drive back and be home before the kids went to bed. I'd thrown my ski gear into the car, but I hoped I wouldn't have to ski. Les had bought it for me one Christmas, even though I'd said I would prefer a weekend at the Canyon Ranch Spa, and I knew it was expensive. Only I wasn't much of a skier. Les flew down double black diamond runs. I stuck to the bunny slopes and preferred après-ski activities like hot tubs and shopping to actual skiing. Skiing was cold and wet, and it mussed your hair, and I almost always broke a fingernail putting my boots on. I was hoping to spot Les at Sneaky's, but if I had to ski to find Les, I'd do it. I wished Charlie were here to be impressed with my preparedness and my can-do attitude.

The slopes were crowded, even midweek, with the sunshine and fresh powder drawing lots of locals away from work, I suspected. Sun glared off the snow, and I teared up. I slid along cautiously, trying to get the feel of the skis. How long had it been since I skied? Three years? Four? I was sure it would come back to me, like bike riding, although, come to think of it, it'd been even longer since I'd been on a bicycle. The scents of new snow, pine, and coffee mingled pleasantly as I got on line to order my latte. The nearest lift ran continually, and I scanned the people standing in line to board, hoping to see Les. No one looked familiar. Giggles and shouts drew my attention, and I turned my head to watch kids as young as three or four zip down the kiddie hill. I wondered if I'd ever been that fearless. I didn't think so.

I had just received my steaming latte when I saw Les. In

the chairlift line, he wore the electric blue parka he'd bought at an end-of-season sale and had goggles over his face. I'd recognize his receding hairline anywhere, though.

"Les!" Several people turned at my call, but not Les. I skied toward the line, coffee sloshing over my ungloved hand. Ow.

Les was chatting with a curvaceous woman a couple of inches taller than he was. In sleek white winter gear, she was a ski goddess, dark hair curling on her shoulders. The chair came up behind them and they sat easily, still talking. Seeing Les with another woman gave me an unpleasant jolt, but a tiny part of me relished the thought of telling Heather-Anne he'd dumped her for somebody else. I didn't have time to think about it, though, as I cut into line with a bunch of "excuse mes" and "so sorrys" and plunked into the chair four behind Les and his snow bunny. It whisked up the mountain.

The passenger beside me was a teen snowboarder who made a point of staring away from me and didn't respond to my "Hi." Fine by me. I didn't have time for chitchat; I needed to keep tabs on Les and his companion. The ground fell away quickly, and I stared down at the sloping white dotted with skiers and evergreens. It might almost have been fun if I hadn't been afraid of losing Les. As we neared the top, I watched Les and his friend gracefully exit the lift and angle toward a trail slightly to the left. I was so busy keeping track of them that I forgot to ready myself for getting off. I snagged the tip of my ski in the snow and jolted forward, landing on my knees and face. My cup went sailing, splattering coffee on two or three people. The skiers behind me grumbled and skied around me as the lift operator dragged me out of the way.

Mumbling my thanks and brushing snow off my fuchsia parka, I slid quickly toward the trail Les had taken. Thank goodness it was only a blue, not one of his double black diamonds. Maybe his friend wasn't an expert skier. Les was skiing easily, cutting from one side of the run to the other in lazy swoops, his electric blue jacket easily visible. I could catch him if I took a straighter line. Not taking time to pull up the goggles around my neck, I pointed my skis downhill, flexed my knees, and pushed off with my poles.

Whee! For a moment, the whoosh of wind in my hair and the speed were exhilarating, but my thighs began to ache almost immediately, and an icy spot made me wobble. I had the uneasy feeling I was out of control, but I was gaining on Les. I straightened to relieve the stress on my thighs, and that slowed me a little. A snowboarder came out of nowhere and slid across the run in front of me, and I dug my poles in to keep from colliding with her. My skis nicked the back of her board, and she cut away, yelling something in a rude voice.

Well! *She* cut *me* off, not vice versa. Still, it wouldn't hurt to slow down a bit. As long as I could keep Les in sight, I could talk to him at the end of the run. Trying to force my skis into a snowplow position with the tips wide, I found my out-of-shape legs weren't up to the task. My right leg skidded, and I windmilled my arms to catch my balance, glad of the loops that secured my poles around my wrists. For a moment, I thought I was going to tumble over, but I got the ski back in line.

Now I was scared. My leg muscles shook, and I knew a fall at this speed would really hurt, even break a bone or two. My ankles throbbed and only the boots kept them from giving out completely. The run took a wide, easy turn to the right, but I couldn't turn my ski tips and bounced off the groomed trail into an area dotted with pine saplings. Oh, my God. Wasn't this how Sonny Bono died?

I squeezed my eyes shut, letting my momentum carry me down the mountainside. I heard shouts behind me, but I knew no one could save me. Something slapped my cheek, making it sting; the smell told me it was a pine branch. My teeth chattered as my skis rumbled over the clumpy snow. After what felt like an hour, but was probably only thirty seconds, the snow smoothed out again, and I dared to open my eyes. I was back on the run, which had curved to the left and intersected my straight-as-an-arrow path. A flash of electric blue told me I'd just passed Les. Before I could yell his name, a boy of maybe five or six stopped at the bottom of the run and paused to wave a ski pole at his parents. If I kept going, I'd plow right through him.

What had my instructor always told me to do when in trouble? Sit down. Before I could think about how badly it would hurt or calculate the chances of breaking some bones, I did my best to force my legs into snowplow position. Feeling my speed drop a bit, I flung myself back. My fanny hit the ground, my skis popped off, and I skidded the rest of the way down the hill on my tush, slowing to a stop as the little boy skied toward his parents, completely unaware that I'd been coming straight at him. I sucked in a deep breath, but before I could expel it in a huge sigh of relief, a man yelled, "Get out of—"

All I could see was the electric blue jacket as Les tried to steer around me. One of his skis lodged under my outstretched leg, and he went down, landing half on top of me. Oof. I was momentarily winded but pushed myself up on my elbows. I fixed a smile on my face. "Oh, Les—"

He turned on his side to face me, scowling and spitting snow. Despite the thinning blond hair, round face, and electric blue parka, he wasn't Les.

Finding Cherry and Moss's house was harder than I'd anticipated. I was sure that if it'd been daylight, I could've driven straight to their development, but in the dark all the gated housing areas looked similar, and I couldn't remember if theirs was called Aspen View, Mountain View, or Eagle View. A recent snow had left the streets snow-packed and slick, and I drove slowly, trying to peer through the gates, every muscle in my body aching from my humiliating reintroduction to skiing. I'd learned to drive on Georgia's red dirt roads, and driving on snow still made me nervous. Rude people behind me honked and zipped past, spinning snow onto my windshield and making it even harder to see.

I breathed a sigh of relief when the guard at the fifth community I stopped at, Ponderosa Heights, recognized the Fitzwaters' names and let me in after writing down my name and license plate number. Aspen trunks shone whitely in the moonlight, and the snow was so pretty it looked fakey, like something you'd see at Disneyland—white and powdery and sparkly. I crawled down the street until I reached the winding driveway leading to Cherry and Moss's. I drove past it and parked half a block up, like Charlie had suggested. She'd told me to stake out the place, see if Les was really in residence, and get photos of him if I could. It'd been my bright idea to try to find him on the ski slopes, thinking I could wrap things up and get back to the kids tonight. Once we knew for certain that he was holed up at the Fitzwaters', we'd call Heather-Anne and let her take it from there. Part of me thought it was unfair to sic Heather-Anne on Les if he was trying to get away from her, but Charlie pointed out that that's what we'd been hired to do.

I gnawed my lip, the heater blowing. I'd stopped at a drugstore for some ibuprofen and taken several, but I still ached all over, and I felt stiff as a fence post. Hotness that wasn't from the heater began to burn through me. Hot flash! Unzipping my parka, I opened the car door and stumbled into the snow, scooped up a handful, and held it to my face. Ooh, that felt good. As the prickly heat receded, I looked around. The moonlight on the snow lit up the neighborhood, and I could see the Fitzwaters' lodgestyle home clearly. Without really thinking about it, I found myself walking up the driveway, my boots scrunching loudly in the snow. If I waited in the car, I'd have to leave to find someplace to pee, and with my track record that's when Les would appear. It would be smarter—wouldn't it?—to investigate the house now and see if Les was really here. Truth is, surveillance, with all that waiting around, and having to pee but not being able to, and freezing because you can't turn on the heater and let the subject know you're there, wasn't my long suit.

Lights flooded the snow-covered front yard as I neared the four-car garage, and I jumped. Someone must have seen me.

I thought about hiding behind the evergreen shrubs and had even started toward them when I realized the lights were motion activated like the ones Les had had installed at our house. Heavens, that had given me a start. My breaths came out in smoky puffs. I didn't see any lights in the house. I felt a little disappointed. Part of me wanted to see Les again. It'd been more than a year since he ran off to South America, and I still missed him. An itty bit. Not his snoring, or the way he ignored me for days on end when he had a big deal in the works, or how he used to slap my fanny if he caught me eating a doughnut or a cookie, but telling him about my day and discussing what the kids were up to, and planning vacations together. We both loved to travel. I remembered that he'd taken his last trip—to Costa Rica—without me and blinked back tears.

I paused near the steps, shivering, trying to work up my courage to walk up to the door. What if Les answered? A happy thought struck me. I didn't have to mention Heather-Anne. I could say I was in Aspen for the skiing and decided to drop in on Moss and Cherry. That would keep him from being suspicious. I climbed the stairs before I could lose my nerve and knocked timidly. I waited, shifting from foot to foot, getting chilled. Butterflies swarmed in my tummy. Zipping my parka, I knocked again, a little louder. Still nothing. Maybe I'd been wrong about Les staying here.

I backed down the steps, looking up at the house, but no lights popped on. I seemed to remember that the huge window to the left of the door looked into the living room. Struggling through knee-deep drifts, I tromped to the window, leg muscles screaming. With my hands cupped around my face, I tried to peer in. Too dark. Cold and wet and tired, head ducked against a strengthening wind, I turned to leave. I should have stuck with Charlie's plan. A sudden flash of movement made me look up. A black shadow had rounded the far end of the house and was aiming for me like an arrow shot from the crossbow my daddy used to hunt wild hogs. About to hyperventilate, I turned to run, but the deep snow pulled at my boots, and I had only managed a couple of steps before something slammed into my back and I pitched face-first into the snow.

5

I struggled to breathe, cold, grainy snow filling my nose and mouth. Something heavy on my back held me down, and when I turned my face to gasp for air, hot, meaty breath blew over my cheek. It was accompanied by a ferocious *grrr*ing and I froze, trying not to think about a news story I'd read recently about a pit bull that attacked a woman going about her daily business and bit her nose off, among other things. I really didn't have money in my budget now for a plastic surgeon.

"Knievel will rip your throat out if you move," a man's voice said.

Despite the edge of fear in his voice, I recognized it. "Les," I said in a small voice, trying not to upset Knievel, whose paws on my shoulders kept me from raising my head. "Les, it's me."

There was silence. "Gigi?"

"Yes!"

More silence, long enough for me to wonder if he'd walked away. I shifted my shoulder, and Knievel growled louder in response. "Nice doggy," I said. "I hope someone already fed you dinner. Les?"

"I'm thinking." After another moment, he said, "Off, Knievel."

The heaviness left my back, and I rolled over slowly, looking for the dog to make sure he wasn't going to pounce on me again. I kept one hand on my nose. When I had managed to sit up, snow and wet all over the front of my parka and velour leggings, I made out Les standing in the shadow of a large spruce, holding a shotgun on me. Knievel, a Doberman pinscher, sat a foot away, ready to chew me into confetti if Les gave the word. "You're a handsome boy," I told the dog. He curled his lip, showing strong white teeth.

I began to shiver. "I'm c-cold," I said. "Can I get up?"

"Of course you can get up," Les said impatiently. "Jeez, Gigi."

"You're p-pointing a g-gun at me."

"What? Oh." He lowered the gun to his side. "You can't be too careful these days."

I didn't know what he meant by that, but I struggled to my feet and brushed snow off myself. Knievel kept his eyes trained on me, looking for an excuse to rip my nose off. "What happened to Bella?" I asked.

"Bella? What the hell are you talking about?"

"Cherry and Moss's bichon," I said. I hoped Knievel hadn't eaten her.

"How the hell should I know? God, Gigi, I'd forgotten how you go on about irrelevancies."

I swallowed hard. "Sorry," I whispered.

Heaving an exasperated sigh, he said, "I guess you'd better come in." He turned and headed around the side of the house, and I followed. Knievel stuck close to me, eyeing me like I was a pork chop he was hoping to sink his teeth into, until Les called, "Knievel, heel." The dog trotted forward then, and I slogged behind them, wanting nothing more than some dry clothes and a bowl of soup. I couldn't even feel good about having located Les so easily and earning Heather-Anne's thousand dollars.

The back door hung open as if Les had been in such a hurry to confront the intruder—me—that he hadn't bothered to close it. Golden light spilled onto the snow, a yellow road leading into the kitchen. Knievel's claws clicked on the hardwood floor as he trotted toward a bowl in the corner and began to slurp. The kitchen was all ceramic tile and warm woods with a stone arch over the six-burner Viking stove; Cherry had redone it in a Tuscan style since the last time I was here. Les laid the shotgun up against the wall and bent to remove his boots. I did the same, stealing covert looks at him from my bent-over position.

He looked about the same as when I'd last seen him. Maybe a little browner. He still combed his blond hair to hide his bald patch, and he still had the mustache Charlie said made him look like Hitler. I'd always liked it; I thought it made him look a little bit like a 1940s movie star, and it tickled when he kissed me. Beneath the too-big jacket he was shucking off—maybe it was Moss's?—he wore a pineapple-printed Hawaiian shirt not at all right for Aspen in February. Its loose fit disguised his little potbelly. With both of us in our stocking feet, he was only an inch taller than me; he never liked it when I wore high heels when we went out together.

"What are you doing here, Gigi?" Les asked suddenly, and I nearly toppled over. "How did you know I was here?"

I straightened slowly, taking my time pulling off my parka so I could try to remember my story. White feathers drifted from a tear on the shoulder where Knievel's claws must have ripped it. I gave the Doberman a look where he lay with his head on his forelegs in front of an old-fashioned iron stove that was putting off a lot of heat and muttered, "Naughty dog." He ignored me. Les didn't offer to take my coat, so I hung it over a chair tucked under the heavy butcher-block table.

Taking a deep breath, I launched into the story I'd settled on. "I'm in Aspen to do some skiing and thought I'd drop in on Cherry and Moss. I haven't seen them since . . ." Since before Les ran off with Heather-Anne.

Les raised his spiky brows. "Skiing? You haven't skied in years, Gigi."

"I was on Snowmass today," I said, trying to make it sound as if I'd schussed down in Lindsey Vonn style. I didn't tell him I was listing my skis and boots on Craigslist as soon as I got home. I was never skiing again.

He gave me a doubtful look. "Are Kenny and Dex with you?"

"Uh, no." I thought quickly. "School. I couldn't take them out of school. They're staying with . . . friends. They miss you." I knew Kendall missed her daddy, although I wasn't so sure about Dexter. He never talked about Les.

He turned away and began to wash his hands in the farmhouse sink. I liked it and wondered whether I shouldn't redo our kitchen. *My* kitchen. Les had insisted on stainless steel appliances and sinks, but I'd always found the metal kind of cold, especially on gloomy, cloudy days—not that we had many of those in Colorado Springs. I remembered I could hardly afford to buy napkins, and my shoulders slumped. When Les didn't respond to my comment about Kendall and Dexter, I said, "What are *you* doing here? I thought you were in Costa Rica or someplace." Trying to make it sound like I didn't know or care where he'd gone.

"Business." Reaching into a cabinet over the stove, he pulled out a bottle of Scotch. Mac-something-or-other; I couldn't read the whole label.

"Where's Heather-Anne?" I asked, suddenly remembering I wasn't supposed to know she wasn't with him.

"Home." He poured a shot, downed it, and poured another without looking at me.

"I'd like some," I said. I was cold, wet, and unhappy. Books and movies always made it seem like a shot of whisky would warm you right up. That's what Saint Bernards carried in those cute little barrels attached to their collars, wasn't it? Or maybe that was brandy.

"You hate Scotch," Les said, turning to face me. Surprise and uncertainty fought it out on his face.

"Not anymore," I said, semidefiantly. "A lot of things have changed since you left."

He looked doubtful, but poured me a shot in a heavy crystal tumbler and walked it over to me. "What else has changed?"

"Well, I'm working now." I tasted the amber liquid and coughed. Nasty.

Les gave me an "I told you so" smirk and I forced myself to take another sip. It wasn't so bad this time.

"I heard," he said. "For that third-rate PI firm I invested in. Stupidest financial decision I ever made."

"Charlie is not third-rate!"

He rolled his eyes but didn't argue. His gaze ran over me, and I was suddenly glad I'd worn the aqua cashmere sweater that brings out the blue in my eyes and the dark purple leggings that make me look svelte. Well, less fat. "You're looking good, Gigi," Les said. "Divorce must agree with you." He moved in a little closer, and I could smell the Scotch on his breath.

Flustered, I tipped the rest of my Scotch into my mouth. It burned down my throat to my tummy, and I felt a warm glow spreading through my limbs. My fingertips tingled. It worked, I thought, just like in the movies. My brain felt a little fuzzy.

"You haven't asked about Cherry and Moss," Les reminded me, his gaze dropping to my lips.

I licked them nervously. "Oh, Cherry and Moss. I was hoping to see them . . . thought I'd drop by while I was here in Aspen. For the skiing. Where are they?" Les had me so rattled I looked around, half expecting Moss to come in with an armload of wood from outside, or Cherry to pop in and suggest we have a *Die Hard* marathon in their theater room after dinner.

"They're in Singapore," Les said, watching me closely.

"Oh, right." I remembered I wasn't supposed to know they were gone. "I mean, I'm sorry they're not here."

"I'm not." Les slipped an arm around my waist and pulled me closer. "I've missed you, Gigi."

I wriggled away, flushing. "Don't say that, Les."

"Why not? It's true. You can't tell me you haven't missed me, too." He plucked the glass from my hand.

"Maybe a little at the beginning." I watched him from the corner of my eyes as he poured us both more Scotch. "What are you doing here?" I twisted my head from side to side; my neck hurt. Noticing, Les set his glass down and moved behind me. He started massaging my neck and shoulders, thumbs digging deep into my aching muscles. It felt good. "Mm."

My eyes wanted to close, but I forced them open, trying to remember what I'd asked him. "Why did you come back?"

"I might have made a mistake."

"You did?" He smelled good, like fresh air and the spicy aftershave the kids got him every Father's Day. The familiar scent did something to my insides, or maybe it was the Scotch, and even though I meant to ask him what kind of mistake, the words didn't make it from my head to my tongue. I turned and pushed against his chest halfheartedly. "What about Heather-Anne?"

"She's—we're kind of taking a time-out right now. I'm not sure . . . You always could get me going, Geej," he said, wrapping his arms more firmly around me.

I wondered briefly if Heather-Anne knew they were taking a time-out. "We shouldn't . . . We're divorced."

"I don't feel divorced right now," he murmured against my ear, his teeth nipping at it in the way he knew made me crazy. Some part of my brain that didn't feel all warm and woolly tried to remind me that I should be asking him what he was doing here, why he wasn't in Costa Rica, or calling Charlie to let her know I'd found him. Then he kissed me, mustache tickling, and pulled me against his body and we fit together just like we used to, and I felt myself melt like butter on a stack of steaming hotcakes.

6

Charlie Swift pointed her pancake-laden fork at Father Dan Allgood, the Episcopalian priest who lived in the rectory next door. "I told you you don't need to keep making my breakfast. I'm well enough to do it myself now." She patted her hip. "Almost good as new."

"You didn't say it very convincingly," he said with a lazy smile, "and since that's your sixth pancake, I get the feeling you appreciate my cooking." With a flick of the spatula, he flipped a pancake off the griddle and slid it onto the stack on his plate. Turning off the gas, he collected his plate and joined her at the kitchen table, his broad shoulders and six-foot-five frame making the table feel smaller all of a sudden. Light gleamed on his blond hair and turned the syrup stream he poured onto his pancakes a luscious amber.

"Who wouldn't?" Charlie mumbled around a mouthful of pancake. She downed half a glass of orange juice. "You're going to make some lucky woman a wonderful husband." Having breakfast together, as they had been since Dan started cooking it for her after she got shot, felt weirdly cozy, and she tossed the joke out to defuse the feeling.

Dan gave her a look from under his brows but didn't respond. He was probably in his late forties, ten years older than she was, Charlie thought, although his rugged build made him appear younger. The expression in his eyes, though, especially when he was staring off into the middle distance, unaware that someone was watching him, made him seem older. For all she knew, he'd already been married three times; they didn't often discuss personal matters. She knew he'd been ordained an Episcopal priest ten years ago and had been the rector at St. Paul's for two years, but she didn't know where he grew up or what he'd done before becoming a priest. She'd been tempted to ask on more than one occasion, but something about the way he stilled when the conversation looked like it was headed in that direction made her back off. It's not like she was eagerly sharing the grimmer details of her air force years or her peripatetic childhood, either.

"We've got a new case," she told Dan, scraping up the last remnant of syrup with her fork. "The bimbo Gigi's husband ran off with wants our help locating him."

"What?" Dan's head came up, and his blue eyes fixed on her face. "Run that by me again?"

Charlie told him about Heather-Anne Pawlusik's descent on Swift Investigations and her unexpected request. "Gigi's got a lead on him; she's in Aspen now trying to track him down. I expected to hear from her last night, but you know Gigi."

"She didn't call?" A line appeared between Dan's brows.

"She probably got busy or forgot her phone." Charlie wasn't concerned; Gigi would be in touch when she had something to report or when she wanted guidance on how to proceed. Probably she hadn't seen Les yet.

"What are you going to do?"

"Track down some phone numbers from Les's cell phone bill and do a background check on our client. I didn't meet her, but I don't quite like the way she just turned up to hire Gigi."

"I thought you liked any client with a bank balance on the plus side," Dan mocked gently.

"Usually," Charlie said, "but this cuts pretty close to home for Gigi, and I want to make sure we don't get blindsided."

"Always thinking ahead." Dan picked up their plates and deposited them in the sink.

"I try."

After Dan left, Charlie finished clearing up their breakfast, filled the bird feeders in her yard, did her physical therapy exercises, and took a Motrin to cut the persistent ache in her gluteus maximus. Reaching for Les's phone bill, which Gigi had left when she swapped her Hummer for Charlie's Subaru, she started to log on to her computer but stopped. There was no reason, she thought, why she couldn't go into the office. She could drive the short distance without bothering her wound, and the place would be empty with Gigi in Aspen. She hadn't been planning on returning to work until the following week, but who knew what business they might lose if the office went unmanned for a couple of days?

Excited by the prospect, Charlie swapped her sweats for corduroys with a bit of stretch, threw a blazer over her white turtleneck, and headed out the front door. Momentarily dismayed to see Gigi's Hummer sitting where her Subaru ought to be, she returned to the house for the right set of keys, gritted her teeth, and climbed into the taller vehicle, regretting the stretch through her ass. Settled in the seat, she felt like she was driving an M1A1 tank. She drove cautiously at first, slowing through the curve that passed a string of hotels, then picking up speed as she turned onto Woodmen Road. The massive vehicle handled like a snowplow, and Charlie could practically hear the gasoline evaporating from the tank, but at least she'd be the victor in any traffic accident involving anything smaller than a semi.

Parking in front of Swift Investigations five minutes later, Charlie unlocked the door and took a deep breath. It felt like coming home. It felt like the old days, before Gigi descended on her. No coffee smell from the coffeemaker Gigi had insisted on, no tinkling of Yanni or the pan flute guy from Gigi's CD player, no need to make conversation or explain what she was doing. Heaven! Beelining for the minifridge tucked behind her desk, Charlie liberated a Pepsi and took a celebratory swig. She sat behind her desk and smoothed a hand over the calendar blotter.

After a few moments of reveling in the feeling of being back at work, and alone, Charlie busied herself with the background checks for Danner and Lansky; she'd found the folders on Gigi's desk. Reports drafted, she began to dig into Heather-Anne Pawlusik's background. Sitting for too long made her ass ache, so she set the computer keyboard atop the file cabinet and typed standing up. Forty-five minutes later, she paused for another Pepsi, hoping the caffeine would help her make sense of what she'd found.

Heather-Anne's history in Colorado Springs seemed clear enough: She'd rented an apartment on the northeast side and broken the lease about a year before she ran off with Les, worked as a personal trainer for the Y and Gold's Gym, had an overdrawn Ent checking account, had been involved in a traffic accident a year ago, and paid utilities and cable bills mostly on time. She wasn't registered to vote and didn't seem to belong to any civic or professional organizations.

Trouble was, when Charlie tried to find out something about their client's earlier life, including records of her birth, education, and former employment, she ran into a brick wall. Apparently, Heather-Anne Pawlusik hadn't existed before showing up in Colorado.

7

When I woke up, my eyes were gummy, my head hurt, and my mouth felt like I'd been eating cotton balls. I wasn't sure where I was or why I felt so stiff. Forcing my eyes open, I found myself staring at a black doggy snout at eye level. "Oh!" I wriggled backward until the sofa back stopped me, watching the large nostrils work, before I recognized Knievel. His brown eyes were fixed on me hopefully, and his stubby tail wagged. Cherry and Moss's. Les. Last night.

"You're looking a little friendlier this morning," I said, reaching out a hand to pat his head.

He danced back a few steps, trotted halfway toward the door, then looked over his shoulder at me. I recognized the routine: It's just what Nolan does when he needs to do his chores. I sat up, and the plaid afghan over me slipped to my lap, reminding me I was naked. "Just a minute," I told an impatient Knievel, wondering where Les had gotten to. Memories of the night before brought a smile to my face. I'd forgotten how sweet he could be when he wanted to, and he certainly remembered how to push my buttons.

"Grrr-rowr." Knievel scratched impatiently at the door.

I found my bra under the coffee table and put it on. My panties had disappeared—hadn't we made love the first time in the kitchen?—so I pulled up my leggings, shrugged into my sweater, and padded barefoot to the door. The floor was cold.

When I opened the door, a blade of sunlight magnified by brilliant snow cut into my aching eyeballs, and Knievel shot out before I could worry about whether or not he'd run off. He was a black blur against the snow, and a flock of small birds twittered upward as he charged toward them, barking. He disappeared into a row of evergreens, and I hoped he knew better than to run into the street. "Knievel?"

He didn't come back, even though I held the door open for another two minutes until my freezing feet and hands forced me to close it. He'd scratch when he wanted back in. I visited the powder room, wishing I had a toothbrush, and then wandered toward the kitchen, looking for Les and a bottle of aspirin.

"Les?" The kitchen was cold and deserted. The iron stove had gone out. My brow puckered, and I searched the ground floor, not finding any sign of Les in the formal dining room, the theater room, or the gated wine cellar with its cute little bistro table and chairs where Cherry and Moss and Les and I had played spades until the wee hours one night while drinking wine nonstop so I woke up feeling a lot like I did right now. Les must be sleeping upstairs. I climbed the stairs, my cold feet grateful for the plush carpet.

"Les?" I called again. No answer. My tummy began to hurt. Where could he be? I poked my head into the beautifully decorated guest rooms to the right of the landing. The tropics-themed decor in one room beckoned me in, and I wondered where Cherry had gotten the cute little monkey sculptures on the dresser. I was running my hand over the bamboo-patterned duvet when my headache reminded me I hadn't found any aspirin yet. Les wasn't in the master bedroom, either, but I found some painkillers in the medicine cabinet and swallowed them, feeling guilty about invading Moss and Cherry's room and stealing their aspirin.

Tiptoeing down the hall the other way, I found an office, a room full of exercise equipment and mirrors that reflected my ash blond hair sticking out stiffly—oh, my heavens—and another bedroom with attached bath. A damp towel was crumpled on the floor of the bathroom, but there was no razor or deodorant on the sink. I picked up the towel, folded it, and laid it over the towel bar. Les had showered this morning, and then . . .

I moped toward the large window that overlooked the front yard and leaned my forehead against the cold pane. It felt good. I looked down, hoping to spot Les or Knievel or I didn't know what. Nothing moved except a magpie gliding from the tippy top of a spruce tree to the snowy lawn. He landed in one of Knievel's paw prints and pecked at something. Then the bird hopped toward the driveway, where car tracks made ugly ruts in the snow. It took me a moment to realize. Tears pricked at my eyelids. Those tracks hadn't been there last night when I came up the driveway. Someone had driven out . . . and the only someone around here besides me was Les.

I ran back downstairs, as if it were still possible to keep Les from leaving—again—and stopped in the foyer. Not thinking it through, I opened the hall closet beside the front door, planning to grab a coat. An alarm panel met my startled gaze, a red light on it blinking angrily. Uh-oh. I knew what that meant because we had a similar security system at home; at least, we'd had one until I discontinued the service because I couldn't afford the monthly fees. Forgetting about the coat and Les, I opened the front door a crack and peered out to see an Aspen Police Department car charging up the driveway, lights flashing.

8

As Charlie puzzled over Heather-Anne's unusual lack of history, the door opened, and she looked up. Albertine entered, saying, "Gigi—" before noticing Charlie.

"Charlie!" She bustled forward, her coral and turquoise tunic top molding to a massive bosom and full thighs. She enveloped Charlie in a huge hug. "I thought you weren't coming back until next week."

"Gigi had to go to Aspen on business, so I thought I'd return a day or two early," Charlie said with a smile, cheered by Albertine's greeting, the long fingernails painted turquoise to match her top, and her brisk, no-nonsense demeanor.

"She's chasing after that no-good ex-husband of hers, isn't she?" Albertine asked. "More fool she."

"We've got a client," Charlie said, slightly taken aback by Albertine's disapproval, "although I did tell Gigi I thought we should turn down the case."

"Damn right, you should've." Albertine shook her head, her towering pile of braids, whorls, and curlicues tilting dangerously, despite enough shiny hair shellac to prevent wispies in gale-force winds. "Gigi's not really over that larcenous jackass, and I'd hate to see him take advantage of her again. As for that skank he took up with . . . well! If my Tyrone brought home someone like that, I'd take him by the ear and beat some sense into him with a broom."

Charlie laughed. She'd only met Albertine's son once when he visited from New Orleans, but he was a six-foot-three former LSU offensive lineman. Still, she didn't doubt Albertine could cow him into submission. "Gigi said she can handle it."

"Hmph" was Albertine's only response. She gave Charlie's shoulders another squeeze, then said, "I'm expecting a delivery of okra, so I've got to get back. Come on down for a bowl of the best gumbo this side of the Big Easy later on."

"Will do," Charlie promised. Just the thought of Albertine's rich gumbo made her stomach growl.

Albertine had barely walked out the door when the phone rang. "Swift Investigations," Charlie answered.

"Oh, oh, Charlie! I tried you at home and you weren't there and then I thought maybe, just maybe, you'd gone into the office, and I'm so happy I caught you!"

"Calm down, Gigi." Charlie struggled to make sense of her partner's words through the Georgia accent that got more pronounced whenever Gigi was agitated. "What's wrong?"

A gulping sound came over the phone. "Well, there's good news, bad news, and worse news," Gigi said, sniffling.

Charlie suppressed a growl. Gigi's inability to relay information succinctly drove her crazy. "Just cut to the chase."

"The good news is that I found Les."

"That's great! So—"

"The bad news is that he's gone again."

"Well—"

Gigi drowned Charlie out with a wail. "And the worse news is that I've been arrested!"

By the time Charlie got Gigi calmed down enough to get a coherent story from her about finding Les at her friends' house, she'd made it halfway through a new Pepsi.

"So then I noticed the alarm had gone off—Les must've set it when he left and I set it off when I let that evil Knievel out to do his chores—"

"There was a stuntman staying at the house? I thought he was dead."

"What?" Gigi asked, sounding totally bewildered. "I'm not talking about a movie. This is *real*."

"You just said something about Evil Knievel shoveling the walk or something."

"Knievel's the *dog*," Gigi said, sounding as testy as Charlie had ever heard her.

"Right." Charlie knocked back the rest of her Pepsi, figuring she would need the caffeine in her system to make it through the rest of the day.

"Anyway," Gigi continued, "the police came and they accused me of breaking in and of stealing things—you know I would never steal anything—and then they brought me down to the police station and, oh, Charlie, I don't know what to do. *Please* come up here and fix it!" Gigi ended on another wail.

Charlie couldn't ignore Gigi's plea. "Of course I'll come. I just need to figure out how I'll get there since I can't drive that far yet." She cycled friends through her head. Albertine had a restaurant to run and couldn't spend the day jaunting off to

Aspen. Dan might be able to do it if he didn't have any parish commitments. She thought about Connor Montgomery, the Colorado Springs Police detective she had some sort of relationship with. The confusing sort that occurred when one party was wary of involvement due to memories of an adrenaline-junkie fighter-pilot ex-husband who had too much in common with a certain gorgeous four-years-younger-than-her homicide detective whose kisses lit her up like every star in the Milky Way compressed into a snow globe. Maybe Montgomery wasn't working—

"Did you hear me, Charlie? I said Dexter could drive you."

That jolted Charlie out of her reverie. "Dexter? Your son?" She tried not to sound appalled but wasn't sure she'd succeeded. She'd only met the seventeen-year-old Dexter twice, but on both occasions she'd had to restrain herself from slapping the kid or pulling a gun on him because of his air of entitlement and the way he treated Gigi.

"Of course my son," Gigi said, sounding so relieved to have come up with a solution for Charlie's transportation difficulties that Charlie didn't have the heart to tell her she'd rather walk to Aspen. "I'll call him and have him pick you up at your house. If you leave right now, maybe you can get me out before I have to spend the night in jail. I'm not cut out for prison life, Charlie."

Charlie had no trouble believing that and did her best to reassure Gigi before driving home to pack an overnight bag. She'd barely tossed her toothbrush in when a honk from out front made her peer out the window. A shiny red BMW 325i sat in her gravel driveway, the lanky blond Dexter leaning on the horn. With a growl, Charlie finished packing, locked the house, and stalked to the car. Rap music with an insistent bass beat vibrated the Beemer and was probably scaring away every bird, bunny, bobcat, and bear in earshot, Charlie thought sourly. Dexter didn't emerge as she approached and yanked open the back door to toss her bag in. "You've never heard of knocking?" she asked as she opened the front door and slid into the passenger seat.

Dexter Goldman gave her a sullen look. Wearing a ratty T-shirt advertising a band Charlie had never heard of but was sure she would hate, he slouched in the driver's seat. His streaky blond hair brushed his earlobes. Psychedelic jams hit just below his knee, the lime and puce and orange reminding Charlie of some of Gigi's more lurid clothing combinations. The poor kid had inherited his mom's fashion gene. Despite the near-freezing temperatures, he had flip-flops on his feet. He was handsome in a way Charlie was sure appealed to foolish teenaged girls; he reminded her of a young Brad Pitt, à la *Thelma & Louise*. She reached over to click off the stereo.

"My tunes!"

"Drive," Charlie ordered.

The teen put the car in gear and stomped on the gas, spewing gravel as he tore out of Charlie's driveway. Charlie shut her eyes briefly; it was going to be a long trip.

Dexter's passion for speed and his total lack of consideration for other drivers made the drive shorter than Charlie had anticipated. She spent the trip on her cell phone and laptop, trying to locate Gigi's friends in Singapore. It seemed to her that the quickest way to get Gigi out of jail was to have the Fitzwaters tell the police she had their permission to be in the house. Accordingly, Charlie had dialed their home number to hear their message for herself and then the cell phone number Gigi had given her for them, without much hope. She was right; apparently the Fitzwaters' cell plan didn't include coverage in Southeast Asia. She was reduced to Googling hotels in Singapore and calling them to see if Cherry and Moss were staying there. Since the time difference made it early morning in Singapore, she dealt with a variety of sleepy desk clerks who took a long time to deliver the news that the Fitzwaters weren't registered at Hotel X or Y or Z. She didn't even want to consider the possibility that they were staying in a private home or rented condo. She shifted uncomfortably in the seat, her wound complaining.

It wasn't until they approached the outskirts of Aspen as dusk was settling that Dexter suggested, "Why don't you just send them a message on Facebook?"

"What?" Charlie gave him a startled look; the teen had been silent for most of the trip, earbuds blasting the rap music that Charlie refused to listen to, fingers tapping the steering wheel in time to the beat.

"Huh?"

Charlie yanked out the earbud closest to her. "I said, 'What do you mean?'"

"They said they were posting photos on Facebook, so they must be checking it. Send them a message and tell them about my mom." The boredom in his voice said he'd long ago given up hope of finding intelligent life in the generation that preceded him.

"Can I do that without a Facebook account?"

Dexter sighed ostentatiously and talked her through the process step by step. Within half an hour of Charlie sending the Fitzwaters a Facebook message explaining the situation and urging them to contact the Aspen police as soon as possible, Dexter was pulling into a handicapped slot in front of the Aspen Police Department. The police were housed in an imposing two-story redbrick building fronted by a bushy evergreen that soared above the roofline, with a long set of steps leading to wooden doors. Piles of snow were mounded on either side of the neatly shoveled sidewalk.

Charlie was about to suggest to Dexter that parking in a handicapped slot was asking for a ticket when the doors opened and Gigi emerged at the top of the steps, fuchsia parka practically glowing in the dusky light, champagne blond hair fluffed around her face like a halo. "You did it," she cried, spotting the Beemer. "I'm free!" Hurrying down the stairs, she flung her arms around Dexter, who pushed her away after a nanosecond.

"Let's not act like you escaped from Alcatraz," Charlie said, clambering stiffly out of the car and stretching her legs. "I take it the Fitzwaters called?"

"Oh, yes!" Gigi beamed. "They told the police I was a friend of theirs, not a thief, and said they should let me go. So they did. The police were very sweet, really, and very polite."

"Did the Fitzwaters say anything about Les?"

Gigi nodded vigorously. "I asked," she said proudly. "They

said he called them over the weekend and asked if they minded if he stayed at their place for a few days. Cherry said it sounded like he had business in the area. Their caretaker broke four ribs and his wrist snowboarding, so they were happy to have someone to take care of Knievel. Oh, no, what will happen to him now?" Her brow creased with concern. "We could take him with us, but I don't know if he and Nolan would get along."

"I'm not having a dog in my Beemer," Dexter announced, and Charlie found herself sympathizing with the kid for the first time that day.

"I'm sure the police will stick him in a kennel until the Fitzwaters get home," Charlie said quickly, not wanting to get roped into providing a temporary home for a mangy mutt named after a daredevil. "The kennels around here are probably nicer than most apartments in Colorado Springs." Aspen was a ritzy enclave that catered to the super-rich, and its amenities and prices were legendary. Charlie was sure kenneled pets dined on venison fritters and drank Perrier. "Where's my car?"

"It's still at Moss and Cherry's," Gigi said. "They gave me the alarm code and said we could spend the night."

Charlie was relieved; her ass was not up to another four hours on the road. She slid into the Beemer's backseat and stretched her legs out on the seat as Gigi bundled herself into the front.

"Guess what," she said, turning around to look at Charlie, eyes alight. "They put me in the very cell that Charlie Sheen stayed in."

9

Dexter and Charlie didn't have to be so rude about Charlie Sheen, in my opinion. He wasn't convicted, after all. Calling him a "dubious, wife-beating, prostitute-patronizing, profanity-spewing celebrity" was a little harsh. Still, I had a photo of the cell on my phone and was planning to post it on my Facebook page until Charlie told me that publicizing my arrest might not be the best advertisement for Swift Investigations.

We all spent the night at Moss and Cherry's, but Les didn't come back as I was halfway hoping he might. Charlie searched the room he slept in but didn't find anything that would tell us where he went or why he'd left Costa Rica. She asked me if he'd said anything that might be helpful, and I didn't have the nerve to tell her we hadn't talked much, that a little Scotch and kissing had led to other activities I was embarrassed to confess to, especially with Dexter standing there. It was bad enough that he found my panties under the kitchen table. I said they must be Cherry's and was glad he'd never met her, because she's smaller than a midge and definitely wouldn't own a pair of size sixteen pink lace undies. Thank the good Lord Charlie wasn't in the kitchen right then or she would have put two and two together and come up with five, like she always does.

Knievel showed up all wet and mud-covered as we were

sitting down to eat the KFC we'd picked up on the way to the house, and Charlie let me put him in the Subaru when we were leaving the next morning so we could drop him at a kennel on our way out of town. Dexter took off while we were loading up Knievel and locking the house.

"Why do you suppose Les set the alarm before leaving?" Charlie asked as I was arming the system the next morning.

"Habit?" I suggested. "He always set our alarm, even if he was just running to the 7-Eleven for milk."

"Or he wanted to slow you down," Charlie suggested. "Make sure you weren't on his trail again."

It took me a couple of seconds. "You mean he deliberately got me arrested?" I was indignant.

Charlie gave me a "could be" shrug.

I was still huffing and puffing about Les getting me arrested when we arrived at the kennel and handed Knievel over to a slim redhead who cooed at him. Charlie made out like it was a big deal, taking time to drop off the Doberman pinscher, but I could tell she was just as concerned about the dog as I was. He was really pretty sweet when he wasn't knocking you into the snow and threatening to rip your throat out.

I dropped Charlie off at her house round about eleven o'clock. She looked pooped, and I was afraid she had overdone it, but she wouldn't let me come in and make her lunch or anything. I moved my overnight bags to the Hummer, said good-bye to Charlie, who said a long soak in her hot tub would cure what ailed her, and headed for home. On the way, I had to pass the turnoff for Chapel Hills Mall, and somehow I found myself in the parking lot, pulling up in front of Macy's. After the encounter with Les and being arrested, I

deserved a new sweater or pair of shoes. I felt anxiety drain-
ing from me as I breathed in the smell of the store, a mix of
fibers, cosmetics, and stale air from the heater. Oh, yum. I'd
gained two pounds, according to the scale in Cherry's bathroom, so I steered clear of fitted clothes it would depress me
to try on and headed for the jewelry counter.

Rows of sparklies tempted me, and I found myself trying
on earrings and bracelets and necklaces. On sale, they weren't
any of them more than a hundred dollars. Letting them drip
through my fingers made me feel better, helping me forget
how stupid I'd been to sleep with Les and the humiliation of
getting arrested. I particularly liked a pair of drop earrings
set with Swarovski crystals in pink, yellow, and blue. I didn't
have anything to wear them with, but I was sure I could find
something in the cocktail dress section. As I was headed to
the cashier with the earrings and matching bracelet in hand,
I thought about what Albertine would say, and my footsteps
slowed. The earrings weren't on my financial diet. Scrunching my eyes closed, I practically flung them back at the display and dialed Albertine's number.

"Help!" I squawked when she answered.

"Gigi?"

"I'm in Macy's."

"Get out now," Albertine commanded. "Don't touch anything. I'll meet you in the food court in ten minutes."

"Thanks." Hanging up, I almost giggled at how much she'd
sounded like a 911 operator giving instructions to someone
reporting a fire. *Get out of the house. Don't go back for anything.* Still smiling, I made it out of the store without checking
a single price tag or running my hands down a silky blouse or

fuzzy sweater and marched the few steps to the food court without ducking into any other stores. To reward myself, I drifted to the new Baskin-Robbins counter and ordered a scoop of jamoca almond fudge ice cream. Only one scoop, and in a cup, not a cone, so I wouldn't blow my diet. I got Albertine a cup of mint chocolate chip, which I knew she liked.

As I was paying, Albertine arrived in a swirl of scarlet and gold caftan that she definitely hadn't found in Chapel Hills Mall, and I handed her the cup and a spoon. She looked from her ice cream to mine and burst out laughing, a rich sound that made several people look around and smile. "Gigi, you are something else," she said.

"What?"

"You did good to call me." She spooned up some ice cream as we settled at one of the tables.

"Thanks for coming."

"You didn't buy anything, did you? Because if you did, you can take it right back." She peeked under the table, looking for shopping bags.

I shook my head. "Nope. Just the ice cream."

"Good. That's progress. Come on. It's the lunch rush and I've got to get back. I'm walking you out of here, though, to make sure you get out safely. And you're coming down to the restaurant after work to tell me what triggered this."

"Okay," I said meekly, licking the last of the coffee-flavored ice cream off my spoon and putting the cup in the trash.

We parted in the parking lot, and Albertine watched until I made it through the mall exit to Briargate Boulevard.

. . .

Dexter's BMW was in the garage when I got home, and I found him in the kitchen, glugging orange juice from the container. Nolan greeted me with shrill yips of joy and demanded to be let into the yard, which made me wonder if Kendall had remembered to let him out before she left for school.

"Dexter—"

Without answering, he put the juice carton back in the fridge and slouched past me, probably planning to disappear into his bedroom or meet up with some of his friends at the mall.

"Thank you very, very much for driving Charlie to Aspen, honey," I said, reaching out to brush a strand of hair off his forehead. He shook his head like a horse getting rid of flies, and my hand dropped. "I'm sorry you had to miss school. I called your principal and explained the situation. Well, I didn't tell them I was in jail, of course, but I said there was a family situation and—"

"So you saw Dad," Dexter interrupted.

I shot him an uncertain look. "For a little bit."

"I suppose he's going back to South America soon?" Dexter gazed straight ahead. "Did he mention if he might stop by . . . Never mind."

"Oh, honey—" I reached over to touch his shoulder.

"It doesn't matter," Dex said, shrugging my hand away.

I was as mad at Les right then as I've ever been, and mad at myself for falling into bed with him—not that we'd used a bed—instead of kicking him in the balls like he deserved.

. . .

After showering off the jail stink, I styled my hair, put on makeup, and began to feel a bit more cheerful. Right up until I remembered Les and the way he'd walked out on me again. Disappeared. Maybe I should give Heather-Anne her money back and tell her she was better off without him. I was angry with myself for getting my hopes up. I should know better by now. Finding the happiest sweater in my drawer—a lemon yellow angora blend with purple pansies embroidered on it that was long enough to cover my behind—I pulled it on, then had to redo my hair. Then, since it was only about one o'clock, I called good-bye to Dex (who didn't answer) and drove to Swift Investigations.

I listened to the messages off the answering machine and called everybody back. I hated having to tell the people who wanted us to find lost pets that we didn't do that kind of detecting, but Charlie flat-out refused to look for pets. "No one will take us seriously as investigators," she said, "if we spend all our time hunting for Fido and Fluffy." I gave the unhappy pet owners the Humane Society's number and suggested they consider microchipping.

After the pet owners—there were two of them today—I called a man who wanted us to find his runaway teenaged daughter and set up an appointment with him. I offered to meet him that very afternoon, but he said she'd already been gone three months and he wasn't canceling his tee time for an appointment with me. Next week would do fine, he said. I started to tell him that if it was my Kendall gone missing I'd be out there looking for her morning, noon, and night till she was safe at home again, but I remembered in time that Charlie thinks it makes potential clients irritable when we say things like that. Once I'd typed the appointment onto the calendar, I looked around, not sure what else to do. Charlie had finished off the background checks for Danner and Lansky, so I decided to drive those down to the law firm. After that, I returned to the office and made the call I'd been putting off: I phoned Heather-Anne to give her an update.

I hoped she wouldn't be in her room and I could leave a message. She picked up on the first ring.

"This is Gigi," I said, "from Swift—"

"I know who you are, Gigi, for God's sake. Have you found him?"

"Well . . ." I told her about tracking Les down in Aspen and talking to him briefly. I didn't mention sleeping with him, although I wanted to, or the police arresting me for breaking into Cherry and Moss's.

"So you chatted with him a bit and then he disappeared—poof!—like Glinda the Good Witch?" Heather-Anne sounded annoyed and skeptical both.

"Um, yes."

"Of all the incompetent— What are you going to do now?"

Ooh, good question. "We have other leads we're following," I said, reciting the line Charlie gives folks when she's completely stumped. "I'm sure we'll pick up his trail"—that made us sound like hounds on the scent of a possum—"in a day or so."

"That's too long," Heather-Anne snapped. "Tomorrow is—"

When she didn't finish, I asked, "Tomorrow is what?"

"Important."

I thought she was hiding something. "Why?"

She sighed like I'd pushed her to the limit. "If you must know, it's the anniversary of our first date. I didn't want to have to say that, given that you were married to him at the time, but—"

I hung up. My hands trembled and I clasped them together. I was not going to cry; tears would melt mascara all over my face, and I'd end up looking like a rabid raccoon. Then, ashamed of my rudeness, I dialed her back and got a busy signal. Maybe she was still spilling the details of their first date, not realizing I'd hung up. I called again and asked the hotel operator to connect me with voice mail, where I left a very nice message about being sorry we got cut off and promising to be in touch as soon as I had more information. Nasty task completed, I locked the office and headed down to Albertine's. I needed a drink.

Albertine's sits at the far end of the strip mall from Swift Investigations, and it's the cutest little place; it brings back memories of the one and only time I was in New Orleans for Mardi Gras. I went with my friend Lacey and her brother the year after I graduated from high school, while I was still at beauty school and before I met Les. I still have some of the green and gold beads the Mardi Gras king and queen tossed from the float, and I can still remember throwing up in an alley behind some bar after Lacey's brother bought me one too many Southern Comfort and Cokes. Mostly, Albertine's smells like New Orleans, all shrimpy and spicy, although it sounds like New Orleans, too, with Dixieland-type jazz playing in the background and a live combo on Saturday nights. It was crowded at happy hour on a Friday evening, and I was happy for Albertine, who'd been wondering before Christmas if she might have to close up. Of course, Mardi Gras was coming up on Tuesday, so that might explain some of the crowd.

Albertine saw me come in and motioned me to a stool at the bar. By the time I got there, she had a chartreuse margaritatini, her special concoction, poured into a sugar-rimmed glass and garnished with a lime wedge. Yum. Sinking gratefully onto the stool, I took a long drink and licked my lips.

Albertine smiled widely. "Now, what was that almost shopping spree this morning about?"

"I got arrested," I said, finishing off the drink in record time and licking sugar from the rim.

"Say what?" Albertine's eyes bugged out, and she pulled up a stool on her side of the bar and summoned one of the waiters to take her place at the cash register. Enjoying having such a wild tale to tell, I told her about tracking Les to Aspen, finding him at Cherry and Moss's, and getting arrested the following morning. I left out the bits that happened after the Scotch and before the cops arrived. She exclaimed at all the right places and insisted on seeing my photo of Charlie Sheen's jail cell. Then she fetched us both another drink, studying me closely as I sucked on the lime wedge.

"Oh, no," she said, narrowing her eyes till I could see the silvery apricot shadow on her lids. "Oh, no, you didn't."

"Didn't what?" I could feel myself blushing, so I lowered my head to sip from the margaritatini.

"You did! You slept with that no-good louse who tossed you aside like last week's newspaper—and for that blond bee-otch."

I bit my lip.

Noticing that she had attracted attention from the two

thirty-something men on the stools beside me, Albertine scowled at them and lowered her voice. "What were you thinking?"

"Well, there was Scotch. I never thought I liked it, but I was cold and scared—that was because of Knievel jumping on me—and then Les—"

Albertine held up a hand. "I don't want to hear it, girl-friend."

"But you asked!"

"I asked what you were *thinking,* but it's clear you weren't." Albertine balled her hands on her hips. Her bangles clinked. "I'm going to call Charlie right now so we can stage an inter-vention."

"No, don't!" I put a hand on her arm, even though she hadn't reached for her phone. "Charlie doesn't know, and be-lieve me, it's not going to happen again. I am totally and com-pletely over Lester Goldman." I made myself think of how bad I'd felt this morning when I found he'd disappeared in the night, and how mad I was that he'd hurt Dexter again.

Apparently, it worked, because Albertine's face lost its stern expression and she said, "Are you okay, Gigi?"

I sniffled and drained my second margaritatini. "Um-hm. Peachy."

"You shouldn't be okay. You should be mad. M-A-D . . . mad." Albertine scowled.

"I'm angry that Dexter's all—"

"Not mad for the kids, Gigi—mad for you."

"I can't blow up at him, Albertine. I've got the kids to think about. Les is still their daddy, and he and I . . . we need to get along so that Kendall and Dex aren't . . . don't end up in therapy for years. Dr. Phil says kids can think it's their fault when parents divorce. It's not all Les's fault . . ."

"Say what? The man cheats on you, steals from his partners, and boogies off to Costa Rica in the dead of night and it's not his fault?"

"Sounds like his fault to me," offered the total stranger on my right.

I stared at him, and he gave me a friendly smile over the lip of his martini glass.

"This is a private conversation, Nico," Albertine told him. "Do you mind?" He grinned at her, obviously a regular, and wandered off to join a group near the window. After studying me for a moment, Albertine relaxed against the stool back. "Well, okay then. I can see that we need to find you a new man, a rebound fling, to help you move on."

She swiveled to survey the room, and for one dreadful moment I thought she was going to beckon Nico back. My heart seized up, but she was only watching her waitstaff to make sure they were doing a good job. When she turned back to me, I said apologetically, "I'm not really the fling type." Besides, what man was going to be interested in a chubby, earlyfifties, former stay-at-home mom who was so uninteresting her husband ran off to Costa Rica with a blond bimbo?

"We can fix that," Albertine said confidently.

I didn't know whether to be encouraged or scared.

10

~mn~

Saturday morning, after a brisk walk on the Santa Fe Trail, which ran behind her property and which was frequented by bikers, joggers, and walkers, even on a brisk February morning with the path mucky from melted snow, Charlie decided she needed a plan of attack for making headway on the Les Goldman case. With Les playing least-in-sight after giving Gigi the slip, their client, who had apparently sprung fully formed into existence when she arrived in Colorado Springs two-plus years ago, was the natural source of more information. After giving brief consideration to following Heather-Anne, Charlie decided a full-frontal assault would be the best bet. Surveillance took too long and didn't guarantee results; in addition to which, she couldn't face the prospect of another day sitting on her ass in her car or the hotel lobby.

She dialed Heather-Anne's number at the Embassy Suites and introduced herself when the woman picked up.

"Charlotte Swift?" Heather-Anne's voice was wary. "What happened to Gigi?"

"She's still on the case," Charlie said reassuringly, "but we'll make progress quicker—which I understand is important to you—with both of us working it."

"That makes sense, I guess," Heather-Anne said. "Thank you."

"It would be helpful if we could talk."

"I already told Gigi everything I know."

"Sometimes you know things you don't realize you know. I won't take much of your time, maybe half an hour. If you could come to the office, or I could meet you—"

"I'm doing a training session for an old client," Heather-Anne said, a note of impatient acquiescence in her voice. "At the downtown YMCA. I need the money. I could talk to you after that."

"Great."

Arriving twenty minutes early for her ten o'clock meeting with Heather-Anne, Charlie parked the Subaru in the garage off Kiowa Street and showed her Y membership card to get in. Charlie tried the cardio area first, scanning the treadmills, stairsteppers, and spinning bikes for anyone who might be Heather-Anne. At least three women fit the description Gigi had given her: early thirties, slim, blond, tanned. None of them appeared to be guiding a client through a fitness routine.

Charlie made her way to the adjacent free weights area and immediately spotted her quarry. Heather-Anne, blond hair in a long ponytail, wore black bike shorts with green piping and a matching midriff-baring bra top that exposed a small gold ring in her navel and a significant amount of cleavage, much appreciated, apparently, by her client. From what Charlie could see, he was in his midsixties, portly, and gray-haired and had his gaze fixed on Heather-Anne's cleavage as she demonstrated dumbbell flies. Getting off the bench, she gestured for him to take her place and stood at the head of the bench as he began the exercise. He kept his head tilted back and his eyes on the trainer's taut, tanned midsection.

Charlie had deliberately worn a pair of blue sweats from her air force days and a long-sleeve T-shirt to blend in. To remain unobtrusive while keeping an eye on Heather-Anne, she selected light dumbbells from the rack and began a series of biceps curls. The pull in her muscles reminded her how out of shape she was since getting shot and made her vow to get back in the gym as soon as the doc gave her the all clear. As Heather-Anne directed her client to an exercise ball, Charlie moved to the lat pulldown machine near them, straining to overhear their conversation.

"It was a sad day when you disappeared last year," the client said with a roguish smile. "I hope you're back to stay."

"I didn't 'disappear,' Hollis," Heather-Anne said, her hands resting on his abs as she counted crunches. "I fell in love and moved to be with my sweetie. You've got to be willing to make sacrifices for true love."

Charlie was glad Gigi couldn't overhear the woman's saccharine tone. It was enough to make Charlie barf, and she hadn't been married to Les.

"I'd make sacrifices for someone like you," Hollis said, his face red with exertion.

Heather-Anne smiled flirtatiously. "Oh, Hollis. As a matter of fact . . ."

Hardly able to believe her ears, Charlie listened as Heather-Anne fed the smitten Hollis a story about needing a bit of money to tide her over since her car had been broken into and her wallet stolen from her hotel the previous night. An almost-sob, eyes that looked at Hollis like he was the only lifeguard in sight while she floundered in heavy seas surrounded by Great Whites, a flash of cleavage, and the man was trotting to the locker room to retrieve his checkbook. Charlie raised her brows, realizing she was watching an expert in action.

"Can I work in?"

Startled, Charlie released her grip on the bar, realizing she'd done at least fifty reps while listening to Heather-Anne milk the unsuspecting Hollis, to find a young man motioning to the lat pulldown machine. "I'm done," she said, sliding out from under the thigh pads.

Having learned enough, Charlie exited the Y and returned to her car, loosing her hair from its ponytail and shaking it around her face to change her looks somewhat before meeting Heather-Anne. She kept a duffel in the car full of hats, shirts, totes, and other items that made it easy to change her appearance while on surveillance, and she pulled a red hoodie from her stash. Looking in the rearview mirror, she finger-combed her bangs down onto her forehead, added a flick of mascara and a slick of red lipstick—purely for disguise purposes—and left the car to meet her client.

Standing at the corner of Kiowa and Tejon where they'd agreed to meet, Charlie felt the wind bite through her thin sweats and smelled the familiar downtown scent, a mix of exhaust, coffee from a nearby diner, and wet cement from the damp sidewalks. Saturday shoppers strolled past, studying the wares in boutique windows, and a panhandler worked the corner of Acacia Park across the street. Dark clouds snagged on the mountain peaks to the west promised precipitation later. Charlie hoped for snow; winter rain was too damn depressing.

On the thought, she caught sight of Heather-Anne making her way down the sidewalk from the Y, a windbreaker protecting her torso from the cold, but her long shapely legs still bare. She looked pleased with herself, tossing her honey-colored hair back from her face and smiling a feline smile as she approached the corner. When she was within earshot, Charlie stepped forward, hand outstretched. The younger woman reared back, and fright flared in her eyes. Charlie got the distinct impression that she was planning to run.

"I'm Charlie Swift," she said quickly. "You're Heather-Anne Pawlusik, right?"

Heather-Anne recovered swiftly, running her fingers through her hair. "Oh. Yes. I was expecting someone older, taller." She appraised Charlie through narrowed eyes.

Wondering why the woman had spooked so easily, Charlie said, "Do you want to get a coffee?" She nodded toward a Starbucks.

"No. I miss the cold. Costa Rica's so damned hot all the time. Let's sit in the park." Without waiting for Charlie's reply, Heather-Anne started across the street. Charlie caught up with her, and they found a bench across from the empty bandshell that hosted open-air concerts in the summer. Now a colony of pigeons huddled beneath it, purple and gray feathers fluffed against the cold.

"So," Heather-Anne said, "you said you needed more information. I suppose you don't really trust Gigi to do the job right." She finished with a little laugh.

Charlie was conscious of a surprising surge of anger on her partner's behalf. True, she hadn't wanted to share the business with Gigi, but she was learning quicker than Charlie had thought she would, and she had become quite competent with computer searches. Her stream-of-consciousness thought process frequently led her to data that Charlie would never have uncovered with her more linear approach. It galled Charlie that this snot-nosed thirty-year-old was making fun of the woman whose husband she stole. "On the contrary," Charlie said, careful not to let her anger show. "Gigi's very sensitive to nuances in interviews."

"Really?" Heather-Anne looked unconvinced. "So, what else do you need to know?"

"I'm not sure anyone knows exactly how much money Les embezzled from his various business interests. Was it enough for him to retire on or was he working somewhere?"

Heather-Anne didn't seem offended by Charlie's reference to her lover's criminal activities; indeed, she smiled proudly. "Oh, he made more than enough to retire. More than enough. He works at managing his money, you might say."

"I need help understanding something," Charlie said with an air of bewilderment. "He's got a beautiful girlfriend, plenty of money, no family responsibilities . . . no man would walk away from that without a damned good reason. I have to conclude that something scared him away. What was it?"

Heather-Anne blinked once, slowly. "You're smarter than he said you were. I think his investment in Swift Investigations was a better move than he realized."

"Save the flattery for your marks, Heather-Anne," Charlie

said, pleased to see she'd finally startled the other woman, who looked reflexively over her shoulder as if Hollis were standing behind her. "Or is it even Heather-Anne?"

The younger woman stilled, an animal freezing at the sudden appearance of a predator. Only a strand of hair moved, teased by the wind, catching at the corner of her mouth. She finally brushed it away. "What's that supposed to mean?"

Her voice was harder, older than before, and Charlie was intrigued to see that she didn't rush off in an offended huff. *She wants to find out how much I know,* Charlie thought.

"It means," Charlie said calmly, "that I couldn't find any trace of Heather-Anne Pawlusik before you turned up in Colorado Springs two years ago. Either your entire history's been erased, or you didn't exist before moving here."

Tears sprang to Heather-Anne's eyes. "If you could figure that out, so can he. He'll find me." Her lips parted, and fear crinkled her smooth forehead.

"Who? Les?"

"No, my husband."

Charlie eyed her client doubtfully. "Your husband?"

Heather-Anne nodded. "I left him four years ago. He was . . . is violent, obsessed. I had to leave before he killed me. I drifted from small town to small town in the South, waiting tables, babysitting, doing other jobs where I got paid under the table so I wouldn't leave a money trail. I came here with a boyfriend, and when he moved on, I decided to stay."

Heather-Anne's eyes searched Charlie's face. "I liked it here, thought it was far enough away that he wouldn't find me easily. I thought I was safe here. And I was. I changed my name, got my personal trainer certification, built a new life.

Then I met Les, and I began to think that I could love again, that I could trust again."

The B-movie dialogue was making Charlie nauseous. "Oh, cut the crap, Heather-Anne. You saw a meal ticket."

"You're wrong," Heather-Anne said with quiet dignity. Charlie couldn't tell if she was sincere or acting. "I love Les. He's my soul mate."

Charlie could believe that, given that Les had embezzled from people who trusted him, and Heather-Anne—if her performance with Hollis was anything to go by—was adept at separating men from their money . . . and their wives. Neither one had more conscience than your average anaconda.

The panhandler had made his way around the park and now hovered within arm's reach, his ripe smell drifting toward the bench. For the first time, Charlie noticed a small mutt hovering close to the man's leg. With a sigh—she never knew if she was helping someone or enabling an alcohol or drug addiction—she handed him a five, responded to his nod of acknowledgment with a small smile, and turned back to Heather-Anne when he was out of earshot. "What's your real name?" Charlie asked, "and what does your history have to do with Les's disappearance?"

Heather-Anne hesitated. "Cindy," she said. "Lucinda Cheney. I—I wasn't exactly up front with Les about my situation," she confessed, bowing her head so Charlie couldn't read her face. "He found . . . he found some letters, some documents from my life before. He was hurt, angry. I didn't blame him." She looked up so Charlie could see the anguish and sincerity in her face.

Oscarworthy, Charlie thought. "So, you're saying—?"

"We fought. He accused me of lying to him, said our whole relationship was a sham. I told him I loved him, that my feelings were real."

Charlie rolled her eyes, but Heather-Anne, caught up in her story, didn't notice. "He said he needed some time alone to think things through. I thought he meant an afternoon, an evening, something like that. I went to the beach to give him some space. I spent the afternoon there, just walking, thinking, crying. When I came home, he was gone. No note. Nothing. I didn't know where he'd gone, if he was planning to come back . . . nothing." She held her empty hands out, palms up, as if to demonstrate "nothing."

"So you came here. Why?"

Heather-Anne—Charlie had trouble thinking of her as Cindy—twisted a strand of hair between two fingers. "I thought it was possible he'd come back to Gigi. He was fond of her, you know. Or to see his kids."

Personally, Charlie thought it unlikely that a man who hadn't given his kids a thought in over a year and couldn't be bothered to pay his child support was going to return to his spurned wife and alienated kids after a spat with his new honey. She pulled out a small notebook. "Right. Well, you'll forgive me if I take everything you've said with a grain of salt until I can find some proof. Where did you live before leaving your husband, and what is his name?"

Heather-Anne pulled back with a frown. "I can't tell you that! You'll make inquiries and he'll hear about it. He'll know why and he'll find me. You have no idea what he can do. Look, I paid you to find Les, not to tear my life apart. If that's too much for you to handle, give me my money back and I'll hire a PI firm that wants my business." She held out her hand as if expecting Charlie to count bills into it on the spot.

Charlie studied the younger woman, sure she wasn't telling the whole truth but uncertain where the lies lay. "We're still hunting for Les," she said, "and Gigi's your best shot at finding him fast. She tracked him to Aspen, after all."

"Yeah, and let him give her the slip," Heather-Anne said with asperity. She tossed back her hair with a head jerk.

"Let's come at this another way," Charlie suggested, putting her cold hands between her thighs to warm them. "Les embezzled from a lot of people on his way out of town, and maybe long before that, for all I know. Was anyone particularly mad at him?"

Heather-Anne gave her a disbelieving look.

"I said 'particularly,'" Charlie emphasized. "I'm sure he generated hate mail on a Bernie Madoff level, but is there anyone who stands out? Anyone who threatened him with something more specific than 'I could kill you, you scum-sucking, lower-than-snail-shit slimeball'?"

Heather-Anne was nodding before Charlie finished. "Patrick Dreiser. He and Les were partners in a vending machine company. He had to declare bankruptcy when Les left. His wife left him, and his son had to quit Stanford to get a job. He blamed Les. If he'd had adequate financial controls in place, Les wouldn't have been able to do what he did," she added self-righteously. "That's what Les says."

The old "blame the victim for making someone kill/rape/ rob him" technique. "What did Dreiser do?"

Voice dropping to a whisper, Heather-Anne leaned in. "He threatened to hurt Les's kids, Kendra and Darryl."

"Kendall and Dexter."

"Whatever. The point is, he sent Les this e-mail with photos that were . . ." Heather-Anne shuddered and Charlie got the impression that, for the first time, the woman was sincere. Her horror was genuine. "Who could threaten to do that to kids?"

"What steps did Les take to protect them? Did he tell the police? Warn Gigi?" Gigi had certainly never mentioned such threats to Charlie, but maybe it had happened before she joined Swift Investigations.

Heather-Anne looked baffled. "He couldn't call the police—they would've arrested him! It all came to nothing because Dreiser realized—"

She cut herself off, but Charlie finished for her. "Dreiser realized Les didn't give a damn about his kids, so threatening them wasn't going to get him what he wanted." Not giving Heather-Anne a chance to reply, she asked, "What did Dreiser want?"

"His money back, of course. A couple million and change. Plus ten percent for 'mental anguish.'"

Charlie whistled softly. If Les had made off with two mil from one business, he must have made a total haul of over ten million. No wonder he thought Swift Investigations was small peanuts, not worth embezzling from. Eight figures would finance quite a nice lifestyle in Costa Rica, she imagined, and made it all the more unlikely that he would willingly return to a country where police slavered to arrest him, prosecutors panted at the prospect of tossing him in jail, and defrauded victims waited their chance to boil him in oil.

Heather-Anne stood and twisted to pick up her gym bag. Charlie could see slat marks from the bench imprinted against the back of her bare thighs. "I've got to go—another training appointment. With Les gone, things are a little tight for me." She grimaced. "So, I'll hear from you soon?"

"Absolutely," Charlie said. She watched Heather-Anne sashay out of the park, highlighted hair riffling in the breeze, bare legs drawing appreciative looks from every man within eyeshot. Like trout watching a glittery lure, she thought, making her way back to her car. She wondered if the men Heather-Anne reeled in ever even knew they'd been hooked.

11

Sunday morning, I showed up at the Embassy Suites hotel for a meeting I hadn't known about with Heather-Anne. She had called my cell last night and left a voice mail, but I'd dropped into bed early after a day of shuttling Kendall to skating practice and convincing Dexter to work on his biology project. Spiders, and I'd even helped him catch some in the basement—ugh! I'd also had to move money from my shrinking savings account to pay the utilities bill, which was twice as large as usual due to my leaving the gas grill on accidentally after barbecuing on an unusually nice day in mid-January. I dreamed about being on a Mexican beach, probably because Albertine had suggested we go there when we were giggling about the ideal man for a postdivorce fling after our third margaritatini Friday night. I was holding out for George Clooney, but Albertine insisted Jimmy Smits was sexier. Albertine thought maybe having a fling would be easier if we headed to Cabo or Acapulco over spring break, but my checking account wasn't up to that, even though a girls' weekend with Albertine would've been fun. Sun, sea, shopping, tropical drinks with little umbrellas. It sounded divine.

I hadn't checked my messages until morning, and Heather-Anne hadn't answered when I called back, so I was running late when I arrived at the Embassy Suites. They were hosting a huge art sale, promising "Original Works of Art for Under $99," and I saw several paintings I liked as I wove through the clumps of people looking at stacked canvases. How was I ever going to find Heather-Anne in this crowd? I craned my neck, looking over the heads of the shoppers, and saw a four-foot-square painting of sunflowers in yellows, oranges, and bright blues that would have looked wonderful on the wall above my sofa. I moved toward it before remembering my mission. Maybe Heather-Anne meant for me to meet her in her room? I listened to the message again.

"I heard from Les. We need to talk. My hotel, nine A.M. tomorrow."

Since it was already ten past nine, I headed toward her room. The crowd noise petered out as I walked down the hall. A maid passed me, pushing a vacuum cleaner, and an elderly couple blocked my path as they hauled six or eight bags out of their room on a luggage dolly. I helped them get it pointed down the hall. "They're so awkward to maneuver, aren't they?" I asked, and the old man agreed with a nod, trying to press a tip into my hand.

By the time I made it to Heather-Anne's room, it was almost nine twenty, and I was worried that she'd be mad I was so late. The door was resting against the jamb, like someone hadn't closed it firmly. I left hotel doors like that when I went to fetch ice. Did Heather-Anne expect me to just walk in? I couldn't do that. I tapped on the door. No response.

"Heather-Anne," I called softly. "It's me, Gigi." I shifted from foot to foot. My Joan and David boots pinched. When the door still didn't open, I knocked louder, then leaned my head toward it to see if I could hear anything. Faint voices sounded from within. Had Les shown up? I pressed my ear against the door, trying to hear what they were saying. Scrunching my toes in the boots, I lost my balance and banged against the door, which popped open. I fell into the room with a thud.

I lay flat on the floor for a few seconds, winded, before pushing to my knees. This was more embarrassing than the time my bathing suit top came untied at the Fassendilbers' pool party. "I am so sorry, Heather-Anne, I didn't mean—" I stopped as I straightened up and realized no one was in the sitting room area. An old *Quincy* rerun played softly on the television.

"Heather-Anne?" I inched farther into the room. "The door was open, so I—" I wasn't about to go into the bedroom. What if Les really was here and they were . . . ? I sidestepped to my left so I could see through the open door. I squeaked.

Heather-Anne Pawlusik lay on the floor, her head by the door, a spangly scarf pulled so tightly around her throat that her face was blotchy and swollen. Her eyes, her tongue . . . The gruesome details hit me like someone was driving nails into my eyes and I screamed.

An answering scream sounded from just behind me, and I whirled, screaming again when I came face-to-face with a round-cheeked maid holding a pile of towels. She shrieked again and crossed herself awkwardly around the towels. We took turns screaming for another couple of seconds before the maid looked past me and screamed louder. *"Está muerta. Asesina!"*

I didn't speak Spanish—well, not more than it took to ask for the *baño*—but her expression made me think she'd just called me an assassin. Which was plain silly because—

"You keeled her!" she clarified, stabbing a finger toward Heather-Anne. "Dead!"

"Yes, she's— No! I didn't—" The maid turned and fled, dropping the towels, before I could tell her I hadn't killed Heather-Anne.

"Why did you tell Ms. Herrera that you killed Ms. Pawlusik if you didn't?" the detective asked. She was tall, skinny, and skeptical in a blue-gray suit that flattered her pale complexion and reddish hair. We were in an unoccupied suite at the hotel, four doors away from Heather-Anne's room, and herds of police and hotel officials were coming and going. They'd made me sit in this room by myself for more than an hour with a cop watching me from one of the dinette chairs. I was tired and scared and had already cried so many times I knew I must have a mascara trail down to my chin. Poor Heather-Anne!

"I didn't tell her that," I insisted, rubbing my feet together. I wished I could take off the painful boots, but I couldn't imagine being interrogated by the police in my stocking feet. "I just agreed with her that Heather-Anne was dead."

Detective Lorrimore cocked an eyebrow and I got the feeling she didn't believe me. "'Heather-Anne?' So you had a relationship with the victim?"

"I knew her, if that's what you mean," I said. "She was a client."

"A client?"

"I'm a private investigator."

"Really?" Disbelief sent her eyebrows soaring.

I couldn't much blame her for that reaction; I'm sure most PIs don't dissolve into puddles of tears when they find a dead body. "Yes. She hired us to find her—" How did I describe her relationship to Les? "Her boyfriend," I said.

At the mention of a possibly estranged boyfriend, the detective perked up and readied her pen over her notepad. "His name?"

"Lester Goldman."

Detective Lorrimore started to write, then stopped, staring at me from under her brows. "Didn't you say your name was Goldman?"

Her eyes narrowed in suspicion, and I knew where she was going. I felt like I was sinking in quicksand. "Do you know Detective Connor Montgomery?" I asked in desperation. He was a homicide detective who was a friend of Charlie's, and I'd met him several times.

"Montgomery? Wait a minute . . . Do you work for Charlie Swift?"

"We're partners."

"You're the one that set fire to the Buff Burgers last year, right? And blew up the meth lab?"

"I didn't—" Before I could explain what really happened in both those cases, she was gesturing to a uniformed cop and whispering something to him. They both laughed. Keeping her eyes on me, Lorrimore dialed a number on her cell. "Montgomery. Get your ass down to the Embassy Suites. Your girlfriend's partner turned up in a hotel room with a homicide victim." She flipped her phone closed, leaned her shoulders against the wall, and folded her arms across her chest. "Oh, this is going to be good."

Her smile made me uneasy. I couldn't decide whether to worry about ending up in jail for the second time in two days or what Charlie would say if she heard someone refer to her as Montgomery's girlfriend.

12

~wm~

"'Girlfriend' is a revolting term," Charlie said some hours later, pointing the business end of her grout trowel at Detective Connor Montgomery to emphasize her point. "It's Barbie and Ken. Middle school." She slapped more grout onto the tile and smoothed it with rapid, angry strokes.

"Would you rather I referred to you as my lover?" He was behind her, but she could hear the lazy smile in his voice.

"But I'm not."

"Yet."

His certainty sent tingly warmth from her midsection to her extremities, and she had to re-grip the trowel after a moment's pause. "Don't count your chickens," she recommended.

He laughed. Glad that the hair falling around her face hid her expression, Charlie pretended to concentrate on her tiling, deliberately not looking up to see how his lean face lit up when he laughed, how his brown eyes warmed. With his dark hair and tall, athletic body, he reminded her of the actor Clive Owen, only with a better sense of humor.

When he spoke again, his voice was serious. "It's not looking good for Gigi."

Charlie swiveled her head to stare at him. "You can't seriously believe that Gigi would—could—plan and carry off a murder."

Montgomery helped himself to a beer from the fridge; surprisingly, Charlie didn't resent his familiarity. Her lack of resentment worried her.

"Plan? Probably not. Strangle her in the heat of the moment . . . The woman stole Gigi's husband, Charlie. That sounds like a pretty good motive to me. Gigi's a large woman, strong; she could have overpowered Pawlusik physically."

"I don't think it's Pawlusik," Charlie said, standing, rubbing her ass absently, and crossing to the sink to wash grout off her hands. When Montgomery arched his eyebrows, she explained how she'd tried to check out Heather-Anne's background and come up with a blank. "When I called her on it—"

"Why am I not surprised?" The hiss of air escaping the bottle as he twisted the cap accompanied his comment.

"—she said her name was really Lucinda Cheney and she was on the run from an abusive husband. She wouldn't give me his name or tell me where she'd been living, although she mentioned traveling through the South. My guess? Cheney isn't her real name, either."

"Lorrimore will track down her real identity through fingerprints," he said. At Charlie's questioning look, he said, "It's not my case. Conflict of interest. Everyone knows you and I are—" Charlie's baleful look made him reconsider his word choice—"whatever we are. Gigi works for you—with you—so I'm out of the loop."

"You must still know—"

"Uh-uh. It's strictly by the book on this one, Charlie. I can't give you anything. No lab results, no autopsy findings, no hints about what Lorrimore's thinking. She's a good cop. She'll get to the truth without your help."

He gave the final word an ironic twist, and Charlie stuck out her tongue. His hand flashed out, snagged her around the waist, and pulled her hard against the length of him. Before she could even think about breaking free, he'd pressed a hard kiss on her lips. When he would have pulled back, she stopped him with her hands on his face, and the kiss deepened. It was several minutes before they broke apart, both breathing heavily. Montgomery's gaze fell to Charlie's swollen lips, and his eyes glittered. "We could—"

"Uh-uh." She turned away, trying to regain her composure as she tucked her T-shirt back into her painter's overalls. "There's work to do."

"You don't even have a case anymore," Montgomery said, coming up behind her and wrapping his arms around her. "Your client's dead."

"That may be," Charlie said, disentangling herself reluctantly, "but she paid us in advance to find Les, and if Lorrimore suspects Gigi had a hand in Heather-Anne's death, Les may be the only one who can prove otherwise."

"How?" Montgomery accepted defeat, let his arms drop, and returned to his beer.

"He can testify that Heather-Anne had a deranged husband after her. Reasonable doubt. He can explain why he decamped from Costa Rica and ended up in Aspen. You know"—she paused, furrowing her brow—"we don't even know for sure that Heather-Anne was the intended victim."

"What, someone mistook her for someone else? Come on, Charlie."

"No. She said one of the men Les cheated threatened to hurt his kids. Maybe Heather-Anne's murder is a message to Les."

"Thin."

Charlie rounded on him. "My partner's a murder suspect. I'm going to do what it takes to clear her." Her own vehemence and concern for Gigi startled her. She hadn't wanted Gigi as a partner, but the woman was growing on her. Damn it. "Because it reflects badly on Swift Investigations, of course, to have one of the partners on trial," she added loftily. "It's bad for business."

"Of course."

89

The amused understanding in Montgomery's voice made her want to hit him. Or kiss him. Or . . . She shooed him out the door, beer bottle in hand, so she could get to work.

13

~~~~

I wasn't under arrest. That happy thought bounced through my brain as I drove home from the Embassy Suites Sunday afternoon. That didn't mean the police wouldn't change their minds and nab me any minute. Detective Lorrimore had talked to me for what seemed like hours, going over the same questions again and again, like I was going to change my story the eighteenth time I told it. I knew she wanted to put me in jail and throw away the key. I'd been relieved when Charlie's friend, Detective Montgomery, had stopped by and dragged Lorrimore into the hall for a few minutes. I'd tiptoed to the door, hoping to overhear something, and been embarrassed when a uniformed cop came through the door while I had my ear pressed against it. The officer almost knocked me on my fanny, and the door bruised my forehead. Looking in the rearview mirror, I tried to arrange my hair to cover the bruise. A horn blared beside me, and I jerked the Hummer's wheel so I ended up back in my own lane, giving the scowling woman an apologetic smile.

Passing the exit for Fillmore, I suddenly realized I didn't

want to go home. I wanted to talk to Charlie. Whipping the Hummer toward the exit, I waved guiltily at the two lanes' worth of people honking at me. A quick left on Fillmore and another left into the merge lane had me headed north on I-25 again within minutes. I got off at Woodmen and worked my way back toward Charlie's house. A couple of police cars and a few news vans sat outside the Embassy Suites, and I ducked down in the seat as I passed it.

"Glad to see you're not getting fitted for an orange jump-suit," Charlie greeted me when I ding-donged.

"Orange is so not my color," I said. "I can*not* go to prison. What would the kids do?" Kendall would probably move in with her friend Angel, and they'd become groupies, following that band they were obsessed with around the country. She'd never finish high school and would end up shacked up with some loser in Schenectady or Amarillo when the drummer tossed her aside like a used Kleenex, penniless and alone in a strange town. Dexter might well end up in the jail cell next to mine for doing something dangerous and stupid with his dangerous and stupid friends. I sighed.

Charlie beckoned me in, and I followed her through to the kitchen. She grabbed two Pepsis from the fridge, tossed one to me, and led me back to the living room. I flopped into her oversized armchair, thinking that the earth-toned decor was nice but a little dull. Maybe I'd get her a yellow wall clock or a colorful mobile for her birthday. I'd seen one in shades of bright purple and lime at the Fine Arts Center gift shop last week. Thinking about it made me realize I didn't know when Charlie's birthday was. "Charlie, when's—"

She interrupted me. "What did the police say?"

I ran through it, taking great gulps of the Pepsi and wishing it were hot cocoa with plenty of whipped cream on top. "So they finally let me go, but I know that Detective Lorrimore suspects me," I finished. "What did Detective Montgomery say?"

"That he can't tell me anything." Charlie looked annoyed. Her dark bangs flopped in her eyes, and she flipped them out of the way impatiently. "He doesn't think you murdered Heather-Anne, though."

"He said that?" The thought pleased me.

"No, but he's sharp enough to realize that you couldn't pull off . . . that is, that you would never kill anyone."

"You were going to say I'm not capable of planning a murder, weren't you?" I don't know why the thought riled me, but it did. I could kill someone!

"Not being a murderer is a good thing, Gigi," Charlie said. "Have you talked to a lawyer?"

"You think I need one?"

Her silence answered my question.

"The only lawyer I know is my divorce lawyer," I said morosely. "Considering how that turned out, I think I'd rather throw a dart at the Yellow Pages than call him."

Charlie laughed, and the sound surprised a smile out of me. She has a great laugh. "It won't matter," she said, "because we're going to track down Les and get to the root of this so that you won't need a lawyer. First, I'm going to talk to the people who knew Heather-Anne, or whatever her name was, when she lived here: her roommate, her co-workers. I need to get more of a feel for the woman. You need to get on the computer and find out what you can about Lucinda Cheney, which is what she said her real name was. I don't know where she lived, but she talked about the South, so start there."

I made notes, happy to have a plan of attack. "I'll think about where else Les might be, too," I said, "since he might know something about who would want to kill Heather-Anne." The look on Charlie's face startled me. It took me a moment, but then my eyes widened. "No. Oh, no, Charlie. He wouldn't."

She arched her brows skeptically. "He took up with a tramp, stole money from tons of people, dumped you, and abandoned his kids."

"That doesn't make him a murderer!"

She just said, "Who else would want Heather-Anne dead?"

The first thing that came to me—wives of the men she'd lured away—wasn't a good answer given that I was one of those wives. "Serial killer?"

Charlie gave me a look.

"The ex-husband that was after her!" I offered triumphantly. The more I thought about it, the better I liked that idea, mostly because it didn't involve me or Les.

"We don't even know that there really was a husband, ex or not. I wouldn't exactly bet my paycheck on Heather-Anne's truthfulness."

She didn't push it, but I could see that Les was her prime suspect. I was too tired to argue with her about it, and, truth to tell, I'd be happy to have the police looking at anybody besides me.

14

Charlie arrived at the downtown YMCA before eight o'clock on Monday morning. Her butt cheek was feeling much better; it didn't even twinge as her guide led her past elliptical machines being used by exercisers whose grim faces suggested they were working to repel a Communist invasion rather than a few fat cells. She scanned the room but didn't see Hollis, Heather-Anne's client from Saturday.

Her guide, a middle-aged woman with graying hair pulled back in a ponytail, knocked on an office door with a sign that read SANDRA SECHREST, DIRECTOR. She pushed it open to reveal a desk, two metal chairs with padded seats, and a doctor's-office-type scale. "Sandy, this is Charlotte Smith—"

"Swift."

"She's a detective, and she needs to talk to you about Heather-Anne Pawlusik." Curiosity vibrated in her voice.

"Thank you, Maureen," the woman said, rising. Charlie edged past Maureen, still blocking the doorway, to shake hands with the taller woman. In her early forties maybe, a few years older than Charlie, she had a distinct air of command; Charlie wouldn't have been surprised to learn the woman had been in the military before becoming the Y's director. She wore a blue YMCA golf shirt over close-fitting black slacks. Maureen hadn't budged, clearly interested in hearing what Charlie had to say about Heather-Anne, and

Sandy dislodged her with a "Close the door on your way out, Maureen."

As soon as the door clicked shut, she turned her narrowed gaze on Charlie. "Heather-Anne Pawlusik has not been employed by the YMCA for going on eight months now," she said, "so if there's a complaint—"

When the woman didn't finish her thought, Charlie prompted, "What kind of complaint would you expect?"

Sandy covered her discomfort by sitting behind her desk and motioning for Charlie to sit. As she did, she scanned the desk for clues to Sandy's interests, but the two framed photos faced inward, and the inspirational prints on the office were standard YMCA fare and had probably been there well before Sandy moved in. "Well. I just figured there must have been a complaint of some kind if the police were showing up to question a former employer."

Interesting, Charlie thought, that she would immediately assume a criminal complaint had been lodged against Heather-Anne. "I'm not with the police," she said, handing over her business card. Colorado didn't license PIs, so the best she could do for identification purposes was the card. "I'm a private investigator."

The YMCA director arched well-defined brows. "You're not a cop?"

Charlie shook her head. She wasn't above letting interviewees think she was a cop on occasion, but Sandy Sechrest struck her as the type to demand a badge before saying anything. Sandy rose again. "Then I'm afraid I can't talk to you." Her posture and expression made it clear she was inviting Charlie to leave.

Charlie relaxed into her chair—hard to do with its inhospitable metal back digging into her neck—to make it plain she wasn't leaving yet. "If I were a cop, what would you have told me?"

"Why is a private detective looking for Heather-Anne?" Sandy countered, admitting temporary defeat by sitting again. A small diamond on her left hand caught the light as she smoothed back her maple-syrup-colored hair.

No wonder she was slim, Charlie thought, with all that up and down. "I'm not looking for Heather-Anne. She's dead."

"What!" Sandy popped up again. "Dead? Who killed—? How—?"

"Why would you assume she was killed?" Charlie asked.

"I assumed . . . I mean, she's so young and healthy, so I assumed—" She sank back into her chair.

"You were right the first time," Charlie said. "Someone strangled her."

"Here? I mean, in Colorado Springs? I thought she'd moved on, gone to Belize or someplace. I'd never been more grateful to see the back of someone in my life." The shock of hearing about Heather-Anne's death was loosening Sandy's tongue.

"Costa Rica. Why were you glad she left?"

"Because—" Sandy's eyes narrowed as she assessed Charlie. "I really can't talk about an employee."

"Former employee," Charlie reminded her. "Dead former employee."

"Even so."

"Were you ever in the military?" Charlie asked.

"What does that have to do with anything?"

"I spent seven years in the air force, OSI. I just thought you might have served."

"Navy," Sandy admitted after a moment. "Five years. Pay-back for Annapolis."

"A grad, huh? I went the ROTC route. Why'd you leave?"

"I never intended to stay. I joined for the education, did my time, and donated my uniforms to the thrift shop without a single qualm. Six to nine months at sea, followed by a year or so in San Diego or Norfolk or the Pentagon, didn't have much appeal. I applied to the Naval Academy solely to get out of Liverpool. That's West Virginia, not England." Sandy whiffed out a sharp breath.

Just when Charlie was congratulating herself on the success of her "build rapport with the witness" strategy, Sandy stood again with a finality that told Charlie she was on the verge of eviction. "None of which has anything to do with the case at hand," Sandy said. "I can't talk about Heather-Anne or the pending litigation." Walking past Charlie to the door, she pulled it open.

Charlie rose stiffly and unconsciously rubbed at her hip. "Thanks for your time," she said, moving toward Sandy and offering her hand once again.

"What's wrong with your leg?" Sandy asked, sharp eyes assessing Charlie's gait.

"A bullet in my gluteus maximus," Charlie said, grinning slightly. "Or, as Forrest Gump would say, in my but-tock."

"I trained as a physical therapist after I left the navy," Sandy said. "Come back if you want help getting back in shape."

Charlie had no doubt Sandy Sechrest could run her into the ground. "Thanks," she said. "I just might do that."

She stepped into the hall, but a half-motion or a slight sound made her turn back to face Sandy Sechrest. After a brief hesitation, the woman said, "You might want to talk to Robyn. She was here when Heather-Anne was hired; I didn't arrive until almost a year after that."

"Thank you," Charlie said with real gratitude, recognizing that the Y director was trying to help her without compromising her organization. Employers needed to be cagey about releasing information about their employees for fear of lawsuits.

Robyn, apparently another personal trainer, was with a client but would be done in fifteen minutes, Maureen informed Charlie when she stopped at the front desk. Charlie jotted a quick note for Robyn and decided to wait for her outside. Propping her shoulders on the wall beside the exit door, Charlie gazed at the parking structure that held her Subaru and wondered what tack to take with Robyn. Clear skies and a brilliant sun added up to an almost springlike day, one of the things Charlie liked best about living in Colorado. Even though it could get bitterly cold, it didn't stay that way. It might snow three feet one day, but the sun would almost certainly pop out within a day or two, so you were never trapped at home for long, unlike spots in Minnesota or Michigan or the Dakotas where the snow might fall in late September and still be on the ground in May.

The door beside her squeaked open and a pair of businessmen exited, followed by a short, muscular woman wearing one of the ubiquitous blue golf shirts and a puzzled look. "Miss Swift? You wanted to talk to me?" She waved the note Charlie had left.

"Call me Charlie. You must be Robyn."

The woman jerked her head down once, setting brown corkscrew curls threaded with gray bouncing. "Is it true Heather-Anne's dead?"

Charlie nodded.

The older woman fidgeted, one hand tugging at her ear, the other fingering the YMCA name tag pinned to her blue shirt. She looked like she was dying to gossip about Heather-Anne but couldn't quite bring herself to speak ill of the dead.

"Are you on break?" Charlie asked. "I could buy you a cup of coffee."

Robyn chose the Pikes Perk on Tejon, several blocks from the Y, and Charlie wondered if she picked a coffee shop that far away to avoid running into co-workers. Charlie paid for her muffin and Robyn's chai tea, thinking that it smelled like Christmas with its heavy cinnamon and clove scent, and carried them to the table where Robyn sat. Blinds-filtered sunlight striped the warm wood. The personal trainer fussed with the tea after Charlie set it down, giving Charlie a chance to study her. Fiftyish, or maybe a bit more, she had a plain face with slightly chipmunky cheeks and skin that showed traces of long-ago acne problems. Scraggly brows made an almost straight line over makeup-less eyes, but her mouth was surprisingly pretty, full lipped and with a natural pink color that warmed her whole face. Her body was fitness-champ tight and ripped, making a good advertisement for her personal trainer skills.

"Were you and Heather-Anne close?" Charlie knew at once she'd made a mistake as Robyn snorted.

"Do I look like a rich old guy who thinks with his dick?" she asked.

"Only around the ears," Charlie shot back, surprising a tiny smile out of the other woman.

"Well, if you weren't male, and willing to hand over the password to your bank account for a little flattery and silicone tits rubbing up against your arm while she showed you how to do lat pulldowns, and maybe more outside the Y for all I know, then she didn't know you were alive."

Charlie occupied herself with tearing a bite off her banana nut muffin, not wanting to interrupt the flow of Robyn's words.

They sprayed out of her like soda out of a shaken bottle. "I knew she was trouble when she first walked through the door two years back. Trouble with a capital *T*. But Jake—he was the director then—he hired her on straight away. She said she had all sorts of personal trainer credentials, but I never believed it. I was studying for my AFAA certification then, and when I tried to get her to quiz me before an exam, it was clear she didn't even know what the IT band was." Robyn said it as if Heather-Anne had failed to recognize the name of the nation's first president.

"IT band" sounded like something to do with computers to Charlie.

"Iliotibial band," Robyn clarified, looking pleased with

her knowledge. "It runs— Never mind. Just believe me when I say Heather-Anne should have known what it was, and she definitely didn't. I might as well have been talking about rubber bands, for all she knew. Most of the women who work at the Y, especially the other trainers, agreed with me that she didn't know shit from shinola, but the men all thought the sun shone out of her perky little ass." She rolled her eyes at the gullibility of men. "Things got a little harder for her when Sandy took over from Jake." Robyn smiled with remembered satisfaction. "Sandy went through all the personnel records and noticed that some employees, Heather-Anne among them, *of course,* didn't have documentation of their degrees and certifications and such. She insisted that everyone update their records. Heather-Anne had one excuse after another, and it was just about then that the first of the complaints trickled in."

She paused, clearly wanting Charlie to respond. "What complaints?" Charlie asked.

Robyn leaned forward, pushing her mug aside, to whisper, "A member's wife alleged that Heather-Anne had stolen ten thousand dollars from them."

"How?" Charlie asked skeptically. "Climbed in their bedroom window, broke into their safe, and ran off with a bag full of cash? Stole a checkbook and forged their names?"

"Just what I said," Robyn said, leaning back with a satisfied expression. "From what I saw, men were more than happy to *give* Heather-Anne money. That's probably what happened in this case: Some poor shmuck let Heather-Anne weave her wiles and bilk him out of ten grand and then didn't have the balls to tell his wife what happened. There were some other complaints, but my friend Cass who worked in the front office and overheard a lot of this left, so I'm not quite so up on the details. A lot of it faded away after Sandy let Heather-Anne go, too."

"Can I talk to Cass?" Charlie jotted a few notes.

"She's in Laos with the Peace Corps."

A group of five women, clearly co-workers from a nearby office, squeezed past their table carrying mugs and pastries. A heavyset brunette laughed at something one of the others said and tilted her cup so coffee dribbled on Charlie's blazer. Charlie endured the flood of apologies and hands swiping at her with napkins, surveyed her jacket ruefully, and turned back to Robyn when the group had settled themselves at a corner table.

"Heather-Anne was training some guy named Hollis at the Y on Saturday; I saw her."

"Get out! That's the guy. The one whose wife said she stole their money. Hollis Sloan. Sandy would shit a brick if she knew Heather-Anne was using the Y to train clients. I wonder how she sneaked in?" From the expression on Robyn's face, Charlie knew the first thing she'd do when she got back to the Y was tell Sandy.

"Did you know any of Heather-Anne's friends? Did she ever talk about a boyfriend?" Charlie needed more people to interview about Heather-Anne, preferably someone who might even know her real name and where she'd come from.

Robyn was shaking her head before Charlie finished the question. "With Heather-Anne, there was a new boyfriend every week. You couldn't much blame them," she added with an air of trying to be fair. "I mean, there she was, looking like Jennifer Aniston and treating them like they were God's gift to the female race. What man wouldn't cave? I'm sure some of them were married, too, from the way she got all sly when she mentioned them. Toward the end there was some guy named Len Something who seemed to be sticking around longer than most of the others, which probably just means he had more money than they did. Dumpy little guy."

"Les. Les Goldman."

Robyn snapped her fingers. "Yeah. I saw them together a couple of times. He was way gone on her. Oh! She had a roommate, too. A guy. I got the feeling they'd known each other for a while but that there was nothing romantic going on."

"Name?"

"Al. I don't know if that's short for Alexander or Alan. His last name was—" She narrowed her eyes, trying to dredge up the memory. "Started with a B. Broadman? Broadwell? Sorry. I only met him once." She shrugged, then looked at her watch. "I've got to get back. I've got a client in ten minutes."

Charlie stood with her. "Thanks for talking to me. If you think of anything else, please give me a call." She handed Robyn her card.

"You bet." Robyn swept Charlie with a professional gaze. "If you want to get back in shape, give *me* a call. You're holding up pretty well but starting to get a bit soft. Middle-age spread is a bitch, isn't it?" She walked away.

Charlie stared after her, incensed. *Middle-aged?* Thirty-seven wasn't middle-aged! She wasn't soft, either, just less hard than usual due to the bullet in the butt that had severely limited her workouts. A bullet she'd taken saving a young teen's life, thank you very much. Arms crossed over her chest, she glared after Robyn until a patron said, "Excuse me," and tried to squeeze past her. Charlie sucked her abs in and headed for the door and sunshine.

15

I overslept and only woke up Monday when the doorbell rang. Who in the world—? "Dexter, get that," I called before looking at the clock and realizing the kids were already at school. I hoped. The bell rang again, playing that stupid classical piece—*duh-duh-duh-DUH*—that Les had thought was so clever. It drove me batty.

"Coming!" I leaped out of bed, avoided looking at my sleep-mussed hair and the bags under my eyes, and threw on the pink velour robe hanging from the back of my door. It didn't match my nightie with the parrots on it, but I tied the sash around my waist and headed down the stairs as *duh-duh-duh-DUH* sounded again. How much would it cost to get my doorbell ringtone changed? I was wondering who I could call to find out when I pulled the door open to find Detective Lorrimore and two uniformed police officers standing there. I gaped at them.

"Good morning, Mrs. Goldman," Detective Lorrimore said politely. She wore a tan pantsuit that did nothing for her—you'd think any woman who'd ever seen a photo of Hillary Clinton would ban pantsuits from her wardrobe—and had her reddish hair held back with a tortoiseshell headband. One of the cops behind her slipped his sunglasses on and nudged his partner. I looked down to see that my robe had come open and my yellow nightie fluttered in the morning breeze. I gave him an indignant look: The parrots weren't *that* bright.

"Would you like to come in?" I wanted to bite my tongue as soon as the words were out of my mouth. My southern upbringing tripped me up every time. If I invited the police in, was that the same as giving them permission to search my house? Is that what they were here for? I eyed them uncertainly.

"Actually, Mrs. Goldman," Detective Lorrimore said, "we were looking for your son, Dexter. Is he here?"

"Dexter?" I caught my breath, feeling suddenly dizzy. "Why do you want Dexter?" My mind flashed to the other times the police had shown up looking for Dexter. There'd been the shoplifting charge that Les had fixed by talking to the store owner, the time he'd been clocked doing 120 on the Hancock Expressway—Les had nearly blown a gasket over that one—the misunderstanding with the Lockes, and that Halloween incident a couple of years back. "Let me get my checkbook," I said, resigned.

Detective Lorrimore's brows twitched together. "We need to talk to your son."

Something in her voice told me this wasn't about somebody's light-up Christmas reindeer rearranged in "lewd positions that undermined the family values of the entire cul-de-sac," as the homeowners association chairwoman put it. My mouth felt dry. "Why?"

With a heavy sigh, the detective said, "We think he might have some information about Ms. Pawlusik's death."

I slammed the door shut and leaned my back against it. My heart beat faster than a hummingbird's. What kind of information could Dexter have about Heather-Anne's death? The doorbell played again, and fists hammered on the door. Sheepishly, I opened it to see the three police persons staring at me incredulously.

"Sorry," I said. "I had to sneeze." I dragged a shredded tissue from my pocket and sniffled into it. "Uh, Dexter's in school," I said. "Can we make an appointment for this afternoon?" That would give me time to—

"No." Detective Lorrimore sounded as firm as my Nana Fitterling when she told me and my brothers we couldn't have five dollars to visit the Pet Parlor and host a neighborhood goldfish-swallowing contest. "You may accompany us to the school and sign Dexter out. I'll wait here while you dress." She signaled to the patrol officers, and they climbed into a police car and departed. I craned my neck to see if any of my neighbors were watching. Detective Lorrimore crossed to her SUV and sat in the driver's seat with the door open.

"I'll be just a minute," I said, seeing no way out of it.

My brain fizzed with questions as I got dressed, did my hair, and put on my makeup. I chose the red-and-white-striped Hilfiger sweater because red makes me feel braver. Kendall says it makes me look like a candy cane, but I think candy canes are fun. My hair needed washing, but I didn't have time. A few minutes with the curling iron would have to do. Feeling rushed and only half put together, I hurried down the stairs, grabbed a slice of lemon pound cake from the kitchen, and burst out the front door. Only twenty-seven minutes had gone by. Detective Lorrimore looked at her watch in a "what took you so long?" kind of way and started her engine.

I followed her to Cheyenne Mountain High School in the Hummer. She let me go first as we entered the school, and I approached the student sign-out window nervously. "I'm Gigi Goldman, and I need to pick up Dexter for . . . for an appointment," I said, conscious of Detective Lorrimore listening to every word. A bell rang just then, making me jump, and high schoolers poured into the halls.

The woman behind the desk, who doesn't think much of Dexter, looked at me over the top of her reading glasses. "Mrs. Goldman, Dexter isn't here today."

"What?" I glanced over my shoulder at Detective Lorrimore, who had stiffened. "But he has to be; it's a school day."

She shook her head, the chains that dangled from her glasses clicking. Shuffling through a pile of papers, she pulled one out. "Your daughter turned in this note, signed by you, saying Dexter was ill today. Scarlet fever, it says," she added in a snippy tone, accusing finger pointing to the phrase.

The signature looked a lot like mine, and I wondered how often Dexter had signed my name to similar notes and not been found out. "Oh," I stuttered. "Um, can I speak to Kendall for a moment?" The attendance lady sent a student runner to find Kendall, and I turned around to face Detective Lorrimore.

"I heard," she said, before I could say anything. "Do you have any idea where he could be?"

I shook my head miserably.

"This looks bad," the detective said. "If he's done a runner . . ."

"He hasn't 'done a runner,'" I said, getting more worried by the second. "Maybe Kendall—" My daughter came around the corner then, biology book (which I'd never seen before) tucked under her arm, blond hair French-braided.

"Your hair looks cute, honey," I said, leaning over to kiss her.

She turned her face away with a "Mo-om" and gave Detective Lorrimore an interested look. "What's up? It's Dexter, I'll bet."

"Where is your brother?" I asked.

She shrugged. "Dunno. He dropped me at school and took off. Said he had something to do."

"Why didn't you call me?" I asked.

She gave me a disgusted look. "I'm not a tattletale."

Detective Lorrimore stepped forward. "Your brother could be in serious trouble, Miss Goldman. If you know where he is—"

"I don't," she insisted, eyes widening at how stern the detective sounded. "Are you a cop? What's he done now?"

Detective Lorrimore studied her for a moment and apparently decided she was telling the truth. "Okay, you can go on to class."

"I can help you look for Dex," Kendall volunteered.

"Thanks, sweetie," I said, kissing her before she could duck away, "but it's nothing for you to worry about." I crossed my fingers, hoping against hope that I was telling the truth.

Detective Lorrimore and I left the school, and I let the bright sun on my face cheer me for a moment, right up until the detective said, "I'm not prepared to issue an APB and get every cop in the state looking for your son. Yet. But I need you to promise you'll bring him in the second—the *second*—he shows up." She stood beside the open door of her car, fingers drumming on the roof.

I nodded vigorously and almost made the cross-my-heart sign. "I promise." As she slid into the car, I asked, "Why do you need to talk to Dex? What do you think he's do— What do you think has happened?"

Giving me a look that was straight out of one of those *Law & Order* shows, she hesitated for a moment, then said, "Follow me to the station and I'll show you."

Show me?

16

~~~

Standing outside the Pikes Perk, Charlie had flipped a mental coin to decide whether to track down Hollis Sloan and see what he could tell her about Heather-Anne or to get a line on the woman's former roommate. Deciding to cruise past the house Heather-Anne had lived in before decamping with

Les—Gigi had supplied the address, which her lawyer's investigator had provided—Charlie had headed east on 24 to Powers and then north to a newish housing area called Wolf Ranch. Her MapQuested directions took her around a traffic circle and past a fountain with water cascading down a ridged rock wall. The housing area was built on former prairie and lacked the mature trees that made the downtown area so gracious. Charlie hummed "Home on the Range" as she looked for the house number on a street called Adamants.

It was a pale tan stucco with a rock garden instead of a lawn. Actually, calling it a "garden" was mischaracterizing it, since the two dusty junipers and one skinny aspen sapling in the sea of rock hardly constituted a garden. Charlie liked xeriscaping, the art of landscaping with plants and materials that didn't require much water, but this looked more like someone had backed a dump truck up to the curb, let the rocks slither out, and then raked them into perfunctory evenness. Charlie wondered if that meant the homeowner was lazy, unimaginative, or simply not that interested. She drove slowly past the house, noting the pulled-down blinds and closed garage door. There was no hint the house was occupied: no seasonal pennant, skateboard on the sidewalk, or petunias in a planter on the stoop.

Driving past as slowly as she dared, Charlie rounded a corner and parked down the block, then sat thinking. Most of the other houses looked lived in, with the sound of a daytime drama drifting from one and a woman scrubbing a barbecue grill in the backyard of another. The Wolf Ranch covenants didn't allow fences, so Charlie's view was unobstructed. She gazed across several yards to the house where Heather-Anne had lived and pondered what approach to take. There was no guarantee that Heather-Anne's former roomie—Al, according to Robyn—still lived in the house. If he did, would he respond better to the truth, or would a little improvisation yield better results? Charlie had nothing against the truth; it had its place. Frequently, though, a little creative manipulation of the facts garnered more information.

Decision made, she wriggled out of her blazer and reached over the seat to rummage through the box of clothes she kept for occasions like this. She thought she had . . . yes! Triumphantly, she pulled out an oversized purple and gold LSU sweatshirt. That shouted "Deep South" in a big way. Exchanging her low-heeled pumps for a pair of worn-down athletic shoes, she mussed her dark hair a bit and patted on pale face powder to make herself look wan. Not perfect, she thought, looking in the rearview mirror, but she could pass for a woman on the run from an abusive boyfriend, a woman who was hungry, scared, looking for an old friend.

Leaving her purse tucked under the seat, Charlie took a deep breath and headed toward Heather-Anne's former house. The twinge deep in her ass didn't bother her, and she took a deep breath, surprised at how happy she felt to be embarking on her impromptu charade. She'd missed investigating while she was laid up, she realized. Missed the zing of adrenaline when heading into a sticky situation, the mental challenge of tracing a runaway's route or sorting the lies from the truth in an interview. She had to concentrate on adopting a slumping posture and making her steps weary, since she felt more like skipping. *Shit,* she chastised herself mentally. *Only animated characters, children, and Gigi skip.*

Hesitating at the driveway, she wondered if anyone was watching her. Even though the house seemed emptier than a Popsicle carton in an elementary school lunchroom, she had the feeling that someone was in there. Reminding herself to stay in character, Charlie trudged up the driveway to the front door, paused a moment as if unsure of herself for the benefit of anyone watching, and pressed the doorbell. It buzzed deep in the house, sounding a bit like a rattlesnake's warning. Charlie stepped back and waited. After a long moment, she heard footsteps approaching. They stopped, but the door didn't open. Charlie and the unknown person stood on opposite sides of the closed door, unmoving. Interesting, Charlie thought.

She knocked timidly. "Hello? Cindy?" If she were posing as a friend from Heather-Anne's past, she thought it best to pretend that she'd known "Lucinda Cheney" rather than Heather-Anne, who, Charlie suspected, hadn't existed before the woman arrived in Colorado Springs.

The door swung inward. Charlie found herself facing the most handsome man she'd ever seen, a man straight out of a Calvin Klein underwear ad or the cover of *People*'s Sexiest Man Alive issue. Just over six feet tall, he had black hair that brushed his shoulders, strong cheekbones and jawline, a straight nose, and eyes of such a light green Charlie figured he was wearing contact lenses. His olive skin was lightly tanned, and his physique—which was on display since he wore only a pair of gray sweatpants that sagged from his pelvic bones— testified that he spent many hours in a gym. Once the shock of coming face-to-face with a sex god wore off, Charlie gave an artistic start and stepped back. Channeling Gigi, she affected what she hoped was a generic southern accent. "Oh! I was looking for Cindy."

"There's no Cindy here." The man's voice didn't match his looks; it was light and pitched a shade high. He started to close the door.

"She's got to be," Charlie said, infusing desperation into her voice. "Lucinda Cheney? I don't have anywhere else— She said I could find her here if I ever broke it off with Trey and needed to get away."

The man's green eyes assessed her. "And you are?"

"Charlene," Charlie said. "Are you Al? Cindy mentioned you."

"She did?" Displeasure twitched the man's face. Charlie thought he might be about her own age, certainly a few years older than Heather-Anne. "You'd better come in."

Charlie crossed the threshold. The oak-floored foyer opened into a great room lined with wall-to-wall mushroom-colored carpet. The room held nothing but a sophisticated-looking weight set and benches and an elliptical machine. Drapes closed off what would have been a decent view of the Front Range. Stairs curved upward to a second story. Al, if that's who the man was, stalked toward a kitchen that was all gray granite and white paint and poured a glass of water. Charlie stayed in the foyer.

"If Cindy's not here," she said with assumed nervousness, "I should go."

Al took a swallow of water and leveled a look at her from under dark brows. "Hea— Cindy's dead."

Charlie gasped and dropped her purse. "Oh, no! She can't be. I—"

"How did you get here?" Al asked, unperturbed by her seeming grief and confusion. "I didn't see a car."

"Uh, I hitched to the 7-Eleven over there"—Charlie pointed vaguely south—"and then walked." She bent to retrieve her purse and collected an escaped lip balm.

"Where did you say you knew Cindy from?"

The suspicion in his voice told Charlie he wasn't buying her story. "I don't believe she's dead," she said, putting a little more aggression in her voice. "You're just saying that so I'll go away. I understand if her circumstances have changed, if you and her are—whatever, and she isn't able to help like she said, but you don't have to lie to me." She hitched her purse higher on her shoulder. "I'm sorry I bothered you."

"The police were here this morning to talk to me about Cindy. They knew her as Heather-Anne Pawlusik," Al said, sounding a bit less hostile. He rested his elbows on the counter and leaned forward. "I'm sure you can read about it in the paper. It'll be the article about a woman strangled at the Embassy Suites." His magnetic eyes watched her as he delivered the news.

"Strangled? Was it— Did her husband catch up with her?"

Al clapped lightly. "Oh, very good. You're very good. Your only mistake was in saying 'Cindy' offered to help you in some way; Heather-Anne never offered to help anyone in her life. Now, do you want to cut the crap and tell me why you're really here, or shall I call the police? Given that Heather-Anne was murdered yesterday, I think they'd be very interested in meeting you."

Charlie shot the man an assessing look, then walked toward him with her business card held out. "Charlie Swift," she said in her usual crisp voice. "I'm a private investigator. I was working for Heather-Anne."

The man's brows soared, and he took the card. "That's only marginally more believable than your first story," he said, "although you look more like a PI than a mousy, abused wife."

Charlie wasn't quite sure how to take that. "And you are?"

"Alan Brodnax," he said, offering a ringless hand for her to shake. His nails were filed and buffed, and she wondered what he did for a living. His grip was firm. "Call me Alan. Heather-Anne was the only one who called me Al, and she only did it to piss me off. Why did she hire you?"

"What was your relationship with her?" Charlie countered. They eyed each other.

"We were roommates," Alan finally said. "Platonic roommates. We got to talking at the gym. She mentioned she was looking for a new place, and I needed a roommate to help with the mortgage, so she moved in. It wasn't until after she'd lived here a few months that she mentioned her homicidal husband might show up on the doorstep. It explained a lot about how anal she was about locking up and not leaving windows open, and the way she checked the backseat of her car every time before she got in. And she hired you because—?"

"She wanted me to find Les Goldman, the man she was living with in Costa Rica." A muffled sound came from above Charlie's head, and she looked at the ceiling, startled. "Is someone—?"

"I left the TV on," Alan said easily, not bothering to glance up. "I was checking the stock market report when the doorbell went. I'll turn it off—you sit." He gestured toward the only seating visible, two webbed lawn chairs parked under a glass-topped bistro table in the kitchen nook. He trotted up the stairs, and Charlie sat, looking around at the kitchen, which was totally devoid of personality and appliances. Holes gaped in the counter where a fridge, stove, and dishwasher should have stood. Alan was back in under a minute, still sans shirt. He refilled his water and offered Charlie one as well. "I don't have anything else," he apologized, setting the glass down with a clink, "and no ice. You were telling me about looking for Les . . ."

Charlie found herself slightly distracted by the man's defined pecs and the way his biceps flexed as he lifted his glass. She wondered if his tan was natural or the spray-on kind and if he made a habit of answering the door shirtless. She decided he probably did. "My partner and I tracked him to Aspen, but he eluded us," she said, seeing no harm in admitting that much. "Do you know Les?" Something about the way he'd said Les's name so familiarly made her think he did.

"We met once or twice, before he and Heather-Anne took off for points south. I must admit I didn't understand what Heather-Anne saw in him."

"Did you know she was leaving with him?"

A smile crooked his lips, revealing, as Charlie expected by now, perfect white teeth. The man spent more time on his appearance, she was convinced, than a lounge-full of drag queens. "Actually, no. She stiffed me on the rent. That's what happened to the furniture." He gestured to the empty house. "I was in a slump, jobwise, and I had to sell it to make the mortgage for a couple of months."

"What is it you do?"

"I'm a researcher. I've got an office upstairs"—he jerked his cleft chin toward the ceiling—"and clients around the world."

"It seems a waste." Charlie challenged him with her gaze.

"What does?"

"All that effort"—she waved her hand up and down to indicate his well-muscled body—"wasted sitting behind a computer all day, not another person in sight. I'd've figured you for a model or a salesman . . . something a bit more social."

Alan laughed, a surprisingly infectious sound. "I get out," he said, a glint in his eyes. "Maybe you and I should get together sometime."

The idea was not totally without appeal on a purely carnal level, but Charlie put her libido back in its cage and said, "Mm. Maybe when this case is sorted. Who was Heather-Anne before she became Heather-Anne?"

He gave her a surprised look. "Lucinda Cheney. I thought you knew that since you came in here looking for 'Cindy.' "

"Was that her real name?"

"As far as I know."

"She told me her husband was abusive and she came here to escape from him. True?"

"Absolutely. She was scared to death of him." Alan's eyes took on a somber light. "She used to check the online newspapers for Gatlinburg several times a week to see if he was mentioned. I think she was looking for a wedding announcement, hoping he'd remarry and forget about her."

"Do you think he caught up with her?" Charlie took a swallow of her water, watching Alan closely. Since busting her as a PI he seemed to be comfortable with her, answering her questions in a straightforward way, but she got the feeling he was playing with her.

"Oh, God, I hadn't thought of that." Alan looked thunderstruck, his mouth falling open a half inch. "Of course that's what happened."

"How did you and Heather-Anne mee—?"

A slight click, like a door closing, was quickly followed by a rumbling sound, and Charlie jumped. She struggled to get out of the saggy webbing that had her trapped. The lightweight aluminum chair shot back several feet as she jolted out of it. "Someone's here."

Alan didn't look alarmed; if anything, he relaxed into his seat, a smirk smudging his handsome face. Clearly the noise wasn't made by an intruder; he'd known someone else was in the house all along.

Not knowing which door led to the garage, Charlie rushed into the front room in time to see a silver sedan, make unidentifiable, swing around the corner and zoom away. The garage door gaped open, displaying a glossy black Saab. She stalked back into the kitchen, making the muscles around the bullet wound complain. "Who was that?"

Arching his brows, Alan rose and put their water glasses in the sink. "A friend. Once she heard you say 'PI,' I couldn't convince her you weren't after her."

It took Charlie a bare ten seconds to work out what he was saying. "You had a woman friend up there. Someone who thought her husband had hired a PI to document her fling."

Alan clapped again. *Like I'm a performing seal*, Charlie

thought, annoyed. This pretty boy was really beginning to tick her off.

"I told her to just stay put, that I'd get rid of you, but she was convinced you'd come charging up the stairs, camera in hand, to immortalize our little tryst on film."

Charlie forced a laugh, determined not to let Alan Brodnax see that he'd riled her. "I don't do divorce work—too sordid. Everyone involved is sleazy." *Take that,* she thought, as his eyes narrowed with anger.

"I wish I could help more," he said mendaciously, striding toward the door in a way that told Charlie she'd be on the sidewalk in seconds, "but I've got an appointment."

Probably time to redo his spray tan, Charlie thought, or bleach his teeth again.

"What did the police want?" she asked as he swung the door wide.

He smiled, his strong white teeth reminding her of a wolf. "Why don't you ask them?"

The door closed in her face with a force just shy of a slam. Overcoming the temptation to stick out her tongue at it, Charlie turned away and trekked to her car, her mind churning through the information Alan had provided and possible avenues of investigation. Gatlinburg was in Tennessee, wasn't it? She'd start there.

17

~~m~~

I followed Detective Lorrimore into a small conference room at police headquarters, shutting my eyes involuntarily as I went through the door. I half expected someone to jump out and accuse Dexter of stealing garden gnomes, knocking over mailboxes, or tipping a porta-potty. Or maybe something new. When no one yelled at me, I slowly opened my eyes to find Detective Lorrimore staring at me as she pointed to a chair at the table. I sat, relieved to see there was no one-way mirror like they have in all the cop shows. Detective Lorrimore fussed with a DVD player, cussing a little when it didn't play right away, and then backed away from the television as the picture came on.

I looked at her, but she only gestured to the screen. "Watch."

Grainy gray-tone images popped up. People, a bit fuzzy around the edges, walked down a hall. A digital clock in the lower right-hand corner supplied the time. Crinkling my brow, I tried to figure out what I was looking at. Just as I realized that it was the Embassy Suites hotel, the hall where Heather-Anne had stayed, a tall figure slouched around the corner, backpack hanging from his shoulders. I felt a tickle of unease. His face was hidden until he reached the door he wanted; then he looked up and down the hall, directly at the camera, before knocking. I gasped.

Detective Lorrimore looked at me as if she expected me to comment, but I folded my lips in and watched my son disappear into Heather-Anne Pawlusik's room. He came out five and a half minutes later, turned left, and started to walk away.

Freezing the image, Detective Lorrimore asked, "Did you know your son was acquainted with Ms. Pawlusik? Did you know he visited her the morning of her death and was, perhaps, the last person to see her alive?"

"Besides the murderer."

"Possibly."

My heart thudded in my chest, and I put a hand over it. Thoughts tumbled through my brain. What was Dexter doing at the Embassy Suites? Did he know Heather-Anne? Had Les had the gall to introduce his bimbo to my children? For a split second, anger drove away worry. Then my eyes landed on the TV screen again with its fuzzy photo of my baby boy, my Dexter, leaving a soon-to-be murder scene. Dexter was a sweet boy at heart. Okay, he'd gotten into a bit of mischief in the last couple of years, mostly since Les left, but I knew he didn't have it in him to kill someone. Not even the woman who took his father away. I didn't know why he'd gone to the Embassy Suites, but I knew my son, and there was no way on God's green earth that he killed Heather-Anne "Home Wrecker" Pawlusik.

"I did it," I announced.

"Pardon me?"

"I did it. I strangled Heather-Anne."

"Really? Why?"

Did I have to spell everything out? "Because she slept with my husband. She broke up my family. She left my kids fatherless and stole all our money. She was a Grade A, world-class,

A-number-one, fake-breasted bitch. A tramp. A . . . a slut!"
Boy, it felt good to get that out of my system. I almost smiled
until I remembered I was confessing to murder.

"Uh-huh." Detective Lorrimore popped the DVD out of
the player and turned to face me. She didn't seem as thrilled
as I'd thought she'd be to have my confession. "Where was the
scarf when you came into the room?"

"The scarf? Uh, around her neck."

"She was wearing workout clothes."

"Accessories can improve any outfit."

She just looked at me. "Uh-huh. What did you do with
her laptop?"

"Her laptop?"

"It was missing. The maid mentioned that she had a laptop computer in the room."

Darn, this confessing thing was harder than I'd anticipated.
"I took it." Foreseeing a demand to give them the computer,
I added triumphantly, "But then I remembered I couldn't af-
ford Internet cable anymore, so I gave it away. I . . . I put it in a
Goodwill donation box."

"Generous of you." The detective's tone was wry. She fixed
her gaze on me, and after a moment I began to squirm. "Mrs.
Goldman," she said, her voice surprisingly sympathetic, "I
know what you're trying to do, and I don't entirely blame you.
But you and I both know you didn't kill Ms. Pawlusik. You
don't have it in you."

Why did everyone keep saying I couldn't kill someone? I
was pretty sure I felt insulted. "Neither does Dexter," I burst
out.

"I haven't accused him of anything."

"Then why—"

"It's possible he may have seen something, or that Ms. Pawlusik may have said something, that would help us locate the killer. We need to talk to him." Her voice was implacable.

"I'm going to get him a lawyer."

Detective Lorrimore gave a tiny shrug. "That's up to you, of course. I'm going to station a police officer at the school, although it doesn't appear Dexter spends much time there, and at your home."

"What!"

"Your son seems to come and go pretty much at will; I want to make sure he doesn't slip in without anyone noticing." She smiled a thin smile. "We don't want this to drag on for any longer than necessary, do we?"

My stomach felt like it did that time when we went to the u-pick-'em peach farm when I was a girl and I ate more peaches than ended up in my bucket.

"Does your son have a car? I'll need the license plate number. I'll also need your son's cell phone number, Mrs. Goldman. In fact, why don't you try calling him right now."

Her eyes bored into me, and I sensed "No" was not an option. Reluctantly, I pulled out my phone, feeling somehow as if I were being asked to help trap my son. I didn't see any way out of it, though. I dialed. His cell rang, and with each ring my hope and my fear built. Finally voice mail kicked in, and I let out a long breath. "Dexter . . . honey, this is Mom. Um, if you get this, please call me right away. It's important. I love you." I hung up.

Nodding, Detective Lorrimore said, "Well, I guess we're done for now."

Somehow, I found myself on Nevada Avenue outside the police station a few minutes later, disoriented, unsure where I'd left the Hummer, afraid I'd burst into tears on the sidewalk and be mistaken for a crazy homeless person. Of course, most homeless people weren't wearing Hilfiger with True Religion jeans, but still.

I really wanted to go shopping. There were some cute boutiques nearby on Tejon . . . No. Dexter needed me more than I needed a shopping fix. I pulled out my phone and called Charlie.

We met back at the office. Sick with worry about Dexter, I'd cried all the way from downtown to our office, except for when I drove through Starbucks and got a pumpkin cream cheese muffin with a Cinnamon Dolce Crème Frappucino. I had to duck into the small restroom to repair the damage to my makeup. With my face back on, I felt a bit braver. Charlie listened carefully as I told her everything about my visit to the police station. "They want to put my baby boy in prison and throw away the key," I finished, swallowing hard.

"It was bound to happen," Charlie said. She kept going before I could object. "First things first: Call a lawyer." She handed me a business card, and I studied it. "He's the best criminal defense lawyer in town. He owes me a favor. Don't let Dexter talk to the police unless he's with him."

"Okay," I sniffed. "Thank you, Charlie."

"This makes it doubly important that we find out who really killed Heather-Anne. It seems to me we've got two tracks to follow. First, we need to locate Les, because he's got to know something. I can't believe his fleeing Costa Rica and Heather-Anne's death aren't related. Second, we find Heather-Anne/Lucinda's husband—ex-husband?—in Gatlinburg and see what he has to say. Heather-Anne's roommate, Alan, made it clear the husband was his nominee for murderer. He says Heather-Anne was still scared to death of the guy. So I'll see if I can get a line on the hubby while you call the lawyer and do what you can to find Dexter before the police do. Call his friends. Send him a message on Facebook."

"That's a great idea." I didn't even know Charlie knew what Facebook was.

I plunked myself down at my computer, slurping up the last of my Frappucino, and immediately logged on to Facebook. Neither of my kids would let me friend them, but I could still send Dexter an e-mail via the site. As I typed, the door opened and Albertine came in, her gold and coral and orange tunic like a blast of sunshine in our dim office.

"Geez, Albertine," Charlie complained, shading her eyes. "Can you dial down the wattage? You'll scare the bears into thinking it's time to emerge from hibernation."

"No can do," Albertine said with a lazy wave. "It's my natural state. You might try upping the wow factor yourself, girlfriend," she added, studying Charlie's sweatshirt and blue jeans. "Although that purple is more color than you usually manage."

"I was undercover, sort of," Charlie said briefly, fingers clicking rapidly on the keyboard. I don't know how she can talk and type at the same time.

"Anything interesting?" Albertine asked.

"Nah. Just a guy who looked like the offspring of Clark

Gable and Angelina Jolie, walking around bare-chested. He asked me out." Charlie kept her gaze on the computer screen, but I could see her fighting to keep back a smile.

"Hot damn," Albertine said, pulling up the uncomfortable wooden chair we keep for visitors. Charlie won't let me replace it with anything comfy or even put a cushion on it; it would encourage clients to linger, she says. Albertine sat, her generous curves overflowing the chair's sides. "Tell me all about it."

Charlie gave her a three-sentence version of meeting Alan Brodnax—I don't know how she does that; it always takes me *much* longer to tell a story—and Albertine pushed her coral-painted lips forward thoughtfully. "He doesn't sound like your type," she finally said.

"What's my type?"

"Not the screw-around-with-married-women type," Albertine said.

"I think she goes more for the law-enforcing type," I put in.

Charlie pretend-scowled as Albertine and I laughed. "Some of us have work to do," she said, making a show of turning back to her computer.

Albertine stood, muttering something about putting on beignets.

"I've got to get hold of Dexter before the police catch up with him," I said, pulling out my cell phone in hopes the phone numbers of some of Dexter's friends would be in there. I'd only ever called a couple of his friends' houses once or twice, needing to talk with their parents about one thing or another.

"The police are looking for Dexter?" Albertine paused, her hand on the door. "I saw—"

"They think he killed Heather-Anne," I said, blinking rapidly so I wouldn't tear up.

"Say what?" She shook her head violently, threatening to topple the tower of curlicues and braids that rose a good four inches above her head. "There is no way that sweet, sweet boy killed anyone."

" 'Sweet'?" Charlie asked. "Are we talking about the same kid? No offense, Gigi, but—"

"I saw him this morning," Albertine interrupted.

I leaped from my chair and ran around my desk. "You did? Where?"

"Here." She pointed to the floor. "He was rattling the doorknob of your office when I came in, oh, it must have been fifty minutes or an hour ago."

Only a little bit before Charlie and I arrived. I'd missed him by minutes. "Did you see where he went?"

"Sorry, sugah," Albertine said. "I'll certainly holler if I see him again." She left.

"Charlie! He was looking for me. He needs me."

"Gigi. Dexter's not a nine-year-old. And he's not dumb, even if he is—"

I saw her bite back a sharp comment.

"If he's done something—and I'm not saying he murdered Heather-Anne," she hastened to add when I opened my mouth. "We know he talked to Heather-Anne. If she said something that upset him, something about Les, maybe, he might need a while to process it. Maybe that's why he took off. He might even be trying to find Les. We just don't know until we talk to him, so stop acting like—" She broke off again. "He'll be in touch."

I blew my nose into a tissue. "Thanks, Charlie."

"Why don't you go home, in case Dexter shows up there. You can call his friends from there, and I'll let you know if I come up with anything. Don't forget to make a list of places Les might be. It'll be okay." She gave me a reassuring look.

I wanted everything to be okay *now*. I wanted Heather-Anne alive—far away, but alive. I wanted Dexter in school where he belonged, without policemen lurking about to arrest him. I wanted Les . . . I wasn't sure where I wanted my husband, my ex-husband. I knew where I didn't want him: in Costa Rica, in jail, or dead. I wrapped a fluffy pink chenille scarf around my neck and put on my Prada sunglasses, the ones that would make me look like Jackie O if I were brunette and sixty pounds thinner. "I hope so."

18

~m~

Outside, I had to loosen the scarf because the temperature must have been in the midfifties. In February! The sun glared off the Hummer's chrome, and I was grateful for the glasses. I clambered up onto the seat and started the car once I'd found the keys in my purse. My friends keep telling me I should get a smaller purse, but it's so convenient to have everything I need with me—flashlight, nail file, extra hose, snacks. I used to watch *Let's Make a Deal* when I was younger, and I just knew that if I ever got on the show I'd win something by being able to pull out a boiled egg or a staple remover or whatever else Monty was after.

Merging into traffic on Academy Boulevard, I had made it to the intersection with Woodmen—the new exits confuse me—when a head popped up behind me. I caught a glimpse of blond hair in the rearview mirror, screamed, and ran the Hummer's driver-side wheels onto a concrete traffic island. I was fumbling at the door, planning to run for it, when a man's voice said, "Jesus, Mom, it's me! Get a grip."

Dexter.

I turned around, openmouthed, to stare at my son. "Dexter! What are you—?"

"Just drive, okay?" He gestured out the window to where traffic was backing up as cars slowed to look at us stranded on the median.

Waving apologetically to the people behind me, I reversed the Hummer, and it thudded onto the roadway. I put it in gear and eased back into traffic. The car seemed okay, thank goodness, since I couldn't afford repairs. Dexter had ducked down again. I made the turn onto I-25 and risked a glance in the rearview mirror. "What are you doing here?" I asked. "Oh, Dexter, there's—"

"The police are looking for me, Mom." He didn't sound so sure of himself now. "They were at the house and—"

"What were you doing at the house? You're supposed to be in school." It was strange talking to him when I couldn't see him.

"I had stuff to do," he said.

I wasn't letting this slide, not this time. "What stuff? I've been to the school and seen the note you got Kendall to turn in. You forged my signature!"

"Yeah, well." He had a shrug in his voice like it was old hat.

"You can't—"

"Mom, the police want to arrest me." I heard fear in his voice, underneath the exasperation, and I turned half around, trying to peer into the backseat.

"It'll be okay," I said, echoing Charlie. A honk made me face front again.

"You don't know—"

"I do. Detective Lorrimore showed me a video of you visiting Heather-Anne's room at the Embassy Suites the day she was killed. Oh, Dexter, what were you doing there?"

"They have a video? Shit."

"Shit" seemed like the right word in these circumstances, so I didn't say anything to him about his language.

"Why?"

There was silence for a moment. "I heard you and Charlie talking about her on the phone. I thought maybe Dad was with her, or she'd know where Dad was." His voice cracked the tiniest bit, and for a moment he seemed more like my little boy than the grown man he almost was.

"What did you say to her?" Curiosity tickled me. What had my son said to the woman who lured his dad away?

"I'd met her before and—"

"You had? When? How?"

"Dad introduced us. We went to Cold Stone and—"

"Kendall, too?"

"Yeah. Does it really matter now?"

It did, and if I caught up with Les I was going to have it

out with him. How could he introduce my children to the woman he was running around with? It wasn't the most important thing now, though. "Tell me what she said." I realized I'd missed my exit and edged right to take the next one.

Dexter seemed to catch on to what I was doing. "You're not going home, are you? You can't. There are cops there."

I'd forgotten. If I pulled into the driveway with Dexter in the backseat they'd haul him off to prison. Unsure what to do, I pulled into a Safeway parking lot, parked as far from the store as possible, and twisted around to face my son. He was lying on the backseat, but he slowly edged up, casting hunted looks out each window. Not seeing any cop cars nearby, he straightened up.

"So Heather-Anne asked me in, being real nice, and even offered me a soda. She asked me if I'd seen Dad, and when I said no, that I'd been hoping he was there—in the hotel with her—she got all snotty and told me to get out. She said he didn't want to see me, that he had a new life, and that he was much happier without us 'millstones' dragging him down and keeping him from achieving his true potential."

I wished Heather-Anne was alive so I could kill her. Detective Lorrimore might not think I was the murdering type, but right then I was.

"Then she kicked me out."

"Did you see anyone as you were leaving?" I looked at him hopefully, hoping he'd say he'd run into a murderous thug carrying a scarf in one hand.

"Nah." His brows came together slightly. "But I kinda thought there might be someone in the other room while I was there."

"The other room?"

"Yeah, Heather-Anne and I were in the living room kind of area, with the TV. The bedroom door was shut. I don't know why, but I thought there might be someone in there. I thought it was Dad, but he'd have come out when he heard my voice, so it wasn't him. And the way Heather-Anne asked me about him, I knew he wasn't in there."

I tried to read my son, but I couldn't. His blond bangs fell across his eyes, and his mouth was set in a straight line. His hands were tucked into the kangaroo pocket of his hoodie, and he kept his gaze on the floor. I couldn't tell if he was angry or hurt or worried, or all of the above. "We need to tell the police," I said.

That brought his head up. His eyes practically bugged out of his face. "Are you out of your mind? They're not going to believe me. They'll think I'm making it up about someone else being there."

That thought stopped me.

Dexter leaned forward, trying to convince me. "If you give me some money, I can leave. David's at the University of Minnesota. He's sharing an apartment with a couple of guys. I'm sure I could crash with him for a while. When this blows over, I can come back."

"What about school?" I asked the question without thinking; I wasn't letting my son leave home to avoid the police. If he left, I might not see him again until he showed up on *America's Most Wanted.* "No. Absolutely not."

"I could get my GED." The thought of missing school lit up Dexter's face, and I could tell he was liking his plan more and more.

I started to hyperventilate at the thought of Dexter on the lam, becoming a grocery clerk or petty thief to support himself, hanging out with David and his frat boy friends who probably spent every weekend binge-drinking, never getting his high school diploma. I thunked the automatic locks down and used the child safety switch so Dexter couldn't run off, then pulled out my phone. I called Charlie's lawyer friend.

Tucker Winston—it confuses me so much when people have two first names, or two last names—arrived in the parking lot twenty-five minutes later. He got out of one of those Jeeps that don't have any doors and walked toward us, a big smile on his face. His very young face. He didn't look much older than Dexter, and I watched his dreadlocks bounce on his shoulders with dismay. Even though he wore a very pricey, very British pin-striped suit that looked like Anderson & Sheppard, the dreadlocks made me nervous. The only other white person I could think of with dreadlocks worked at the Panera where I had lunch at least once a week. I buzzed down the window as he approached.

"Mrs. Goldman?" He had a deep, rich voice that reassured me slightly. "I'm Tucker Winston."

"Do you have a driver's license?"

"It's good to be cautious." He flipped open a thin billfold and handed me his driver's license.

He might think I was making sure he was who he said he was, but I actually wanted to see if he was old enough to be a real lawyer. From his birth date, I figured out he was thirty-three and handed the license back, feeling a bit better. Charlie wouldn't have said he was good if he weren't, but I needed to be sure.

Sliding the wallet back into his pocket, he said, "I've contacted the police, and I think it's best if Dexter and I have a chat with them. They're prepared to be reasonable."

Dexter muttered something that sounded like "I want to go to Minnesota."

"What's 'reasonable'?"

"A very good question." Tucker Winston smiled broader. "Are you sure you're not a lawyer?"

I felt flattered and relaxed even more.

"They're not looking to arrest him at this time. They just want to hear his story. Mrs. Goldman—"

"I'm Gigi. G. G. for Georgia Goldman, get it?"

"Why don't you go into the Safeway and get yourself a sandwich or something while I confer with my client. I think it would be best if I talked to Dexter alone," he added when I started to object.

"Okay." I got my purse, unlocked the door, and looked back at Dexter, who hadn't said anything to me since I made the phone calls. "Will you be okay, honey?"

"Like you care."

His words made me tear up, and I hurried across the parking lot to the Safeway, thinking a one-pound bag of peanut M&M's suited my mood better than a sandwich.

Two hours later, we were done at the police station and Tucker Winston, Dexter, and I were walking out the door. The police hadn't arrested Dexter, although Detective Lorrimore had told him not to leave town. I hadn't been allowed to sit in on the interview, but Tucker Winston filled me in when they got done. Dexter had told the police what he'd told me, and they'd seemed equal parts skeptical and interested to hear there might have been someone in the bedroom while Dexter talked to Heather-Anne. Dexter stood with his arms crossed over his chest, a sulky-scared expression on his face. I'd spent the time in the waiting area, trying to read a four-year-old *Field & Stream* magazine and chatting with a guy as big as Shaquille O'Neal who had so many tattoos he looked like a highway overpass graffitied by gang members. I'd been nervous of him at first, but he mentioned he was there to get fingerprinted for a special ed teaching job, and I'd shared my M&M's with him, and we'd talked about how sad it is that kids can't take peanut butter sandwiches to school anymore since so many kids have peanut allergies.

By the time Dexter and I entered the house from the garage, it was almost four and Kendall was home from school. She was peeling a cucumber over the sink when we walked in and took a large bite out of it before saying, "Where've you been? I had to get a ride home with Eli since Dexter wasn't there, and he asked me to the Spring Fling."

"Did you say yes?"

"Ew. As if. He has pimples, and I once saw milk squirt from his nose when he laughed. Come on—we're going to be late for practice if we don't leave right now."

I noticed she was wearing a long-sleeved leotard and thin sweatpants and her skate bag sat in a lumpy heap on the kitchen table. "Sorry, Kendall," I said, feeling frazzled. "Dexter can drive—"

Without a word he turned and stomped out of the kitchen. I heard him climbing the stairs seconds later. I sighed. "Get in the Hummer. I'll take you."

I returned to the garage and walked around the Hummer to the driver's side as Kendall hopped into the passenger seat and slammed the door. The sound ricocheted through the mostly empty four-car garage, and I winced. I closed my door more gently and put the Hummer in reverse, remembering just in time to raise the garage door. It rumbled up.

"Where's Dex's car?" Kendall asked.

I landed hard on the brake, making the tires squeal.

"Mo-om."

Where was Dexter's car? I started down the drive again, realizing Kendall would be late for skating if I went in to ask Dexter about the BMW. Had he left it in the office parking lot? I closed my eyes, trying to visualize the parking lot. No, I didn't think I'd seen—

"Watch out!"

My eyes popped open, and I swerved to avoid the neighbors' Maine coon cat. She was sitting on the sidewalk, tail swishing as she watched a squirrel chitter from a tree branch. We thudded off the curb, and I gave Kendall an apologetic smile. "Sorry, sweetie. I was thinking about something."

"Well, don't."

We drove to the World Arena Ice Hall in silence. Kendall texted the whole way, and I thought. She was out the door before I could kiss her good-bye. "Angel can give me a ride home," she said, walking briskly into the low building.

Would it kill her to say "Thanks for the ride"? I had more important things on my mind than Kendall's manners, though, and I sped home.

"Dexter," I called as I came through the door. "Dexter!"

When he didn't answer, I trotted up the stairs to his room. Even that brief exertion made me breathe heavy, and I promised myself I'd start using the treadmill again, just as soon as all this was over. I was way too stressed for exercise right now. Dexter's door was closed, and I knocked. "Dex? Honey?" I didn't hear anything from within, so I said, "I'm coming in."

I pushed open the door, and the smell of teenaged boy smacked me. I think it's equal parts musky aftershave splashed on too heavily, spray deodorant, and hormones. Not that I know what hormones smell like, but that's what it must be. All the other parents joke about teens' rooms being disaster areas and compare them to landfills or the mess left after a hurricane, but Dexter keeps his room neat. His bed, desk, dresser, and entertainment center all came from Ethan Allen and had a light cherry finish. I'd tried to talk him into letting me have his room painted a pale tan to coordinate, but he'd insisted on navy blue walls so dark they seemed black. He'd've painted them black except Les put his foot down. His laptop was closed on his desk, his iPod and cell phone charging in a little station beside it. The flat-screen TV had the entertainment center all to itself except for a couple of books from last year's American lit class that looked so new I suspected he hadn't ever opened them. *SpongeBob SquarePants* was on, but Dexter had the sound muted. He lay atop the navy-and-green-striped comforter on his queen-sized bed, arms behind his head, remote in one hand, staring at the TV. He didn't look at me.

After a moment standing beside the door, I moved to block his view of the television. He gave me that long-suffering look from under his brows. "What?"

"Where's your car? The Beemer?"

"Since I only have the one car, you don't need to specify 'the Beemer.'" He craned his neck, trying to see around me.

I found myself wanting to slap him and was so horrified I gripped my hands together behind my back. "Were you in an accident? Is that it? Don't be afraid to tell me." Images of crumpled fenders and repair bills I couldn't afford bebopped through my head.

Dexter snorted, but I couldn't tell if he was snorting at the idea of being afraid of me or at my suggestion that he'd been in an accident. A dreadful thought snuck up on me. "You weren't in a hit-and-run, were you?"

"No!"

He looked offended, and I took a deep breath. "Then what?"

He pushed buttons randomly on the remote and mumbled something.

"What?"

"I said I loaned it to someone."

My mouth dropped open. Pretty much the only rule Les laid on Dexter when he gave him the car was that no one else drove it ever. Up till now that hadn't been an issue since Dexter was never into sharing.

"It's my car, okay?"

"Your dad bought that car, and I pay for the insurance, which isn't cheap for a teenaged boy driver, so—"

"You don't need to make a federal case out of it."

Something about the way he wouldn't look at me and the way he fussed with the remote made me uneasy. "Who did you lend it to?"

More mumbling.

"Not Milo? He's already had three speeding tickets and a DUI, his mom tells me. I know they took his keys away. Please tell me it's not Milo. Or James! He crashed his dad's Lincoln through a fence and into someone's pool. It cost the Mickelsons over twenty thousand dollars, counting the vet bill for that poor cocker spaniel."

"It wasn't Milo or James. If you must know, I loaned it to Dad."

The news hit me like an elbow to the throat at a Black Friday sale. I put a hand on the entertainment center because my knees felt wobbly all of a sudden. "What?"

"Dad. Short guy, mustache, used to live here, remember?"

"Dexter—"

"I knew you'd go all whoo-whoo on me"—he waggled his hands—"so I didn't tell you."

I tried hard to slow my breathing and not get all whoo-whoo, whatever that was. "How—? Where—? When did you see your dad?"

"He called last night, said he needed a car for a few days, and asked to borrow mine. I didn't really think I could say no. He's my dad, you know, and he bought it for me, as he was quick to remind me. So I dropped Kendall at school today and drove to Castle Rock to meet him. He drove me back to the house, but we spotted the po-po from a block away."

"Po-po?"

"The cops. The police car. Dad freaked out. So he dropped me back at that Denny's near I-25 and Academy, and I walked down to your office, you know, to hitch a ride home with you. You weren't even there." He sounded aggrieved.

I couldn't think what to say, so I just stared at him. Les had called him. He'd met Les without telling me. We might never see the BMW again, and I'd have to take the kids to and from school every day, unless Carla Leach would carpool, and I didn't want to do that because her two high schoolers both smoked and the Hummer stank for half a day after they'd ridden in it. "Did he have anything to say?" I finally asked. "Dad, I mean."

Dexter shrugged. "Not really. He was upset about Heather-Anne, which makes sense, I guess, since he was screwing her."

"Dexter!"

"Well, he was. He said he'd seen you in Aspen and wanted to know if you were dating anyone yet."

"He did?" Could Les be jealous? "What did you tell him?"

Dexter gave me a look that said he thought a world-ending meteor would land on the city before I found a boyfriend. "Duh."

"Did he say why he was here? Where he was staying?"

"Business. He didn't say what kind, and I didn't ask. Probably something crooked, like usual. I didn't ask for an address, either; it's not like I think we're going to be all buddy-buddy just because he borrowed my car. I'm not that dumb."

The cynicism in Dexter's voice broke my heart. "Hon—"

"Can you move, please? I can't see the television."

As I slowly left the room, the television sound blared on: "Whooo lives in a pineapple under the sea?"

I called Charlie immediately to tell her that Les had been in the area and that he had borrowed Dexter's car. I started to tell her how inconvenient it was going to be to have to chauffeur the kids to and from school, but she interrupted me.

"Do you have LoJack on the BMW?"

"Of course. Les insisted. We have it on the Hummer, too."

"Then call the police and tell them the car's been stolen. They'll activate the LoJack to locate it and, with any luck, pinpoint Les for us."

"But it wasn't stolen."

"Gigi—"

I hung up and called the police. I hate lying, but I told them the Beemer had been stolen. They promised to track it down and let me know when they recovered it. They called back an hour later, to tell me the LoJack system had apparently been removed from the car or was otherwise inoperable.

I called Charlie back to tell her.

"Would Les have known where the installers put the LoJack unit?" she asked.

"Of course. He watched them do it at the dealership."

She sighed. "Then he took it out. Well, at least the police are on the lookout for the car. Maybe some alert cop will spot it." She didn't sound optimistic.

19

~~~

I dropped the kids off at the high school Tuesday morning
and was late getting to work. I'd had to coax Dexter into going; he'd said that he could work on his GED from prison. I
didn't want to encourage that kind of mopey attitude, so I
told him that if he graduated in June, as scheduled, he could
work on his college degree from prison, if it came to that.
Kendall overheard us—sometimes I think my daughter eaves-
drops on purpose—and wanted to know why Dexter was
going to prison. We hadn't told her about Dexter visiting
Heather-Anne or the police's suspicions.

"If they could put you in prison for being too mean and
ugly to live, he'd have been there long ago. Is it because of
what happened at the bowling alley?"

Dexter shot her a "shut up" look and quickly filled her in.
I didn't ask what had happened at the bowling alley; sometimes being an ostrich with your head in the sand is the only
way to survive motherhood.

"Murder?" she shrieked when he told her. "I'm not riding
with a murderer."

"I'll murder *you* if you don't shut up," Dexter growled.

I couldn't much blame him. "Kendall, honey, you don't
want to go saying anything about this at school."

"Don't worry, Mom," she said. "I wouldn't want people
to know I have a psychopath for a brother. Although anyone

who's met him has probably already figured that out." She got in the front seat and slammed the door.

"She'll blab it to everyone before the end of first period," Dexter predicted, slamming his book bag strap in the Hummer's door and reopening it to yank the strap out. He slammed the door shut again. I was getting a headache and it wasn't even seven o'clock yet. Arriving at work was a huge relief.

Charlie had beaten me in, and I said, "Welcome back," as I shoved my purse under the desk.

She grunted and took a drink from her Pepsi. Charlie's always pretty surly before her second Pepsi. "Was the doc okay with you returning to work full-time?"

She gave me a look from the corners of her eyes, which I took to mean she hadn't asked him. "Charlie—"

"Gigi." She raised her head from the computer and said, "I'm not going to go vaulting over fences chasing bad guys or have to sprint to get away from a bioweapon-wielding terrorist. I'm going to sit here quietly, on my pillow"—she half stood and lifted a striped pillow from her chair—"and surf the Net. I might even"—she paused dramatically—"make a few phone calls. I'll be fine."

I knew when to shut up, so I did, but I knew that she'd be vaulting fences and tackling bioterrorists in a split second if the need arose. The weather had turned cold again, like it did here in Colorado Springs—fifty degrees one day, twenty the next—and I took off my favorite parka and hung it on the coat tree by the door. "Did you see the forecast?" I asked. "The weatherman says we might get a foot of snow."

"You know how to tell when a weatherman's lying, don't you?" Charlie asked without looking up. "His lips are moving."

I laughed but said, "I don't know. It feels like snow." Tucking my angora-blend turtleneck tunic under my hips, I sat and started making a list of all the places Les might be. It was depressingly long. He was a social guy and he got around. Of course, some of these people, the ones whose money he'd run off with, might not be happy to see him. I crossed two names off the list. Then another three.

"How's Dexter holding up?" Charlie asked, popping open another Pepsi. She took a sip and brushed her bangs off her face. "Was it hard for him at the police station yesterday?"

"Oh, Charlie, your friend Tuck—that's what he told us to call him—was wonderful. I have to admit I was a bit nervous at first, his hair and all, but he talked to Dexter and they talked to the police and everything's fine for the moment, although Tuck isn't sure the police bought Dexter's story about someone being in the bedroom while Dexter talked to Heather-Anne. Still, they didn't arrest him, so that's good."

"What's their next step?"

"I don't know."

She picked up the phone and dialed a number from memory. "Montgomery, it's me."

I tried not to listen in on her conversation, but it's kind of hard not to overhear in an office that's smaller than my closet with no doors except on the powder room. From Charlie's tone, it didn't seem to be going well, and she hung up after barely more than a minute, scowling. "He won't tell me anything," she said. "Says he doesn't know what Lorrimore's thinking or doing. Says he got called out on an attempted murder outside Cowboys last night and isn't in the loop on the Heather-Anne case."

"He probably isn't," I said, dismayed by her anger.

"He could be if he wanted to be."

She plopped down in front of her computer again, winced, and tapped the keys so hard they sounded like bullets. "Wait a minute . . . Look at this, Gigi. He lied!"

"Who lied?" I scurried around my desk to peer over Charlie's shoulder. Her screen showed a page from the *Mountain Press*, a paper that advertised itself as being for Gatlinburg, Pigeon Forge, and Sevierville, Tennessee. She was looking at what seemed to be the society page. An article about a fundraiser for the Heart Association showed a color photo of four smiling people in evening wear, two women and two men.

"That strapless dress isn't a good choice for her," I said, pointing to the woman on the far left who looked to be about my age and size. "She needs more support."

Charlie stabbed a finger at the screen. "Not her. Him."

The man she pointed at had a gray-streaked beard and a weathered face, and he was seated in a wheelchair. "He looks kind of like Kris Kristofferson. What about him?"

" 'Sunny and Brian Wilcox, Lisetta Teegle, and Wilfred Cheney share a joke at the Have a Heart fund-raiser at Gatlinburg's Glenstone Lodge,' " she read from the caption. "Wilfred Cheney! That's Heather-Anne's purportedly abusive husband. He's in a wheelchair—he couldn't have strangled Heather-Anne at the Embassy Suites."

"Maybe it's her brother-in-law," I suggested. "My sister May married a man with six brothers, and she's all the time getting calls from people trying to reach one of her nieces and nephews or sisters-in-law."

"I didn't know you had a sister."

145

"Three of them," I said. "Two of them are still in Georgia, but Coretta and her husband live in Houston."

"It's not a bad thought," Charlie said, "except—" She tapped a few keys and a new photo came up, this one from a newspaper wedding announcement. "Ta-da." She leaned back so I could see it better.

A young woman with her dark hair in an up-do, wearing a wedding dress so tight I could practically read the label on her undies, had her arm tucked into Wilfred Cheney's arm. There wasn't so much gray in his beard, and he wasn't in a wheelchair, but it was the same man. I leaned closer and studied the bride, who was younger and plumper than Heather-Anne, and brunette, to boot.

"Do you think that's Heather-Anne?" Charlie asked, eyeing the photo doubtfully.

The bride's hand rested on the groom's arm, and I could make out a flawless French manicure, even in the black-and-white photo. "It's her," I said, pointing out the manicure.

Charlie gave me an incredulous look. "First time I've seen someone make an identification off a manicure. I'll take your word for it." She scrolled up to show the date: almost five years ago. "The Heart Association fund-raiser was two months ago," she said, "so sometime after the wedding, Wilfred ended up in a wheelchair, and Lucinda ran off and became Heather-Anne. What do you want to bet the two events were related?"

"Who lied?" I asked, going back to Charlie's original statement.

"Alan 'I Don't Own a Shirt' Brodnax. He said Cheney's been after Heather-Anne, that she was afraid of him, that he might well have killed her. You can't tell me Brodnax—who is a professional researcher, for heaven's sake—didn't know the man was in a wheelchair and couldn't have been chasing Heather-Anne all over the country, much less strangling her at the Embassy Suites without anyone noticing."

"Maybe someone did," I said. "I mean, maybe someone noticed a man in a wheelchair." The thought excited me: Dexter wouldn't be the prime suspect if Heather-Anne's former husband had been seen at the hotel.

Charlie's brows arched, but before she could say anything, the phone rang. I snatched it up. "Swift Investigations, Gigi Goldman speaking. May I help you?"

An official-sounding voice on the other end asked me if I was the owner of a red BMW and read off a license plate number. It's not like I had my license plate numbers memorized, but I said, "Yes."

Charlie looked a question at me, and I mouthed, "Dexter's car." She scooted closer, and I held the phone away from my ear a bit so she could hear.

The speaker identified himself as a CSPD patrol officer and said, "Your car's been involved in a hit-and-run accident at the First and Main Town Center. Do you know who was driving the vehicle?"

"I reported it stolen last night," I said, grateful that Charlie had made me do that.

"You'll need to come down here and make arrangements to have it towed and deal with insurance issues," the officer said in an uncompromising voice.

"Was Les— was anyone injured?"

"There were no reported injuries. The driver fled the scene, according to witnesses."

"Come on," Charlie said when I hung up. "I'll drive. You're shaking too much to keep the car on the road."

"What could have happened?" I shrugged into my parka and zipped it. "What if Les is injured? Maybe he has a concussion and doesn't know who he is or how to get help. He might need me."

Charlie gave me a not-so-gentle shove out the door. "He divorced you and ran off with another woman, Gigi. He doesn't get to 'need' you anymore."

"You don't stop caring about someone after more than thirty years of marriage just like that, you know," I said, my cashmere gloves making it hard to snap my fingers on "just like that."

Charlie rolled her eyes. "Then the sooner we get there and have a look around, the sooner you can play ministering angel. Although, personally, I'd be more tempted to play Dr. Kevorkian."

20

We got to the First and Main Town Center on the east side of Colorado Springs twenty minutes later. It wasn't hard to figure out where the accident was. A police car with its lights twirling blue and red in the gray morning was parked half on the sidewalk near the Cinemark Theater. A tow truck driver was hooking up to the rear of the Beemer. The front half of the car was covered with a huge COMING ATTRACTIONS sign advertising an R-rated movie with werewolves, aliens, and Adam Sandler. Ick, yuck, and ugh. The sign had apparently fallen on the BMW after it rammed into the metal post holding it. I knew what I would see if I looked under the sign: thousands of dollars' worth of damage I couldn't afford to get fixed.

"Maybe it's not as bad as it looks," Charlie said with false heartiness as we parked and got out of her Subaru.

"Maybe it's worse." I'm not normally a gloomy person, but this week was getting me down. I signed some paperwork for the police officer and the tow truck driver while Charlie walked up to the crippled BMW. I didn't know how I'd tell Dexter that his car had been flattened by werewolves and aliens. I was about to join Charlie when the movie theater manager came up, all waving arms and angry voice, to talk about insurance and getting her sign repaired. I saw Charlie jerk open the car's back door before I let the manager drag me into her office.

When I came out, the police car was gone and so was Dexter's car. Charlie stood on the sidewalk, a zip-up folder under her arm, talking to a stocky man who was leaning toward her in a way that made it look like he was sharing a secret. He wore a lumberjack cap and boots, ready for the snow, and he had dark pouches under his eyes, as if someone had glued on soggy tea bags. I wondered if he knew that Preparation H, the kind you can get from Canada, would help with the puffiness.

He broke off when I got near. "Who's this?" he asked suspiciously.

"My partner," Charlie said in a soothing voice. "You were saying . . ."

"Yeah, then the guy takes off running toward the theater. He didn't even stop to see if he'd hurt anyone, and there were plenty of people around, I'll tell you, including a bus-full of seniors from one of those retirement centers who were here to see that new Sean Connery movie. I thought he was dead. Anyway, like I say, the guy took off running and the guy in the other car—at least, I think it was a guy, although it had those smoky windows, so I couldn't say for sure—zooms up onto the sidewalk and tries to run down the first guy. He gets away by the skin of his teeth and ducks into the theater with the clerks all yelling at him about not having a ticket, and the guy in the black car takes off. Look, you can see the tire marks." The man pointed to marks on the sidewalk, where the water jets would be shooting up if it were summer.

"Do you know what kind of car it was?" Charlie asked.

"Something sporty. Foreign maybe. Black."

"You've been very helpful, Mr. Kimmel." She handed him a card. "Please call if you think of anything else."

"Is there a reward?" he asked hopefully.

Charlie shook her head, and he joined a woman I hadn't noticed earlier, who was clearly waiting for him.

"What was that all about?" I asked Charlie, shivering as the wind picked up.

"I'm not completely sure," she said, staring after the man and his wife as they headed for the Dick's Sporting Goods. "It sounds to me like someone is after Les. From what Mr. Kimmel and another witness I talked to had to say, someone deliberately caused the accident, trying to run into Les's car.

I don't know if they were trying to stop him or kill him, although my money's on the former since it'd be hard to kill him in an area this congested and hope to get away."

A frown puckered my brow. "I hope he's okay. Where do you suppose he is?"

"Watching the latest *Hangover* movie?" She nodded toward the theater, then grabbed my arm as I started in that direction. "Not really. He probably ran straight through the building and out the back exit. He could be anywhere in the city, or halfway to Albuquerque by now."

Snowflakes started to fall, and I stuck out my tongue to catch one as we returned to the car. "What's that?" I gestured to the folder under Charlie's arm.

"Ah, this." She held it up. It was a simple black leather-look folder, letter sized, that zipped around three sides. "It's not Dexter's, is it?"

I shook my head. "I've never seen it."

Charlie smiled triumphantly. "Then it must be Les's. He bolted from the Beemer so quickly he didn't think to grab it."

"What's in it?"

"Let's find out."

We got in the car, and Charlie cranked the heat up. The zipper stuck when she tried to open the case and then gave with a ripping sound. "It's better than Christmas," I said, leaning sideways to peer into the case.

It contained a tablet of paper elastic-banded into place on the right-hand side and a pen slotted into the middle. On the left-hand side, letters and papers poked out of two flat pockets. We shuffled through the four or five sheets of paper, most of which seemed to be hotel receipts. "Doesn't look very useful,"

Charlie said. She pulled out the last item, an envelope addressed to Les in Costa Rica. When she shook it, a newspaper clipping fell out.

I stooped to pick it up and held it so we could both read it. I'd noticed recently that I was having to hold things farther and farther away to read them. The tiny, smudgy print on the newspaper clipping was especially hard. I'd bought a couple of pairs of reading glasses and hunted through my purse for some now. Charlie was done with the article by the time I pulled out the retro cat's-eye-shaped pink glasses with a rhinestone pattern on the corners. If I had to look old, at least I could have fun doing it.

"Interesting," Charlie said as I read the brief article. It was about a murder in Cheyenne, Wyoming. Robert Eustis, a wealthy rancher, had been poisoned with brake fluid, apparently mixed in his Long Island iced tea, and died. Due to the ranch's remote location and the brutal winter weather, the body had gone undiscovered for what might have been weeks. The police were calling his death a homicide and were looking for Eustis's wife, Amanda. "We need to make sure she's safe," the local sheriff said, "and see what she might be able to tell us about Mr. Eustis's unfortunate demise."

I turned the clipping over but couldn't find a date on it anywhere. "Whyever do you suppose Les had this?" I asked. "He was never interested in any of those true crime shows."

"Good question." Charlie put the car in gear and backed out. "Is there a return address on the envelope?"

I picked up the slightly worn business-sized envelope and turned it over. "Nope." Peering at the postmark, I tried to read it. "It looks like it was sent from here, though. I can make out 'ings, CO.'"

"Can you read the date?"

"Uh-uh."

"I suppose Les could have been carrying it around for months, but I'll bet it was sent sometime the week before he disappeared. Why else would he bring it with him? I say we get back to the office and see what we can find online about this murder and Mr. Robert Eustis," Charlie said, speeding up once we got back on Powers Boulevard.

The computer search was disappointing. We dug up the article and discovered that it had been published in January three years ago. Further searching led to a couple of brief follow-up articles and an obit with a photo of Robert Eustis. "He looked nice," I said, studying the photo of the gray-haired man, who had been sixty-three when he died. He had gentle eyes and slightly overlapping front teeth. "Says here he's survived by his wife, Amanda, two children, and three grandbabies. So sad. He was predeceased by his first wife, also named Amanda. Now, that's weird."

Charlie had printed out the follow-up articles and was reading them at her desk. "They never solved the murder, and they never located Amanda Eustis the Second. I think a call to the sheriff might be in order."

She found a phone number in a matter of seconds and was talking to the sheriff moments later. I listened in but didn't get anything out of it other than Charlie's one- or two-word responses. She was on the phone less than three minutes and had a thoughtful look on her face when she hung up.

"Well? What did he say?"

She gave me a considering look. "It's what he didn't say that interests me." She paused. "Are you up for a trip to Wyoming?"

I stared at her in dismay. "What? Why?"

"I think we need to talk to Sheriff Huff in person. He was cagey on the phone, wouldn't tell me anything we didn't already know from the newspaper articles. It's clear, though, that there's more to the story. I think he might give up more face-to-face."

"But, Charlie, this rancher's murder might not have anything to do with Les's disappearance or with Heather-Anne's death or anything."

"Maybe not, but my intuition says otherwise. I think this clipping is key. I think it's the reason Les left Costa Rica. A trip to Cheyenne will only cost us a day. I asked the sheriff to fax us a photo of Amanda Eustis, but he says there isn't one. She only married Eustis a few months before he died, and apparently she was camera-shy."

I ignored the last part. "I can't be away overnight again. What will I do with the kids? And now that Dexter doesn't have a car to drive . . ."

"I'll go," Charlie said.

"You can't drive all that way on your own," I objected. "Not yet. Your bullet wound!"

She sucked in her upper lip, and I could see she was thinking about telling me she'd be fine, but then she caved. "You're right. I'll find someone to go with me, do the driving. I'd ask

Montgomery, but he's made it as clear as vodka that he's not coming near this case. Maybe Albertine or Dan."

"I'm sorry I can't go," I said, feeling guilty. "I'm not pulling my weight."

"Don't worry about it. You went to Aspen, and there's plenty you can do here. You might start by talking to Hollis Sloan, the guy I saw Heather-Anne with at the Y whose wife accused her of theft. Then you can track down Patrick Dreiser and see what he's been up to recently, like maybe plotting revenge on Les and killing Heather-Anne to get back at him. On second thought"—she gazed at me assessingly—"that can probably wait until I get back."

"I can talk to him," I said, drawing myself up straighter. Dreiser might make me a little nervous—he was obnoxious and threatening after Les left—but I could talk to him in a public place. It's not like he'd get back at Les by doing anything to me, I thought sadly, since Les had divorced me and obviously didn't care what happened to me. If he'd cared, he would have left us a little something more than the house, the Hummer, and a half interest in a just-scraping-by PI firm. "Should we give the newspaper clipping to the police?"

"Good idea. Fax it and the other papers from Les's folder to them and tell Detective Lorrimore about someone trying to mow down Les. I doubt she'll be able to do anything without more info, but you never know what piece of data might bust a case open."

I made a note. "Thank you for doing this, Charlie," I said. "I know we're not even getting paid to find Les anymore."

She shrugged away my gratitude. "It's not like we have any other big cases at the moment. If we have to find the real killer in order to keep Dexter out of prison, that's what we'll do." When I teared up, she added, "I can't have my partner distracted by running off to the state pen twice a week to visit her son. Think of all the billable hours we'd lose."

"I wouldn't—"

She walked past me and shrugged into her navy peacoat.

"Where are you going?"

"To find someone to drive me to Wyoming, and to visit Mr. 'My Pecs Are Bigger than Your Boobs' Brodnax to find out what else he wasn't telling me."

21

Charlie headed for Brodnax's Wolf Ranch house, keeping one eye on the sky. The snow had stopped for the moment, but steel-wool clouds obscured the top of Pikes Peak and the Front Range. The forecast predicted the bulk of the snow for tomorrow, and Charlie wanted to be out of Cheyenne well before the first snowflakes fell. She called Albertine as she drove, but the woman turned down the opportunity to drive to Wyoming in the face of an approaching blizzard.

"Can't, Charlie," she said. "I've got a private party booked tonight—rehearsal dinner—and I've got to be here to oversee things. Otherwise, there's nothing I'd like better than trying to outdrive a monster snowstorm. Mother Nature doesn't like it when you taunt her, sugar. Just look at what happened to those poor folks in New Orleans who didn't evacuate for Hurricane Katrina. Now, if you ever want to drive to Vegas, I'm your woman."

Charlie hung up and tried Dan. He surprised her by accepting immediately. "I need a break," he said. "We're having renovations done in the office spaces, and it's so noisy I can't hear myself think. I don't have anything scheduled until Friday morning. Mel can handle whatever comes up while I'm gone."

"We'll be back by tomorrow evening at the latest," Charlie assured him. "I'll swing by in an hour and a half to pick you up."

She flipped the phone shut as she pulled up to the curb in front of Brodnax's house. Getting out, she surveyed it grimly. She'd printed off the photo of Wilfred Cheney and thought she'd start by showing it to Brodnax to gauge his reaction. Marching to the front door, she stabbed the doorbell. No response. She listened for a moment but heard nothing. The wind gusted, raking branches against metal gutters at the house next door, but no sign of life came from within Brodnax's house. Standing on the front stoop, Charlie got the feeling the house was deserted.

She walked to the garage, which sat perpendicular to the house, stood on tiptoe, and cupped her hands around her eyes to see into the window. The dark, cavernous space was empty. Not just no-cars empty—totally empty. Not a half-full paint can, not a rake, not a bicycle or lawn mower or bag of deicing salt. Brodnax was gone; he'd cleared out. Charlie could feel it.

She held her windblown hair off her face with one hand

while evaluating her options. She could go home and pack and hit the road for Wyoming. She could canvass the neighbors to see what they might know about Brodnax and/or Heather-Anne. Neighbors were inherently nosy and tended to know a lot more than people thought they did about what went on next door or across the street. Or she could gain entry to the house with the picklocks Gigi had bought on eBay, which Charlie had been practicing with while she convalesced, and see what she could learn. The thought brought a spurt of adrenaline. With the latter plan in mind, Charlie traipsed around to the back of the house. The drapes were drawn as before, and she could see nothing. However, a child jumping on a trampoline in the next yard, and the lack of concealment in the form of fences or shrubs, discouraged her from using the picklocks. She consoled herself with the thought that if Brodnax had cleaned out the garage so thoroughly, he certainly hadn't left anything in the house.

Glancing at her watch, Charlie decided she had time to chat with the neighbors on either side, if they were home, before meeting Father Dan. She crunched across the rock bed that separated Brodnax's house from the house with the trampolining child. The sound of a vacuum drifted through the front door as she rang the bell. The vacuum cut off, and footsteps approached. Charlie stepped back and pasted a nonthreatening smile on her face.

The wooden door opened and a young woman appeared, holding the storm door firmly shut. In her late teens or early twenties, she had flax-colored hair and equally pale brows that made her appear to have none at all. "Yes?" she called through the glass.

Charlie approved of the girl's caution. "Hi. I'm a Realtor, and I was supposed to meet with your neighbor, Mr. Brodnax, about selling his house, but he's late for our appointment. I don't suppose you know when he left or how I can get hold of him?"

"I'm the au pair," the girl said, and Charlie noticed a faint trace of Dutch or German accent. "I just take care of Evie. I only arrived last month, and I don't know any of the neighbors except the lady two doors down whose daughter plays with Evie. Sorry." She closed the door before Charlie could ask anything else.

One down. Charlie surveyed the nearby houses, trying to decide which looked most promising. She finally decided on the one across the street because someone had pulled up the blinds since she'd arrived, probably to scope her out. Promisingly snoopy behavior. She crossed the street. Before she could ring the bell, the door swung open.

"I've been watching you," the thin, midforties woman announced, arms akimbo. She wore a USAFA sweatshirt and jeans and had thick brown hair cut in something perilously like a Dorothy Hamill wedge. She looked like the prototypical soccer mom, able to shuttle four kids to a variety of sports practices and games, plus run the PTA and hold down a full-time job. "The covenants don't allow door-to-door sales."

"I'm a Realtor," Charlie said, smiling until her cheeks ached. "I had an appointment to talk to Mr. Brodnax across the street about selling his house, but he's not there."

"Oh, really?" The woman narrowed her eyes.

Nodding, Charlie said, "Did you see him go? Did he maybe leave a change of address with you?"

"You're lying."

The woman didn't pull her punches. "I'm—"

"I know you're lying because we own that house and Alan was renting it from us. It isn't his to sell."

Oops.

"I'm going to call the cops. You're probably— What do they call it? Casing the place. You're looking to see who's home and who's not and what kind of alarm systems we have so you can rob us. For your information, we have a very active Neighborhood Watch and you're not going to get away with it." Give her some tights and a cape and she could have been Subdivision Savior Woman who vanquishes petty thieves, teenaged vandals, and HOA scofflaws with her prying eyes and dialing finger.

Charlie would have cut her losses and left except the soccer mom had been Brodnax's landlady and undoubtedly had lease paperwork or rent checks with addresses, employment, or next-of-kin information that might prove important.

"Wait," Charlie said, holding up her hands in an "I surrender" gesture. "You're right. I'm not a Realtor." She handed the woman one of her cards. "I'm a private investigator, and it's vital that I find Mr. Brodnax. Look, Mrs.—?"

"Carrie Barbiero. How do I know you're not lying now?"

"I guess you don't," Charlie admitted. She nodded at the woman's sweatshirt. "Are you stationed at the Academy? I was in the air force for seven years."

"My husband teaches in the math department." She studied Charlie for a long moment. "Oh, come on in. I'm an excellent judge of character, and you don't really strike me as a thief. Frankly, I'd be happier than a pig in shit if you'd locate Alan Brodnax. He stiffed us on two months' rent and sold the appliances."

She led the way through a foyer littered with volleyballs, hockey sticks and skates, and snow gear in sizes ranging from tot to teen. Charlie appreciated that she made no apology for the clutter as she stepped over a skateboard and into a family room that looked lived in. Others might say it looked like Visigoths had rampaged through overnight, but Charlie was feeling charitable since she had high hopes for the interview. Gallon-sized plastic Baggies filled with rectangular strips of cardboard dotted the floor and puzzled Charlie.

Carrie noted her look. "I'm in charge of the box tops collection committee at Ranch Creek," she said, sinking cross-legged to the floor with the ease of a woman half her age. "I can count while you talk. What's Alan done to set someone else on his tail?"

Charlie pushed aside a flotilla of Star Wars spacecraft and sat on a denim-covered ottoman. She told her about Heather-Anne's death and the woman's connection to Brodnax. "She used to live in your rental house. Did you know her?"

Looking up from the stack of box tops in her hand, Carrie said, "Oh, my God, yes. We were shocked when we read about her death. We thought she was living the high life in some tropical paradise." Her eyes widened, and Charlie noticed they were a rich brown with hazel flecks. "You don't think Alan killed her, do you?"

"I don't really know," Charlie said. "How would you describe their relationship?"

"That's a damned good question." Carrie leaned back, bracing her palms on the floor behind her. "At first, I assumed they were lovers; I mean, they're both so damned gorgeous it's hard to imagine them keeping their hands off each other. But I saw Heather-Anne go out with a couple different men during the months she lived here, and as for Alan . . . my God, he went through women the way my kids go through Cheerios. Not that I'm spying on them or anything," she added self-consciously. "It was hard to miss. Every time I drove out or walked to the mailbox in the evening, there'd be another car pulling up or leaving. So I guess they were just housemates, friends. We didn't have any complaints with him as a renter until we discovered he'd taken off in the middle of the night and sold off our appliances to boot."

"Do you have a rental application or a canceled check—anything that might have Brodnax's former address or employer's information on it?"

Carrie crinkled her brow. "I'm pretty sure he worked for himself. At least, that's what his application said: self-employed. My husband chatted with him once when he went over to fix the garbage disposal and said he really seems to know his way around computers, that he's some kind of analyst or researcher. Maybe he's a day trader? Anyway, we don't have anything about an employer. All we have"—she rose in one fluid movement and crossed to a cluttered desk tucked between a treadmill and a recliner—"is this."

She came back and handed Charlie a rental application form. Charlie immediately noted a Social Security number and a former address. *Cha-ching!*

"He paid the rent through an automatic deposit, so we

don't have any bank information. It's not illegal to give you that, is it?" She looked like she might snatch the form back.

"Not at all," Charlie said, folding the form and tucking it in her purse. "I promise to let you know if I locate Brodnax. You can start legal proceedings against him even without knowing where he is," she added to distract the woman, who still seemed inclined to ask for the form back. "That will speed the process of getting a judgment against him. You can also file a police report about the theft of the appliances."

"We don't even know when he left," Carrie said. "We've been gone for about ten days. My father-in-law died, and we were in Missouri for the funeral and to deal with estate stuff. He could've left more than a week ago and be God knows where by now."

"I talked to him yesterday," Charlie told her, "so he hasn't been gone long."

Eyeing her suspiciously, Carrie said, "Sounds like you made him leave. What did you say to him?"

"I asked about Heather-Anne, that's all. The appliances were already gone, though, so he may have been planning to disappear for a while."

Carrie's eyes lit with interest. "It sounds like he has something to hide, doesn't it?"

Indeed, Charlie thought, taking her leave of Carrie Barbieri. *But what?*

Forty minutes later, Charlie tooted the Subaru's horn outside Dan Allgood's rectory. She had scooted back across town, tossed a few necessaries in a gym bag, and faxed Gigi Alan

Brodnax's rental application with directions to run his Social Security number and see what she could find out about the man.

Dan emerged from the house toting a bag even smaller than Charlie's. His six-foot-five frame filled the doorway, and his blond hair riffled in the slight breeze. A down-filled vest and rugged work boots made him look less priestly than usual. Charlie was relieved that he wasn't wearing his clerical collar. He said something, and Charlie rolled down the window. "What?"

"I said, if I'm doing the driving, we're taking my truck."

"Fine," Charlie said. "I'll pay for the gas. It's a business expense."

Dan nodded and disappeared into his garage while Charlie returned the Subaru to her driveway and walked back. Dan's blue Ram 2500 idled at the curb. It had a topper over the bed and, Charlie was happy to see, snow tires. She opened the door and tossed her overnight bag behind the seat. "Nice."

"It's been too long since I've been on a road trip." Dan put the truck in gear, and it rumbled toward I-25 with a powerful growl.

Charlie made a blade of her hand and chopped it forward. "Cheyenne, ho."

22

As soon as Charlie left, I set about trying to find Hollis Sloan. I know it was chicken of me, but I was less nervous about talking to him than to Patrick Dreiser, so I hunted up his phone number. Before I became a PI, I assumed they had super-secret databases or sources for finding people. Really, though, the phone book works best. I found a home number for Hollis Sloan and an office number. Apparently, he was an orthodontist. No wonder he could afford to toss money and gifts at Heather-Anne, I thought, remembering how much we'd paid to have Dexter and Kendall's teeth straightened. Kendall still had six months or so to go on her braces, and I'd be over the moon when she got them off and I could stop sending a monthly check to Dr. George. That money was enough for a couple of facials, which I'd mostly given up since Les left, or weekly manicures, or . . . or the utility bill, I told myself, trying to focus on my new budget resolutions.

I figured I'd be more likely to catch Hollis Sloan at the office than at home on a Tuesday morning, so I dialed his office for directions and set off in the Hummer. His office was off of Galley Road, not too far from Mitchell High School. Convenient. He probably put braces on half the freshman class and they could walk to his office for monthly wire tightening. Three or four teens and tweens, all with their mothers, sat in the waiting room when I walked in. Everyone in the room was texting or talking on a cell except for one mother flipping through a *Good Housekeeping* magazine. A male receptionist greeted me with a look and a little smile.

"My name's Georgia Goldman," I said, approaching the counter. "I was hoping I could speak to Dr. Sloan for a few minutes."

"Do you have an appointment?"

I shook my head, conscious that the waiting moms and teens could hear every word. "No. I was hoping he could maybe squeeze me in between appointments. I only need a few minutes."

Shuffling through some file folders, the receptionist said, "We only do exams by appointment, Ms. Goldman. If you're thinking about braces—"

"Braces! I'm—"

"—for your overbite, then—"

I didn't have an overbite! Did I? My tongue pushed against my top teeth. "I'm not here about braces," I said thickly.

"Oh." He studied me, taking in my plum-colored mohair jacket and my gold Bob Mackie tank top. "A sales rep. Dr. Sloan only meets with salespeople on—"

"I'm not in sales, either. I'm a private investigator." I like telling people that. The hum of conversation behind me quit, and I glanced over my shoulder to see everyone in the waiting room staring at me. I handed the receptionist my card and lowered my voice. "It's a private matter."

The receptionist looked uncertain. A smocked assistant emerged from the back and called a couple of names off a clipboard. Two of the kids in the waiting room followed her back. Then an older, silver-haired man I knew at once must be Dr. Sloan approached the counter, laid a file on it, and scribbled something on a sticky note. Tanned and a little thick around the waist, he looked to be in his early sixties.

"Dr. Sloan," the receptionist said, "this woman—"

I held out my hand and gave him my friendliest smile. "Georgia Goldman. Gigi. I just need—"

He peered at me, head cocked. "Hm, something for your overbite?"

I was about to inform everyone in the office once and for all that I did not have an overbite when the doctor added, "I can squeeze you in now. Come on back."

I shut my mouth and followed him to an exam room with a wallpaper border that had galloping horses. He gestured me to the full-length, loungelike padded chair with the powerful light suspended over it. I perched on it and swung my legs up, making sure my skirt didn't slide too high. "I'm really—"

"Open, please." He pressed at the corner of my jaw and I opened.

"Aw weelly ere oo ahsk ahout Hedder-Anng."

"Um-hm." Inserting an angled mirror, he inspected my molars. After a second, he pulled it out and rolled his chair toward the counter to make notes.

Seizing my chance, I sat up straight, banging my forehead on the light fixture he'd pulled low to examine my teeth. "Ow." I put a hand to my head but continued, "Dr. Sloan, I'm here to ask you about Heather-Anne Pawlusik."

He jolted and the pen slipped from his hand, clinking to the floor. He swiveled. "What? Who are you? You're not here about braces."

"I tried to tell you I'm not," I said. "I'm a private investigator."

"Oh, my God." He dropped his face into his hands. "Did my wife send you? Is this—"

"Your wife? Heavens, no. We don't do divorce work. Well, not unless we really, really need the money."

"Divorce? She wants a divorce?" He looked up, panic in his eyes.

"Dr. Sloan! Hollis. I don't know your wife. She didn't hire us. Heather-Anne did."

Sucking in two deep breaths, he said, "I don't understand."

"I'm trying to tell you." Sheesh, the man went on and on. "Heather-Anne hired us—"

"Who's 'us'?" Suspicion glimmered in his gray eyes.

"Me and my partner, Charlie Swift. We own Swift Investigations. Heather-Anne hired us to find my husband, well, my ex-husband, and—"

"What? You're not making any sense. I've got patients to see." He stood up, looming over me on the exam chair.

I could tell he was going to walk out any moment and I'd never get another crack at him. "When Heather-Anne was killed, the—"

"What?" He turned Casper-pale and sagged like a puppet whose strings had been cut. He slammed a hand onto the counter to keep himself from falling. "Killed? You mean . . . she's dead?"

"You didn't know? I'm so sorry I broke the news to you like that. Here, let me get you some water." I slid off the awkward chair and got one of those little paper cups dentists give you to rinse with and filled it from the sink in the corner. Dr. Sloan took it with a trembling hand and drank. I refilled it twice before he regained control. "Better?"

He nodded. "Tell me what happened. No, wait." He crossed to the open door, looked both ways down the hall, and closed it softly. He turned to face me. "Okay."

As briefly and gently as possible, I told him about Heather-Anne being strangled.

"Oh, my God." He ran his hand down his face, dragging the flesh down so he momentarily looked like a basset hound.

"Were you and Heather-Anne . . . friends?" I asked.

He gave a snort of bitter laughter. "I thought so at one time. But then I found out she had more 'friends' like me, and I broke it off."

"More friends like you?"

"I wasn't the only man she was seeing. I know of at least one other. There may have been dozens, for all I know. Dozens of men of a certain age and income dazzled by that smile, that hair, that body, and the thought that she found them attractive. Well, there's no fool like an old fool, as my wife tells me," he said.

"You're not old."

He gave me a cynical look. "I'm older now than I was this morning, Ms. . . . . Gold, did you say?"

"Gigi."

"At first, being with Heather-Anne made me feel younger, vital. Then . . ." He trailed off.

"So if you'd broken things off, why did you work out with her on Saturday?"

He stiffened. "How did you know—? My wife *did* hire you! You've been spying on me." He made for the door.

I hurried after him and put a hand on his arm. "No! My partner was meeting Heather-Anne, and she saw you at the YMCA."

Turning, he looked down at me, and I realized my hand was still on his arm. I quickly drew it away.

"Heather-Anne called me. She said she was back in town. I knew she'd been in Nicaragua or some such place with that crook she ran off with."

I gulped back an objection at his description of Les. "And?"

"She said she was back in the training business, that she'd missed working with me and hoped we could get together." He rubbed his eyebrow. "We got together for a training session, nothing more. She said she needed money. I felt sorry for her, so I gave her some. End of story."

"I'm sorry, but did your wife know you'd given Heather-Anne money again? I heard she accused her of stealing from you." I winced as I said it, expecting him to explode.

"Leave Myra out of this. In fact," he continued coldly, "I don't know why I'm talking to you. I'd like you to leave now." He pulled the door open. One of his technicians stood there, arm raised to knock. She stepped back and looked from Hollis Sloan to me and back again.

"Uh, the Braisten boy is ready for you, Doctor."

"Mrs. Gold has decided she doesn't want orthodontic intervention," he said, not even looking at me. Without a good-bye, he hurried down the hall toward his waiting patient.

The technician escorted me to the waiting room. "Are you

sure?" she asked. "Dr. Sloan is the best orthodontist in the city. He could take care of that overbite in no time."

"I don't have an overbite!"

Back in the Hummer, I examined my smile in the rearview mirror and thought of all the things I should have asked, like who was the other man that Hollis Sloan knew had been sleeping with Heather-Anne, and had she said why she was in town again, and where had he—and his wife—been on Sunday morning when Heather-Anne was getting strangled. Hollis Sloan had seemed genuinely shocked to hear that Heather-Anne was dead, but for all I knew he did community theater productions in his spare time and was an accomplished actor.

I headed back to the office, planning to do some research on Alan Brodnax. After that, I guessed, I'd have no excuse for avoiding a meeting with Patrick Dreiser. The thought made me sigh. I craned my neck and looked up through the windshield. Angry clouds the color of pencil lead made the sky look closer than it had been earlier. I hoped Charlie got to Wyoming and back before the storm hit.

23

The Laramie County sheriff didn't look at all as Charlie had envisioned him after their phone conversation. She'd been thinking tall cowboy, big gut, late middle age. The reality was shorter, slimmer, and younger. Sheriff Hadley Huff was maybe five-nine, 145 pounds, thirty years old, and looked like a marathoner in a crisply ironed white shirt and olive-brown uniform slacks. He shook Charlie's hand when she was shown into his office and surveyed her with frank interest.

"Former military?" he asked.

When she nodded, he said, "Me, too. Army. Six years. Artillery. You?"

"Air force. Seven years. Office of Special Investigations."

They spent a few minutes discussing their respective military careers before Huff opened a file folder. "The Eustis case, huh? I've got to tell you, this one eats at me. I'd only been in office a couple months when Robert Eustis's body was found. As I told you on the phone, the case is still unsolved. Bugs me. After you called to say you were coming up, I made you a copy of the case file. I wasn't sure if I'd hand it over, but—"

He slid a manila envelope across the desk to Charlie. She flipped through the crime scene photos and autopsy report for a moment, then looked up to find Huff's gaze on her. The Wyoming state seal on the wall behind him dominated the office.

"You're being awfully helpful to an out-of-town PI," she observed.

He smiled thinly. "I'd give assistance to anyone I thought stood a chance of making progress on this case. You seem like a better bet than most."

She looked a question at him, and he amplified. "You're not a quitter. I've run twenty-two marathons, and I can stand at the starting line and look at the people lined up at the tape and say, 'quitter, quitter, quitter.'" His finger pointed a different way on each "quitter," as if he were singling out individuals. "I can see it in the way they hold themselves, their expressions, something in their eyes." He shrugged. "I think that once you sink your teeth into something, you keep after it. Ever run a marathon?"

"Once."

"Finish?"

"Three hours and fifty-two minutes."

He nodded with satisfaction. "Knew it."

Charlie felt vaguely uncomfortable at being analyzed so astutely by a young man she'd known for only fifteen minutes. "Are you saying you've quit on the case?"

He smiled broadly, not one whit offended by her question. "By no means, but I've got plenty of other cases in this jurisdiction and limited manpower. I'm viewing you as an extension of my force, if you will, because I know if I share what I have with you, you'll share what you learn with me." He made it a statement.

"Absolutely," Charlie agreed, seeing no reason she wouldn't be happy to pass along what she found out to Sheriff Huff. She returned the reports to the envelope and set it aside. "I appreciate the documents, but I'm more interested in your impressions of the case, the nuances that probably aren't on any of those forms. Did you have any suspects?"

"Two." He held up his index and middle fingers. "Eustis's son, Robert Junior." He folded down one finger. "According to everyone we interviewed, he was mighty pissed off about his father remarrying and hated the new wife."

"Amanda Two."

"Right. He'd persuaded his father to insist on a prenup and was working hard to ensure that Robert Senior didn't change his will in her favor. In that scenario, Amanda Two is dead."

"If he hated the new wife, why wouldn't Junior just kill her? Why kill his father?"

Sheriff Huff gave her an appreciative look. "Rumor—confirmed by several sources, including the local bank manager—has it that Robert Junior was running the ranch into the ground. Robert Senior was on the verge of taking back financial and day-to-day control of ranch operations. The son blew up at his dad when he told him and threatened to kill him, in a café just down the road." The sheriff nodded to his left. "Did I mention that was less than a week before the coroner estimates Robert Senior was poisoned? I guess he couldn't stomach the humiliation, or the downsizing of his lifestyle, or both."

"Your second suspect?" Charlie already knew what he was going to say. "Amanda Two?"

"Bingo. As near as anyone can tell, there's about three-quarters of a million missing from old man Eustis's bank accounts. He'd added Amanda's name to the accounts right after marrying her, and large withdrawals of cash were made starting shortly thereafter. Could have been cash payments for a new bull or piece of ranch equipment, or mismanagement by Robert Junior, but it looks suspicious. At least, Robert Junior insists it's suspicious. In that scenario, Amanda killed her husband to keep him from realizing she was siphoning money out of their accounts, or *because* he'd already found her out, and ran off to start a new life elsewhere."

"Is this her?" Charlie passed Sheriff Huff the newspaper photo of "Lucinda Cheney's" wedding, the only picture she'd been able to find of Heather-Anne.

"I wouldn't know. I never met the woman, and no one could produce a photo of her. I understand she was a platinum blonde, though that's nothing a box of hair dye wouldn't fix."

"Is there anyone around who would know if this was Amanda Two?"

"Robert Junior. I'm sure he'd be more than happy to see you and give you his 'evil stepmother' spiel." From the way Huff said it, Charlie could tell he was no great fan of Robert Junior.

"I'd appreciate it if you could give him a call and ask if he'll see me."

Ninety seconds later, Huff gave her a nod as he hung up. "Robert's out of town, but his wife says she'll see you. Her name's Tansy, and she knew Amanda Two. The ranch is east of here, north of Thunder Basin. Let me have my secretary print you some directions."

Accepting the directions a few minutes later, Charlie let Huff walk her to the door. She turned to face him, the weak

175

sunlight streaming through the glass doors highlighting skin damage on his face from too many hours, Charlie presumed, of marathon training in the harsh sun of a Wyoming summer. "If you had to make a guess, would your money be on Robert Junior or Amanda Two?" In her experience, cops frequently had strong opinions about guilt, even if they didn't have enough evidence to convince a DA to prosecute.

Huff bit his upper lip and strained air through his teeth. "I'd have to flip a coin."

From the parking lot, Charlie phoned Dan to let him know she was done with the sheriff. Dan had opted to drive around Cheyenne rather than horn in on her meeting with Sheriff Huff. "Three's a crowd," he'd said when he dropped her off. Hugging her navy peacoat around her after ascertaining that Dan was less than ten minutes away, Charlie stared at the city. At roughly six thousand feet, Cheyenne was the same elevation as Colorado Springs, but postage-stamp flat, as far as Charlie could see. Broad streets stretched flatly into the distance, and the landscape on the drive into the city had consisted of tan plains pocked by fence posts and the occasional bovine. She was pretty sure this part of the state was so flat she could see all the way north up I-25 to Montana. She bent over and touched her toes, trying to stretch her buttocks and hamstrings, stiff after the almost-three-hour drive. Dark hair spilling over her face, she held on to her toes for a count of thirty, ransacking her brain for "flat" synonyms to describe eastern Wyoming. She straightened when she heard a horn honk.

Dan's truck pulled to a stop beside her. She jumped in and cranked the heater up a notch.

"Did you get anything useful from the local law?" Dan asked, handing her a Wendy's bag that smelled temptingly of french fries. A similar bag gaped between his spread thighs.

Thank God he'd known better than to get her a wimpy salad. Unwrapping the paper around her burger, Charlie told him what Sheriff Huff had said.

"So we're making a side trip to Thunder Basin?" Dan cast a look at the sky. "I was listening to the weather report, and the storm's moving in faster than expected."

"We can spend the night, then," Charlie said. "Play it safe."

Dan shook his head. "I'd rather not. I got a call from a parishioner's husband. She's been ill and isn't expected to live out the night. She's asking for me."

"Okay," Charlie said. "We'll do a hit-and-run at Eustis's ranch and get on the road back to Colorado Springs. If we leave Thunder Basin by six or six thirty, we can be home around ten. With any luck, we can outrun the storm. If we have to stop in Fort Collins or Denver, it's no big deal and you'll still get back sooner. Even if the hotels are packed with stranded travelers and we have to share a room, I'm safe with a priest, right?" She slanted Dan a grin and handed him the directions to the ranch. A gust of wind rocked the truck, and Dan put it in gear.

Dan's gaze held Charlie's for a moment before he turned his eyes to the road. "I guess that depends on your definition of 'safe.'"

24

After all my worries about getting together with Patrick Dreiser, he refused to meet with me.

"I'm tired of the whole damn thing," he said, sounding more angry than tired when I phoned him on his cell, using a number I'd gotten from Les's files. After talking to Hollis Sloan I'd gone home for a snack of leftover lemon cake and to find Dreiser's number. "I know damned well I can't get blood from a stone or money out of you, sweetheart, so I'm not going to waste my time talking about that criminal, defrauding, embezzling ex-husband of yours. Why, my blood pressure's gone up fifty points just talking to you on the phone." He slammed the receiver down.

Well! I might be a teensy bit afraid of Patrick Dreiser—I'd never much liked him even when Les and I socialized with him and his wife, back in our happier days—but I was determined to talk to him. If he wouldn't agree to meet, then I'd have to use my summons-delivering techniques to take him by surprise. I'd gotten pretty good at finding summons recipients and handing over the paperwork they didn't want to receive. I dialed Dreiser's secretary.

Since Les ran off with Dreiser's money, he'd been forced to let a lot of his staff go. Apparently, his secretary was one of the casualties. A kid who didn't sound any older than Kendall answered the phone.

"Dad's on a maintenance call," she said. "Can I take a message?"

"Why aren't you in school?" I asked, hoping that Dexter and Kendall were in class.

"I graduated last year," the teen said, not sounding surprised or offended by my question. "Now I work with my dad."

"Oh. Great. Congratulations. Well, do you know where he is?"

"That gas station just off I-25 at Garden of the Gods."

"Thanks."

I hung up and headed upstairs to change. The soft blue sweater I had put on this morning didn't say "force to be reckoned with." If I was going to take on Patrick Dreiser, I needed a power outfit.

Wouldn't you know it, there were several gas stations just off the I-25 exit at Garden of the Gods Road, and, of course, I hadn't asked Dreiser's daughter which one he was working at. I cruised through three of them, getting tangled up in traffic crossing under the freeway, before I found Dreiser at a fourth station about a quarter mile west of I-25. The vending machines—a soda machine and a snack machine—were outside, adjacent to a men's restroom that smelled strongly, even through the closed door, of one of those scented cakes that goes in a toilet bowl to keep it clean. The front of the drink machine was opened wide, and a pair of work-booted feet showed beneath the door. I parked the Hummer in one of the slots in front of the convenience store, next to a hatchback that was vibrating with the force of the rap music thudding through it. The skinny woman smoking a cigarette in the driver's seat, elbow resting on the rolled-down window and seat reclined like she was waiting for someone, didn't even look at me as I hustled past. I ducked my head against the wind as I trotted around the side of the building. Luckily, it blocked most of the wind.

"Mr. Dreiser?" Even though Les and I had gone out with Dreiser and his wife as business colleagues a couple of times, I'd never felt comfortable calling him Patrick. He didn't like Pat. Mostly, I'd called him nothing.

He leaned back to peer around the open door. His iron gray hair stuck out from under a Dreiser Vending baseball cap. It was inches longer than when I'd last seen him, and I cringed to think that maybe he couldn't afford a barber anymore. He wore a plaid wool shirt under denim overalls and still had the paunch I remembered. At least he wasn't starving to death. He held a large wrench in one gloved hand. He'd always been proud of being a "self-made man," which I'd always thought was a silly term.

"You." He scrunched up his face like he'd taken Robitussin or tasted spoiled milk. "What are you supposed to be? Mrs. Claus?"

I guessed my power outfit of quilted scarlet vest over a cherry-colored turtleneck paired with a shin-length red skirt and cream-colored high-heeled boots—I didn't have any red ones—wasn't having the right effect. I felt let down; all the fashion magazines said red was *the* power color.

Dreiser went back to working on the machine, wrench clanking against metal innards.

"Mr. Dreiser—" I edged around the door, having to step off the curb to get around it, and stepped back up on the sidewalk on his other side. "I'm trying to find Les, and—"

"How bloody likely is that?" he asked, pausing in his work to glare at me from under brows that reminded me of a prickly hedge. "And if you were, why would you be talking to me? I must be the last person on earth Goldman would get in touch with. Besides, he's in Costa Rica."

"No, he's here in town." I knew I'd made a mistake when Dreiser stiffened. Straightening, he turned to give me his full attention.

"Are you saying that piece of shit who wrecked my business and my life is here? In Colorado Springs?" He was practically drooling, and his grip on the wrench tightened so his whole arm trembled.

I stepped back. "Well, he was."

A calculating look came into Dreiser's beady eyes. "Look, Mrs. Claus, he screwed you over, too. You've got to be mad at him. How 'bout we make a deal? If you find him, you let me know where he is. I'll get something out of him for both of us—you can't tell me he doesn't still have the money." He tapped the wrench against his thigh like he was keeping a beat, but he was hitting himself so hard I knew he'd have a bruise.

I shuddered to think what he meant to do to Les. I was mad at my ex-husband, but not put-him-in-the-hospital-or-a-coffin mad.

"Whaddaya say?"

Dreiser moved toward me, and I shrank away, finding myself cornered practically inside the soda machine. Any other time, I'd have found it interesting with all the slots and levers and the shiny aluminum cans stacked one on top of another and a metal container holding coins. Now, though, I was only grateful there was no room for Dreiser to close the door and lock me in there, which he looked crazy enough to do.

"Mr. Dreiser, I guess you haven't seen Les and don't know anything about Heather-Anne's murder, so I'll just be going." I tried to step forward, but he didn't budge.

"Murder?"

Dreiser leaned close enough that I could smell a mix of coffee and alcohol on his breath. Uh-oh. He'd been drinking. That might explain his bloodshot eyes.

"Yes. Les's . . . friend was killed on Sunday." Dreiser's reaction was making me pretty sure he had nothing to do with it.

"He did it," Dreiser said with conviction, still uncomfortably close.

"He wouldn't."

"Hah!" Dreiser barked spittle onto my face, and I tried to push past him. "Not so fast," he said, eyes narrowing. His body penned me in. "I think you know where Goldman is. I think you and he were in it together. You cheated me out of millions, cost me my wife, my—"

I was scared by him, but angry, too. I didn't cheat or steal. I got my hands between us and shoved. I'd have had more luck moving Mt. Rushmore. "You think I'd be worrying about how to pay my utility bill and working as a PI if I had millions hidden away in some bank account? You think Les would have left town with that floozy if we were partners? Get out of my way." The metal innards of the vending machine cut into my shoulders as I leaned back to give myself some momentum to propel me forward and, hopefully, past Dreiser.

"Tell me where the son of a bitch is. I'll get it out of you if—"

I heard a clicking sound, and a lever somewhere near my elbow sank down. A rumbling came from the machine, and suddenly soda cans were spilling out the bottom, falling to the sidewalk, and rolling off the curb and into the parking lot.

"Damn it!" Dreiser yelled, tucking the wrench under his arm to reach for a can with each hand. "Now look what you've done." He grabbed for more cans until he was juggling an armload. One can rolled under the tires of a passing SUV and crunched open with a gush of soda. I scurried away from the machine and Dreiser, sorry about the sodas but happy to make my escape. The river of shiny cans had attracted attention, and a couple of teens were trying to scoop some up while Dreiser ran at them, waving the wrench and dropping the cans he'd collected. A can of lemon-lime soda rolled up against the toe of my boot and began to hiss ominously. Before I could move, a crack opened in the flip-top and warm soda jetted all over my power ensemble.

A blue van rear-ended a hatchback that had stopped suddenly to avoid running into an elderly woman with a walker stooping for a Dr Pepper. Horns blared. A police car turned into the small parking area. I tried to make my way toward the Hummer, but my foot came down on a can and I fell to one knee, putting a hole in my damp tights. I felt frazzled and couldn't help but think this was at least partly my fault.

A shout came from near the gas pumps. "Hey, idiot, you didn't hang the nozzle up right!"

The man was apparently talking to the teenager standing near me, holding at least a dozen cans of soda. The kid whirled around, the long, pom-pommed tail of his knit cap whipping past my nose. A gasoline odor drifted to us.

"Uh-oh," he muttered and ran toward where his car sat, gas flap open. A stream of gas trickled from the hose he'd let fall to the ground in his eagerness to round up some free soda.

A couple more people chased after escaping cans. Dreiser alternated between picking up cans and threatening people with his wrench. The police officer climbed out of his car and lunged toward Dreiser. The cigarette-smoking woman parked next to my Hummer jerked her head in time to the rap beat and made to toss her cigarette butt out the window.

"No!" "Don't!" "Run!" Half a dozen scared voices shouted at the woman, but she bobbed her head to the music and kept her eyes on the store's door. The cigarette butt tumbled, in slow motion it seemed, toward the ground.

Everyone ran.

25

Charlie was tired and her ass hurt by the time she and Dan reached the Triple E Ranch, where Robert Eustis Junior and his family lived. The road out of Cheyenne had been fine, but they'd been on a rutted dirt road for at least ten miles, and the jouncing was not speeding the healing process. As they bounced under the wrought-iron sign proclaiming TRI-PLE E RANCH, Charlie figured the *E*'s stood for Eustis Senior, Eustis Junior, and maybe a brother or sister she didn't know about. She wondered if they realized the words "triple E" brought to mind Victoria's Secret rather than prime rib.

" 'Here you come again, looking better than a body has a right to,' " Dan sang in a Dolly Parton falsetto, making Charlie laugh as she realized they were thinking along the same lines. "Shall I sit in the truck?" he asked, pulling up in front of a weathered ranch house that looked as if it had once been white but was now the same dun color as the surrounding countryside.

"Hell, no," Charlie said. "It's too cold. Maybe being face-to-face with a priest will encourage them to tell me the truth." She swung her legs out of the truck and winced at the pull in her glutes.

"You expect them to lie?"

"I expect everyone to lie," she said. "That way, I'm not disappointed and I'm occasionally gratified by a kernel of truth."

"That's a happy outlook."

"Don't tell me you think most people tell the truth, the whole truth, and nothing but the truth." Charlie gave him a skeptical look over the truck's blue hood, now seemingly frosted with dun-colored dust particles.

Dan gave it some thought as he came around the truck. "I think many people are so busy lying to themselves about what they want and who they are that they can't help but lie to other people. They don't even know they're doing it half the time." He joined her on the walk to the front door.

It opened as they approached, as if the woman who stood there had been watching them. As weathered as the house, she could have been any age between thirty-five and fifty-five. Sandy hair showed an inch of gray roots. Thin, almost bloodless lips split a thin, sun-speckled face. She wore jeans, work boots, and a heavy shearling coat.

"Storm's coming," she greeted them, stepping onto the porch and closing the door. "I've got to feed the stock. You staying in Cheyenne tonight?"

"We're headed back as soon as we leave here," Charlie said.

The woman directed a narrowed gaze at the sky. "You might make it." Holding out a bony hand, she said, "I'm Tansy Eustis."

Charlie introduced herself and Dan.

"A priest, huh?" Tansy's gaze swept Dan. "I'll bet you give a mean sermon." Without waiting for a reply, she started across what would have been a yard if it weren't grass-free, packed-down dirt. A dog the size, color, and general friendliness of a coyote emerged from beneath the porch to accompany her.

Charlie and Dan exchanged a look and followed, hands dug into their pockets against the stiffening wind. Inside the barn, a dim space smelling of hay and dung and warm animals, Tansy used a hose to fill the water troughs in each of several stalls. The dog snuffled at a hole that undoubtedly housed a rodent. "I already dropped hay bales in the pastures for most of our herd," she said, rubbing a cow between the eyes. "These are here because they're injured or sick. This one"—she swatted the cow's rump—"got herself tangled up good in barbed wire."

"I know it's a busy time for you," Charlie said, "so I won't keep you long. I have reason to believe that there's a connection between your father-in-law's death and a case I'm working on."

"Oh? What reason?"

Charlie explained about the newspaper clipping sent to Les Goldman.

"Someone sent this Les a newspaper article about Robert Senior's death? What do you think the connection is?"

"I'm hoping you can help with that." Pulling the Internet photo of Lucinda Cheney from her purse, she passed it to Tansy.

"I can't see well without my reading glasses," the woman apologized. She held the photo at arm's length. "This gal's younger, and Amanda had white-blond hair, worn shorter." She chopped a hand at jaw level. "In fact, she looked a fair bit like Robert's first wife. Her name was Amanda, too."

Charlie nodded. "Could this be your Amanda?" She wished more people paid attention to face shape and the way ears were set against the head and brow prominence—things that were nearly impossible to change—rather than to hair and eye color.

"She's not *my* Amanda. Best I can tell you is it's possible," she said, passing the photo back. "Amanda was on the plump side, and she wore glasses, so it's hard for me to tell. But it's possible."

Charlie remembered what Gigi had said about the photo of Lucinda Cheney. "This may sound silly," she said, feeling ridiculous, "but did Amanda get manicures?"

Tansy gave her a strange look but said, "Here she was, a

rancher's wife, afraid to get her hands dirty or break a nail." Tansy held up her own work-roughened hands with their short, unpolished nails. "She always had her nails done so the tips were bright white with a clear coat over the rest of the nail. You should have heard her squawk if she ever broke one." She shook her head in disgust.

Score one for Gigi, Charlie thought, prepared to accept that Amanda was, indeed, Heather-Anne.

"You said Amanda looked a lot like your husband's mother," Dan said, earning a surprised look from Charlie. "How long after the first Mrs. Eustis passed did your father-in-law remarry?"

"Within the year," Tansy said, the corners of her mouth tightening. "My Robert was fit to be tied."

"He didn't like her?"

"He wouldn't have liked anyone his father married." Tansy moved away from the stall and ducked into a feed storage room, emerging with a brimming bucket. "But, no, he didn't like Amanda. He didn't like that she knew nothing about ranching and was useless on the ranch. Other than her baking—she was just as good with her pie crusts and cakes as Robert's first wife, who used to win prizes—she didn't have much to offer."

"Robert Senior must have thought she did," Charlie observed. "Where did they meet?"

"Funny enough, at the stock show and rodeo in Denver. That's where my husband and youngest son are right now, as a matter of fact—been there since Wednesday. According to Robert Senior, he and Amanda got to chatting during the auction, and one thing led to another. They were married less than three months later."

Tiny alarm bells dinged in Charlie's brain. Denver was only about an hour from Colorado Springs. Was it coincidence that Robert Eustis Junior was in the area when Heather-Anne was killed? "Do you think Amanda killed your father-in-law?" Charlie asked, carefully not mentioning that the sheriff thought there was an equal chance Tansy's husband was responsible.

"The way it happened, with brake fluid in his drink and all, I don't see who else could have done it," she said. Her voice was muffled and her face hidden as she ducked down to apply salve to a cow's injured leg.

"Did she inherit the ranch?"

Tansy stood slowly, letting her gaze rest first on Dan and then on Charlie. "No," she said finally. "We did." Taking off her gloves, she slapped them together, and a puff of dirt rose up. "You better hit the road if you're hoping to get home before the blizzard gets here."

Charlie and Dan left Tansy in the barn and returned to the truck, not saying anything about Tansy's information until they were bouncing down the road back toward the highway.

"You think Amanda Eustis, Lucinda Cheney, and Heather-Anne Pawlusik are the same person," Dan said.

Charlie nodded. "I do." She explained about the French manicure. "Why else would someone send that newspaper clipping to Les? I think that was a warning, that some Good

Samaritan was trying to let him know that Heather-Anne's last husband didn't fare too well."

"Do you think she killed Eustis?"

"I don't know." Charlie wriggled on the seat, trying to get comfortable. "Either she did and ran to avoid prosecution, or she didn't and ran to avoid suffering the same fate, probably at the hands of her nose-out-of-joint stepson. I want to talk to him and make sure he was in Denver—and not Colorado Springs—when Heather-Anne was killed."

"Even if Heather-Anne and Amanda were the same person, how would Eustis have known that, and how would he have known she was in Colorado?"

Charlie shrugged. "Beats me. Probably it's just coincidence, but I'd still like to talk to him. You know," she said, smoothing the Lucinda Cheney photo on her thigh, "it might be worthwhile finding out how Wilfred Cheney ended up in a wheelchair."

Dan took his gaze from the road for a long moment to study her profile. "You worried she has a history of disposing of inconvenient husbands, that she tried to kill Cheney but something went wrong?"

Charlie shrugged. "The idea just came to me. I know it sounds far-fetched, but stranger things have happened."

"For my money, the most curious thing about this whole case is that someone sent the newspaper clipping to Les. Assuming they did so because Amanda Eustis became Heather-Anne Pawlusik, who could it be? It'd have to be someone who not only knew that Heather-Anne was in Costa Rica with Les, but also knew that Heather-Anne used to be Amanda."

"Maybe we're on the wrong track here," Charlie said

slowly. The long gray ribbon of I-80 appeared in the distance. "The clipping was sent to Les, after all, so maybe Les is who we should be focusing on. Other than being Gigi's husband and the father of the two most obnoxious teens in the tri-state area, what do we know about him?"

Dan raised his brows to invite her to continue since it was clear she had an answer in mind.

"We know he's a cheating, swindling, embezzling criminal," she said. "What are the chances he and Eustis were in business together somehow?"

"From what I know of Les, he was no more the ranching type than Amanda was."

Charlie waved an impatient hand. "He wasn't the PI type, either, but he still owned part of my business. He was a wheeler-dealer. I don't think he much cared what a business's product or service was as long as he thought he could make money off it."

"I guess he was wrong in at least one instance."

Charlie backhanded his shoulder.

"So you're saying we wasted a trip out here?"

"Not necessarily. I need to get Gigi started on researching Eustis's business relationships to see if there's any overlap with Les's interests. If they were in business together, I'll bet you a bottle of Lagavulin that Les ran off with some of his money."

"Could even be that's where the missing cash from Eustis's bank accounts went."

Charlie gave him an approving look. "You're not half bad at this investigating thing, Allgood."

"This isn't investigation," he pointed out. "It's speculation."

Charlie tried to reach Gigi as the truck merged onto the blessedly smooth asphalt of I-80. Dan hit the gas and the truck surged forward, rocking her back in her seat and jolting the phone from her hand. She gave him a look. "I thought I was riding with Father Dan Allgood, not Father Dan Andretti."

In answer, he pointed out her window to the north. A sea of roiling charcoal clouds advanced toward them, lightning flickering in their depths, snow falling so heavily it was like someone had drawn a curtain across the northern half of the state.

"What are you dawdling for?" Charlie asked.

26

~~~

Nothing exploded. I had ducked behind the concrete-walled convenience store and scrunched my eyes shut, waiting for the boom, but it never came. Cautiously, I opened my eyes, stood up, and peeped around the corner. A fat man in a white shirt with a plastic name tag, who might have been the manager, stood by the big red button that cuts off the gas flow, his hand still on the switch. If the ice cubes and Coke-colored liquid were anything to go by, someone had dumped a Big Gulp on the cigarette butt. Another gas station employee was sprinkling sawdust on the spilled gasoline and sweeping it into a dustpan. Whew.

I edged around the corner. Some of the soda stealers had scattered when it looked like the gas station was going to go kablooey, but I noticed a man in a suit peering into the vending machine to see if any sodas remained in it, and the elderly woman with the walker was still trying to reach her Dr Pepper. In a half squat, one hand clutching the walker for balance, she looked like maybe she was stuck. I helped her up, handed her the Dr Pepper, and earned a "Thank you, dear," for my trouble.

"It's her fault," Dreiser said when he saw me. He stood by the squad car, apparently in custody, cap missing, hair mussed. "She let those cans loose." He pointed a bony finger at me. The police officer, splotches of dark soda on his shirt, gripped Dreiser's upper arm and had taken his wrench.

I gasped as employees, drivers, and Dreiser glared at me. "I didn't—"

"Spilling cans isn't a crime," the officer said. "Threatening people with a deadly weapon is. Come on." He nudged Dreiser toward the squad car. Dreiser glared at me with a fury that would've stripped paint off a tractor.

"I'm sorry," I said. "I didn't mean—"

Shrill yapping from a white Pomeranian in the nearest car drowned me out. I shifted indecisively from foot to foot and finally decided I had nothing to gain by hanging around. I certainly wasn't going to get anything else from Dreiser, who was shouting something about ". . . payback . . . get you . . . find Goldman . . ." as the police officer locked him into the backseat. I climbed in the Hummer, grateful for once for its size and bulk, and drove out of the small parking lot, hearing someone call after me, "Don't come back!"

I stewed about the injustice of it all—it wasn't my fault Dreiser cornered me in his machine, and it wasn't my fault that the careless boy hadn't hung up the gas hose, and it wasn't my fault that woman wanted to kill herself by smoking cigarettes—but got over it by the time I reached the office. No one needed to worry that I was going back to that gas station. I was never showing my face there again. Come to think of it, I'd never gotten gas there anyway, so it wasn't much of a sacrifice. Thank goodness no one got hurt.

Back at the office, I wriggled out of my ruined tights in the bathroom and tried to blot the soda stains off my clothes. Maybe my dry cleaner could do it. He'd worked miracles on my blue satin blouse when I got raspberry sauce on it. Seated at my desk, I unzipped my boots to ankle level and sighed with relief. They were the teensiest bit too tight around my calves. Even though they were cuter than cute, I didn't wear them too often because by the time I'd had them on for an hour, they cut into my calves something awful. However, one must suffer for fashion sometimes. I'd said that to Charlie once and she'd looked at me like I was crazy. At least the boots didn't hurt as much as the tank top whose sequins rubbed the insides of my upper arms raw whenever I wore it. Massaging the red line around each calf, I listened to the messages on the answering machine. One was from Charlie, asking me to find out how Wilfred Cheney ended up in a wheelchair and telling me that she and Father Dan were on their way back. I brewed a pot of coffee, more because I liked the smell than because I wanted a cup, and Googled Cheney.

Before I could study the results and find a phone number, Albertine breezed in. An emerald green caftan shot through with silver threads drifted around her. It was a light silk, and I wondered if she wore long underwear under it.

"You look like you need a drink, girlfriend," she said. "Come on down to the restaurant."

I glanced at the computer screen, tempted. "I need to get hold of someone for Charlie," I said, "but then I'll be down."

"Let Charlie do it herself. With everyone waiting on her hand and foot since she took a bullet in her posterior, that woman's getting lazy."

Charlie was the least lazy person I knew, and I knew Albertine knew it. "She's not back yet."

Albertine arched her penciled-on brows. "You don't mean she went to Wyoming after all, do you? In this?" She waved a hand at the window, and I saw the snow had started. It fell steadily, like confectioner's sugar from a sifter.

"They've already started back."

"They?"

"Father Dan drove."

Albertine's brow smoothed out. "That's okay, then. I'd trust that man in a tight spot. If terrorists overrun the city or the Yellowstone caldera blows and everything north of Boulder gets buried in lava and ash, I want him in the bunker or shelter next to me."

"He's a priest."

She gave me a pitying look. "Honey, he may be a priest now, but his eyes say he wasn't always one." Helping herself to a cup of coffee, Albertine plunked down behind Charlie's desk. "What are you doing?"

"Trying to figure out how to ask a man how he ended up in a wheelchair." I sighed. Asking that kind of question felt rude and intrusive. I was pretty sure any PIs in Atlanta or New Orleans must have moved down from New York or Chicago, since southerners didn't ask those kinds of questions. It just wasn't polite to pry like that.

"Can I do it?" Albertine surprised me by asking. "I've always thought it would be a kick to be a PI."

"You want to do it?"

She nodded, setting the beads worked into the three skinny braids that fell down beside her face clicking. "Sure."

"What would you say?" Even as I asked the question, I was pulling up a Web site that provided phone numbers for a fee. Swift Investigations subscribed to it.

Albertine straightened up. "I'd say, 'This is Albertine Dauphin from Swift Investigations in Colorado Springs. Could you please tell me how you came to be in a wheelchair, sir?'"

"You'd ask him straight out like that?" Albertine was brave.

"Give me the phone number."

I read it off to her, and she dialed, using a pencil to protect her long green nails. "Put it on speaker," I whispered as the phone began to ring on the other end.

A man answered with a brusque "Hello?" and Albertine introduced herself, sounding self-confident and professional. Once the man confirmed he was Wilfred Cheney, she asked him her question.

His reaction was immediate and violent. "I knew it! You're with the insurance company. Well, I've had it with you mother-fu—"

"Sir, there's no call for that kind of language," Albertine said.

"Oh, yes, there damn well is," he spat. "The accident was

two years ago! I filed a perfectly legitimate workman's comp claim, and you assholes have dragged your feet and—"

"I can't abide profanity. I'm going to have to hang up if you can't moderate your language," Albertine said, sounding stern. I wished I could talk that way to Dexter and Kendall.

I shook my head to keep her from hanging up as Wilfred Cheney blasted the kind of language that got my brother's mouth washed out with soap, then banged the phone down. Albertine replaced the phone more gently and pursed her full lips. "I don't know how you and Charlie do it, Gigi, I really don't. How can you put up with that kind of rudeness day in and day out?"

"Not everyone's that way. I can't imagine it's much worse than some of your customers." I'd heard customers rag on Albertine before, complaining about soup that was too cold, music that was too loud, shrimp that tasted "off."

"Yeah, but my customers are paying me, so it's easier to tolerate their 'tudes. Maybe I'd better stick with cooking and restauranting and leave the PI'ing to you." A guilty look crept over her face. "I guess I really pissed him off. He probably won't talk to you now. What will you do?"

"He said something about an accident two years ago . . ." My fingers tapped at the keyboard, and a newspaper article popped up. It showed a mangled truck with EPB OF CHATTANOOGA stenciled on the side, upside down in a creek, a bridge with a busted railing above it. Everything in the photo had a sort of shimmer to it, and it took me a moment to realize the landscape was coated with a thick layer of ice. Pretty.

"Looks ugly," Albertine observed, having crossed the

office to peer over my shoulder. "That man's lucky he's alive, although if he uses that kind of language around me again, he won't be for long."

I skimmed the article. "It says he worked for the electric company and he was inspecting lines after an ice storm when his car slid off the bridge and ended up in the creek. A Flight for Life helicopter saved his life. I guess there's no way Heather-Anne—if she was really his wife, Lucinda—could have made it . . . No, wait! Here at the end the reporter says, 'Cheney insists an oncoming truck forced him off the bridge. He describes the truck as a red pickup and the driver as a white man wearing a high-collared coat and a knit hat pulled low. Police have been unable to find evidence that another driver was involved and ask that anyone with knowledge of the accident call . . .' Well!" I looked up at Albertine.

"Suspicious," she agreed.

I chewed on my lower lip. "It certainly doesn't prove his wife, whoever she was, had anything to do with his accident, though. In fact, if there was a truck involved and a man was driving it, that seems to prove she wasn't."

"Maybe Cheney was wrong. It could've been a woman under that jacket and hat."

Sighing, I printed the article and shut down the computer. "Some days this job makes my head hurt."

"Don't they all? Come on." She bumped her hip against the back of my chair. "It's mojito time, girlfriend."

27

The blizzard caught up with Charlie and Dan south of Fort Collins, Colorado. Charlie had begun to think they'd outrun it when suddenly they were enveloped in snow so thick it was like being on the inside of an eiderdown quilt. She couldn't see more than three feet out the passenger window and knew from Dan's grim expression that he was having similar difficulty, even though the windshield wipers were swiping at warp speed. The truck's powerful engine growled as it plowed through the quickly accumulating snow on the interstate. A flash of blue outside her window caught Charlie's eye, and she realized it was a car that had slid off the road.

"Maybe we should have stopped in Fort Collins?"

Dan's only reply was a brief sideways glance. He gripped the steering wheel in competent hands and drove in silence for another ten minutes as the snow steadily thickened. The high beams made a golden flurry of the flakes that fell in their cone but did little to illuminate the road. A rough vibration indicated they'd strayed onto the shoulder, and Dan corrected, setting the truck fishtailing slightly. "We can't stay on the road," he said finally. "I can't see ten inches in front of us. Either we're going to run off the road, or we're going to be rear-ended by a semi, although with any luck we're the only people stupid enough to still be driving."

The radio, which Charlie had tuned to a travel conditions

update channel, announced that the state police were closing I-25 from north of Cheyenne to Pueblo, Colorado. "I'm sorry I talked you into this trip," Charlie said.

Dan shot her a half-smile. "I'm a big boy. I don't remember you doing any arm twisting. Besides, I'm the one who wanted to get back tonight."

"We'll just get off at the next exit, find a motel—preferably one with a well-stocked bar—and dig in for—"

Flashing amber lights suddenly appeared dead ahead of them, and Dan steered right to avoid the SUV. Despite the measured way he eased his foot down on the brakes, the truck swerved and then began to spin. Catching a glimpse of the SUV as they spun, Charlie tensed against the seemingly inevitable collision. They slid past it with Charlie craning her neck to try to see if anyone was inside the vehicle. Her muscles started to unclench when the tires bit into the shoulder, which crumbled away beneath them. A ditch! Dan wrenched the wheel back toward the left, the engine labored, and for a moment Charlie thought they were going to make it back onto the road. She found herself leaning hard left, as if that would make a difference. Then, with the slow finality of a mastodon falling to its knees, the truck slid into the ditch and toppled over.

They landed with a jarring thud, and Charlie's head banged against the door as the truck settled on its side.

Dan's voice came immediately, sharp and concerned. "Charlie?"

"Fine," she said, pressing her fingers against her head and face to make sure that was true. Her right shoulder hurt as if she'd wrenched it, and her head ached, but otherwise she seemed okay. "You?"

"Operational."

"I'm sorry about your truck." Guilt over dragging Dan on the trip weighed on her.

"It's only a truck."

Cold began to seep into Charlie, and she noticed that snow had already blanketed the windshield so it felt like they were buried. She shivered.

His thoughts obviously in sync with hers, Dan said, "We need to get out of here or they'll be digging us up in the spring thaw."

The prospect of leaving the still-warmish truck for the frigid cold and wind outside did not appeal to Charlie, but she liked the idea of being buried alive less.

Dan pushed at his door, which gave a metallic creak but didn't open. "Must have dented it," Dan said. "Here goes nothing." He cranked the engine, which started, and buzzed down the window. Snow sifted in. Reaching an arm out and around, he dragged himself up sideways, careful not to kick Charlie as he heaved himself out of the truck. Moments later, he was peering through the door, snowflakes frosting his hair and sparkling on his eyelashes. "Take my hand," he commanded.

Charlie reached her arm up and wiggled around until she lay stomach-down on the seat, her feet on the door. She used the console like a climbing hold and levered herself up until her fingers touched Dan's. He pulled; she thrust with her legs, aware of a deep ache at the site of the healing bullet wound, and levered her head and shoulders out the door. Wind tangled her hair and whipped it across her eyes, and she used her shoulder and arms—*like getting out of a swimming pool,* she thought—to pull herself the rest of the way out of the car. She landed in a heap on the snowy ground, stood, and brushed herself off.

"Well," she said.

"Well."

They looked at each other for a moment, then smiled, and Dan began to chuckle. Charlie laughed, too, knowing it was relief that brought the laughter, not anything funny about their current situation. The immediate future seemed to feature hypothermia, frostbite, and possible starvation. Charlie's stomach grumbled at the thought.

"We need to make sure no one's hurt in that SUV," Dan said, "and then we need to find shelter."

Charlie's gaze swept the barren, snow-clad landscape dubiously. "Where?"

"We passed an exit less than half a mile back. There might be a gas station or something there. Come on. Stay off the highway—we don't want to get flattened by any idiots out driving in this."

"Other idiots."

"Exactly."

They took a few steps back the way they'd come, and Charlie could vaguely make out the amber lights blink-blinking through the snow's thick veil. When they reached the other vehicle, they brushed snow off the windows to peer inside. No one.

"No footprints," Charlie observed.

Shrugging, Dan said, "That doesn't mean much. The way the wind's blowing, footprints would be obliterated in less than two minutes. Look." He pointed back where they'd just walked, and Charlie saw that the wind had scoured their footprints to faint, shapeless impressions. "Let's get moving." He headed into the wind, trudging through the ever-deepening snow that had drifted as high as Charlie's knees in spots. She tucked her hands into her armpits and ducked her head against the wind to follow him.

28

I limited myself to one mojito at Albertine's and made it home in time to cook dinner for the kids. "Kendall? Dexter?" I called as I opened the garage door leading into the kitchen and stamped my snow-wet feet on the mat. My unzipped boots sagged around my ankles, and I kicked them off gratefully.

No answer from the kids. I padded into the kitchen and almost immediately felt liquid soaking into my stockings. Yuck. I looked down to see dirty puddles of water tracked across the kitchen tile, ending at the fridge. I balanced on one foot to peel off my wet knee-high stocking, clutching at the counter when I wavered. How many times had I told the kids to take off their boots in the garage or on the porch before coming inside? Did other parents succeed in making their kids *think*? Grabbing a dish towel, I mopped up the wet spots and opened the fridge. Leftover pepperoni pizza called to me, and I slid a slice out of the box and took a bite. Mmm. Heaven.

"Rowf!"

I looked around but didn't spot Nolan, my black-and-white shih tzu. "Nolie?"

The bark came again. I followed the sound to the basement door and opened it. Nolan frisked out, jumping up at me like he hadn't seen me for weeks instead of hours. Or maybe he was leaping for a bit of pizza. "What were you doing down there?" He didn't spend much time in the basement. Dexter must have been down there playing on the Wii. I closed the door and went in search of the kids. They weren't in their rooms, although I thought Dexter might have been home earlier, since Nolan found a couple of Cheetos in the middle of his bed and scrambled up to eat them. He cocked his fuzzy head at me when they were gone, clearly asking for more. Orange powder clung to his chin whiskers.

A little worried, what with the snow and all, I was about to call Kendall's cell phone when I decided to check messages on my phone first. Kendall's voice told me she was spending the night with a friend since District 12 had already canceled classes the next day due to the blizzard. I deleted the message, sighing. I wished she'd asked first. My mother would have skinned me alive if I'd ever gone to a friend's house after school, never mind overnight, without asking permission. I listened to the other messages, but there was nothing from Dexter. Where could he be in this storm? He'd been going to catch a ride home from school with his buddy James, so maybe that's where he was. I'd call over there as soon as I'd changed.

Fifteen minutes later, wrapped in my pink velour robe and wearing the fuzzy slippers with the bear heads on them that Kendall had given me two Christmases ago, I went downstairs to the kitchen. Nolan danced around my ankles. "You're going to trip me," I told him.

He raced down the remaining stairs and stopped at the basement door. "Rrr-ruff."

"Silly dog." I passed him. Should I make fettucine Alfredo, which sounded really good on a cold night like this, or warm up a Lean Cuisine for dinner? I caught a glimpse of the elliptical machine in the living room out of the corner of my eye and guiltily decided on Lean Cuisine. I hadn't used the elliptical since before Christmas. Well, no one can keep up with an exercise plan during the holidays. Nolan stayed by the door and scratched at it with one paw.

"Is Dexter down there?" I asked him. I opened the door, but it was dark. "Dexter?"

No answer. Nolan stood on the top step and barked, and I wondered if maybe we had mice. Not again. We'd been positively overrun by them a couple of winters back when it got really cold, and Les had called an exterminator. Kendall had cried about the poor cute mice and called Les a mouse murderer. She'd offered to catch them herself and release them in the wild. Les hadn't thought much of that plan and had paid the exterminator extra to get here sooner. Kendall hadn't talked to either of us for two weeks. I hoped we didn't have to go through all that again. Leaving the door cracked, I returned to the fridge and was getting out a Lean Cuisine when I decided it would be better to heat up the rest of the pizza. I didn't want it to go to waste.

I set the oven to preheat, positioned the remaining three slices of pizza on the rack, and was looking for James's phone number when I heard a strange noise. A bump. Like someone knocking against a table or chair. I started.

"Dexter? Are you home?" I could see the garage door was locked, so I left the kitchen and crossed the living room to check the front door. Locked. I peered out the window but saw nothing but snow turning the yard into a jumble of white shapes. Nolan had gone with me, but now he trotted back to the basement door. I followed him, tightening the belt on my robe.

I eyed the door uneasily. Scenes from slasher movies I'd stupidly gone to see played in my mind. There was always a scene where the babysitter goes into the basement, even though there are reports of a serial killer on the loose, or the teenaged couple sneak into the basement to make out, even though escaped convicts are in the area. The last thought brought a memory to mind, and I yanked open the door, suddenly more mad than scared.

"Dexter, I'm coming down. If you've got a girl down there, you're grounded until you graduate." Six months ago, Kendall had gone downstairs to play Wii and stumbled over Dexter and a girl (whose name I had deliberately blocked) "going at it" on the couch. She'd said they were naked, but they both had clothes on by the time I got downstairs. Thank heavens! It was the first time I'd really, really wanted Les back in a long time. Chewing out your teenaged son for "going at it" with a naked girl in the basement is a father's job. I'd stumbled through a talk where I think I'd said "too young" at least a dozen times and worked in "respect" and "consequences" and "your sister has to sit on that sofa" a few times each. I don't know which of us was the most embarrassed, although I think it was me.

I hurried down the stairs, feeling clumsy in the bear slippers. Nolan beat me down. "I'm at the bottom of the stairs now," I warned, not wanting to take naked teenagers by surprise. I didn't even want to think about my baby boy naked with a girl, never mind see it in the flesh. I didn't hear anything. No sounds of people dressing, which I took as a good sign.

"I'm turning on the lights now." I flicked the switch. The lights sprang on. No naked teens. No anything, actually. The game room with its sofa, beanbag chairs, Ping-Pong table, and wide-screen TV was empty. "Nolan, you silly dog, there's no one here," I said, almost light-headed with relief. Nolan *arf*ed at me and wagged his tail.

Then I thought about the guest room. The guest room with its queen-sized bed. Surely Dexter couldn't be shameless enough to . . . I hurried down the short hall, not bothering with any warnings now, and flung open the bedroom door. It smacked into the wall, and I winced. Enough light from the other room filtered in so I could tell there was no one here. Unless they were hiding in the closet, and that was just silly.

Letting my breath out in a long *whew,* I smoothed the rumpled coverlet on the bed and decided to answer the call of nature before going back to the kitchen. Stepping into the three-quarter bath in the hall, I put out my hand for the light switch and touched someone's face.

29

~~~

It took Charlie and Dan almost twenty-five minutes to trudge the half mile to the exit, with Dan walking in front to shield Charlie from the worst of the wind. No cars had passed since they'd been walking, and a cell phone call to the state police hadn't given hope of rescue anytime soon.

"We've got half a dozen motorists stranded on that stretch," the helpful officer said, "and we're trying to get to you as soon as possible. We've got a plow making its way down from Fort Collins and another going west on 34 out of Greeley, but it's slow going. Sit tight and stay warm. Don't panic."

Dan had told them what mile marker they were at and said they were planning to walk to the exit. The cop had sounded dubious about their cross-country hike but mentioned there was a small convenience store with one gas pump at the exit. "I doubt old Fred's there, though; he usually closes up when the first snowflake falls. Cantankerous old goat."

Now, shivering with cold despite her heavy coat and boots, Charlie surveyed the featureless white landscape. Blowing snow made it difficult to see more than ten feet in front of her face. When the wind shifted direction for a few seconds, she thought she saw a small building, its outlines blurred by accumulated snow. She pointed. "There. That must be it."

They headed west down a slope that might have been an

access road and reached the convenience store ten minutes later. It was disappointingly dark, with no sign of life. Its single gas pump was almost hidden by a drift. Luckily, the front of the building was out of the wind's path, and the drifts had piled against the rear of the building, leaving Charlie and Dan access to the door. Charlie rattled it. Locked. Making a visor of her hand, she leaned against the window and scoped out the interior. Rows of canned or boxed foods, refrigerator cases, counter and cash register, coffeemaker. And a sign that spoke to her: RESTROOMS.

"Ideas?" she asked Dan.

"I don't think we're likely to get an invitation," he said, drawing a gadget from his pocket that appeared to be a Swiss Army knife on steroids. Snow crusted on his eyebrows, and Charlie wondered if hers were similarly icy. With surprisingly deft fingers, he located the gadget he wanted, scored the glass around the lock with it, and tapped the glass inward.

Charlie's eyes widened. "You carry a glass cutter with you?"

"Habit."

Habit? Charlie asked herself. She didn't know many priests or pastors in the habit of carrying any tool more exotic than a corkscrew to a parish dinner, certainly not knives and glass cutters.

"Never know when it might come in handy," Dan added, reaching through the hole to unlock the door. He pushed it open and they stepped in, closing it behind them. The stillness and quiet were like a warm blanket after the wind's fury. Charlie took only a moment to savor the peace before scuttling to the bathroom. When she emerged, fluorescent bulbs sputtered overhead, illuminating short aisles of chips and Wonder bread, Band-Aids and magazines. Dan stood with his back to her, fiddling with the coffee machine. Even though a warm beverage had some appeal, Charlie headed past him and liberated a Pepsi from one of the refrigerator cases. She hesitated.

"I feel weird about this. Is this stealing?"

"We'll leave money to cover what we eat and to pay for having the door fixed," Dan said. He turned toward her as he spoke, and she found something incredibly comforting in the breadth of his shoulders and his calm expression. "It's an emergency. No one would begrudge us hospitality in such a situation."

Charlie wasn't quite as convinced about the store owner's generosity, but she twisted the cap on the Pepsi and took a long drink. "Much better," she declared, crossing to Dan. He directed a stream of hot water into a foam cup and plunked a tea bag into it. "No coffee?"

"This is quicker."

"It's cold in here."

"Heat's turned off."

Looking around for something to plug the hole they'd cut in the glass, Charlie found a sponge and cleaning rag in a utility closet and stuffed them in. "Better," she muttered, still cold enough to keep her jacket zipped all the way up. "How long do you think we'll be here?"

Shrugging, Dan wandered the aisles, idly eyeing the merchandise and sipping his tea. "A few hours at least." He plucked something from a shelf. "Want a Hostess Fruit Pie?"

Charlie's eyes lit up. "Cherry? I haven't had one of those

since I was a kid." She remembered bouncing in the old truck down the dirt road leading from Grandy and Gramps's farm in rural Washington to Emerson's General Store on a Saturday afternoon and being allowed to pick out one treat. She'd usually gone for a cherry fruit pie, although she liked Ding-Dongs, too. Her Gramps would stand there, shaking his head, a faint smile on his lips, unable to understand how she could want the processed pie when Grandy's pies were justly famed across three counties.

Quickly peeling off the wrapper, she sank her teeth into the still-familiar pastry that was too thick and too sugar-crusted and felt the too-sweet cherry goo ooze into her mouth. "Oh, yum," she said, closing her eyes.

Dan laughed and opened a container of beef jerky. There were no chairs, so they settled with their backs against the counter that supported the coffee machine since it was the farthest away from the refrigerator cases and the doors. They sat with shoulders touching, knees drawn up, and munched in silence for a few minutes, listening to the wind whip at the building. Water drip-dripped from the hot water spout into the spillover tray. The warmth and the food were enough to make Charlie drowsy.

"I could use a nap."

Dan patted his shoulder. "I've been told I make a good pillow."

"Really? Who told you that?" Charlie studied his craggy face with interest, suddenly feeling less sleepy.

Dan hesitated only a moment. "My wife."

Charlie stifled the urge to screech, "Your what?" sensing that Dan's confidence marked a turning point in their relationship. "I didn't know you were married," she said after a moment.

"No reason you should," Dan said, sliding her a sideways look.

"In a galaxy far, far away," Charlie murmured, letting her eyelids sink to half-mast. Who knew slogging through knee-deep snow in a blizzard was so exhausting? Her head drifted toward Dan's shoulder. "What was she like?"

"Passionate," Dan said, his voice level and impersonal, "about all sorts of things, about life. Kind. Loved animals and children."

"Do you—?"

"No."

Charlie couldn't tell if he was sorry about not having kids or not. "I was married once, too," she offered. "His name was Brad. He was a fighter pilot through and through: brash, brave, a touch arrogant. We got married as young lieutenants. It lasted a little over two years, until each of us figured out we didn't really want brash, brave, and a touch arrogant in our partners."

Dan chuckled, his shoulder shaking under Charlie's head.

"Why did you split up?" she asked.

"We didn't. Rilla died."

Charlie sat up and stared at his profile. "Oh, Dan. I'm so sorry."

"It was a long time ago."

"Before you were a priest?"

"Long before." He turned to look at her, his eyes their usual serene blue, his face disturbingly close. "It seems like another lifetime."

Charlie felt flustered by the intensity of his gaze, off balance. She wanted to ask what he'd done before becoming a priest, how Rilla died, whether he'd had any serious relationships since, but something about the intimacy of being snowed in, of their enforced togetherness, made her wary of inviting more revelations. "That fruit pie made me thirsty," she said, getting up awkwardly and stamping a foot that had fallen asleep. "I need some water."

"Get me one, too, while you're up."

"Sure." With a lurching gait, wincing at the prickles in her foot, she headed for one of the refrigerator cases. When she was halfway there, a door at the rear of the store burst open, letting in a blast of wind, a drift of snow, and a man with a shotgun.

30

~~~

"Aaah! Eee-yow!" I ran screaming from the bathroom, looking for something, anything to use as a weapon. My slippers made me clumsy, and I stumbled into the Ping-Pong table. Grabbing a paddle, I looked around for the phone. The kids rarely put it back on its base, and it wasn't there now. Could I make it to the stairs?

A man's figure, arms upraised, came out of the hall. "Don't—" he started.

Nolan danced between us, barking furiously. "Bite him,

Nolie," I yelled, swinging the Ping-Pong paddle in what I hoped was a threatening way. I wished I had a baseball bat or, better yet, my gun, which Charlie insisted on keeping locked in the office safe. Even my Taser would give me a better chance, but Charlie had insisted on locking that up, too, after I tased her by accident. I couldn't believe a little electrocution made her so testy.

"Gigi."

I screamed again.

"For God's sake, Gigi, stop that screeching. And shut that dog up. Jesus!"

It dawned on me that the intruder hadn't moved and that he was saying my name. I lowered the paddle. "Les?"

He stepped into the light. "Of course it's me," he said irritably.

Of *course*? Where did he get off thinking he could just sneak into *my* house? I asked him that, my voice scratchy from screaming.

"It used to be my house, too, Gigi," he said. "Remember? I paid for it. I've still got my keys."

"Well, it's mine now, and you have no business sneaking around in the basement, scaring me to death. What are you doing here, anyway?"

"I need a place to stay," he said. When he stood under one of the track lights, I could see his face was grayish, and dark circles even my Stila concealer wouldn't have hidden made his eyes look sunken. His shirt was untucked, hanging over his paunch. He looked much worse than when I'd caught up with him in Aspen. I stomped on a spurt of sympathy.

"Not here. Kendall and Dexter—"

"The kids don't have to know," he said quickly. "I'll stay down here. It's only for a day or two, until I can get hold of some cash and get out of Colorado. Someone's after me, Gigi." He looked out the window as if a serial killer with an ax might be crouched in our garden.

I leaned sideways and let down the blinds. You never know. "No." I put enough force into my voice that Nolan growled. "You can't move back in here. It will confuse the kids." It would confuse me, too, but I didn't say that.

"I'm not talking about moving in! I'm talking about camping out for a couple of days. Do you have to make a federal case out of everything? In case you haven't noticed, there's a goddamn blizzard raging out there. Do you want your children's father to freeze to death?"

I bit my lip. I didn't want Les staying here, but I could hardly kick him out into a blizzard. "Well, I guess . . . for one night . . ."

He smiled, and some of the old confidence returned to his face. "That's my Gigi." He moved toward me, arms open wide. "Hey, we had fun the other night in Aspen, didn't we? Got the old fires going again pretty good. Since the kids aren't here, maybe we could—"

I smacked him across the face with the Ping-Pong paddle. The force of it tingled up my arms. It felt *good*.

He jumped back, his hand going to his face. "Ow! What'd you do that for?"

"For thinking you can waltz back in here and I'll fall into your arms."

"Well, that's what happened in Aspen." He waggled his eyebrows suggestively. "You haven't been getting any, have you? C'mon, babe, we always had great chemistry—"

Heat surged through me, and I knew it wasn't a hot flash; it was anger. I was mad, mad, mad at Les Goldman for the way he'd treated me. I lunged toward him, swinging the paddle, and connected with his ear. I hadn't known how much anger was bottled up inside me, but now it burst out like floodwaters punching through a levee. Before he could move, I struck again, whapping the tip of his nose, and then a fourth time, getting the bald spot on top of his head as he ducked. "Hi-yaa!" I think I yelled like they do in those martial arts movies. That felt good, too.

Les backed up, arms covering his face. "Okay, okay, I get it: no nookie."

I glared at him, pffing a lock of hair off my forehead with an upward breath. Now that I'd gotten it out of my system, I felt lighter, freer. I wished Albertine could have been here to see me get my mad on. "You are lower than a slug's belly, Les Goldman," I told him. "You cheated on me with Heather-Anne, and then you cheated on her with me. I'm going upstairs to change. You'd better be here when I get back. Then we're going to talk, and you're going to tell me everything you know about Heather-Anne's death and—"

I stopped because he didn't seem to be paying attention. His brow crinkled and he tilted his head up, sniffing. "What's that? Smells like fire."

I sniffed, too, and noticed Nolan doing the same. It came to me in a flash. "My pizza!"

I dashed upstairs and burst into the kitchen in time to see

smoke escaping from around the oven door. Would it be smarter to open the door and fling some water in, or keep it closed and hope the fire didn't spread? My eyes watering from the smoke, I fanned it away from my face and was reaching to turn the oven off when the smoke detectors began to shrill. Nolan, who had followed me up, started yapping fit to beat the band, and the din gave me a headache. Flinging open a couple of windows, I dragged a kitchen chair over and climbed on it, reaching up to shut down the smoke alarm. I punched buttons randomly but couldn't get the thing to stop. My arms ached and I felt tottery on the chair and I had had enough. I ripped the detector off the ceiling and slammed it onto the tile floor. The battery bounced out and the alarm gave one last chirp and died. The silence was heavenly, but I ruined it by slumping onto the chair and breaking into tears.

This week had been too much: finding Les, sleeping with him, getting arrested, finding Heather-Anne's body, *Dexter* getting arrested, Les showing up again and me going after him like some kind of deranged *Fatal Attraction* psycho. Too much. I boo-hooed for several minutes before getting up to blow my nose and splash water onto my face. Pulling a box of frozen éclair minis out of the freezer, I sat at the kitchen table and popped one into my mouth. The room reeked of smoke, and the open windows were letting the blizzard and cold blow through, but I ignored the discomforts, propped my chin on my hands, and ate another éclair.

That's how Les found me. He poked his head cautiously around the basement door and, not seeing anyone—firemen, I guess—he crossed to me and patted my shoulder. I shrugged away from his hand, and he dropped it awkwardly to his side before crossing to the oven and peering inside.

"What a mess."

"Don't start." My voice quavered, so I folded my lips together. I was not going to cry in front of Les.

He held up his hands in a surrender gesture. "Let me clean it up."

I perked up at that. Les clean? He'd never made such an offer when we were married. Maybe I should have whacked him with a Ping-Pong paddle years ago. I watched morosely as he slid the rack with the carbonized pizza out of the oven and dumped the charred disk into the trash, then dug around under the sink for a Brillo pad and cleanser. "You don't have to do that," I heard myself say.

He ignored me. Good. I looked down and realized I'd eaten half the box of éclairs and was feeling a bit sick to my stomach. There wasn't much an éclair couldn't fix, but this situation was beyond the power of Bavarian cream and chocolate. I pushed the box away. The movement reawakened the smoke smell, and I sniffed at my robe. Pee-yew! I smelled like my daddy used to smell when he came in from burning yard trash in the fifty-five-gallon drum in the backyard.

"I'm going to take a shower," I told Les. I didn't wait for a reply but headed upstairs to my room. I had just closed the door when I realized I'd never checked on Dexter. I dialed his cell phone, and he answered. I sighed a little prayer.

"Yo."

"Hi, baby. Are you okay? Where are you?"

"James's. His folks picked us up from school today—they

didn't want him driving in the snow. They invited me to stay."

The way James drove, they shouldn't let him near any vehicle more dangerous than a skateboard, rain or shine. "You didn't think to call?"

"No. Gotta go. It's my turn."

The line went dead. Not bothering to wonder what it was his turn at, and relieved that Dexter wasn't dead, in jail, or coming home tonight, I stuffed my stinky robe in the hamper and stepped into the hot shower.

Half of me wanted to climb under the duvet with a good Barbara Cartland book, but I knew I needed to have it out with Les. When I went downstairs again, dressed in my mauve velour sweatpants and the Prada sweater with the metallic thread through the lavender yarn—I didn't want to give Les any ideas by coming downstairs in my jammies, not now that I'd finally given him what for—I found that he had finished with the oven and was watching Fox News with a glass of Scotch at his elbow. Just like when we were married. I marched to the television and turned it off. Take that, Bill O'Reilly.

"Hey, I was watching that."

"Did you kill Heather-Anne?" I had tried not even to consider the possibility, but now I had to know.

He goggled at me and spilled Scotch on the leather sofa. It would wipe up. His mustache twitched, and he put on a wounded look. "Gigi, I can't believe you'd even—"

"Did you?"

"No! God, no. I threw up when I heard she was dead."
His face had a greenish tinge at the memory.

"Why did you leave Costa Rica? Was it the newspaper
clipping?"

He clanked the rim of the glass against his teeth, and
Scotch dribbled down his chin. "Stop *doing* that. How did
you— Oh, you found my folder in the BMW?"

I nodded. "Charlie's in Wyoming interviewing that family
right now. She thinks your Heather-Anne and the wife in that
clipping may be the same person."

He took a long sip of Scotch without spilling any, and
I knew he'd had the same thought. "I can't believe it."

He didn't *want* to believe it.

He gave me his sincere look. "I should never have left you,
Gigi. I know that now. I didn't realize how good I had it living here in Colorado with you, the house, the kids. Yes, even
the kids. Costa Rica's so effing humid you can't think some
days, like your brain's trapped underwater, and the damn
monkeys are everywhere, like big furry cockroaches."

I tried to keep from laughing, but a little snort came out
my nose.

"You can laugh," he said, gesturing with his glass, "but it's
true. I'd go to sleep at night under layers of mosquito netting
and wish for a crisp Colorado day. I guess we don't always
appreciate what we have until we lose it." His shoulders
slumped, but I channeled Albertine and trampled the urge to
comfort him.

"Who do you think killed Heather-Anne?" I asked. "And
why?"

"It was probably some lunatic, some Ted Bundy–type just passing through."

That wasn't even worth responding to. I sat on the sofa across from Les and crossed my arms over my chest. The wind howled outside, and I reminded myself to call Kendall at Angel's to tell her good night.

"Well, it *could* have been," Les said when I didn't say anything.

"You said someone's after you . . . Who?"

"I wish to hell I knew." He tossed back the rest of the Scotch and rose to get more from the bottle he'd left on the sink.

"You don't have any idea?" I wasn't sure whether or not to believe him. The éclairs had worn off, and I needed real food. I don't think as well when I get low-blood-sugary. I followed Les into the kitchen and pulled the makings of Alfredo sauce from the fridge. Even though it felt like midnight, it was only seven o'clock. "How about Patrick Dreiser or one of the other people you robbed?"

"I didn't rob anybody. I practiced creative accounting. Caveat emptor and all that. I guess it could have been Dreiser— he took my departure badly, sent me threatening notes for months. Do you want me to put the water on?"

I nodded, and he filled a deep pot with water and turned the gas on under it. If he'd been half this helpful when he lived here, I might have missed him more when he left. The thought made me drop the whisk I was using on the cream and butter. I thought I *had* missed Les, but was that true? What had we talked about the past couple of years? Dexter's

221

suspensions, my shopping habits, Les's gripes about some of his business partners. Not much else. Huh. Did I *really* miss Les? I missed the sex—I was menopausal, not dead—even though there hadn't been as much of that in the year before he left. I put the idea away to think about later . . . maybe. What kind of person was I if I didn't even miss my ex-husband?

"Why are you looking at me like that?" he asked. I shook my head hurriedly, and he held up two boxes of pasta. "Fettucine or linguine?"

31

Charlie froze.

"Ah-hah!" the man said. He was shorter than Charlie and dressed like a cross between an Arctic explorer and an 1850s miner, with a furred hood framing a whiskery face and an unzipped jacket showing a plaid shirt and jeans held up by suspenders. She guessed he must be over seventy. "I knew it when I saw the light! Looters! Hands up!"

Charlie obliged. "I'm not a looter," she said, carefully not mentioning Dan. She didn't want to make the enraged store owner any antsier than he was, not with the shotgun leveled at her abdomen. "I got stranded in the storm and had to find shelter."

"What's that, then?" The man pointed at the Hostess pie wrapper sticking from her pocket. "Looter!"

"I was hungry. I was going to leave money—"

"Sure you were." He sniffed and took one hand from the gun to swipe his jacketed forearm under his nose. "Cold gets me every time. You just stay right where you are, missy, while I call the police."

"Look, Fred—are you Fred?"

His eyes narrowed to slits. "How'd you know my name?"

"The state patrolman mentioned it when we—I—called to say I was stuck on the highway. He said what a great guy you were." A lie, but Charlie figured it wouldn't hurt. "Look, can you put the gun down?" She put some emphasis on the word "gun" in case Dan hadn't caught on.

"Uh-uh," Fred said. "You're a crafty one, you are. You might not be much bigger than a snippet, but you've got some wiles. You just march to the aisle by the window and fetch a roll of duct tape so I can make sure you don't try to pull a fast one while I call the cops. I'll bet you know right where that tape is, what with looting the place and all."

Charlie began to walk backward, not wanting to turn her back on the shotgun. "How did you get here?"

"Snowmobile. I live just over the rise"—he jerked his head to the west—"and when I saw the light come on I fired 'er up and headed over here, fixing to catch me a looter. Which I've done."

Suddenly Dan rose up behind Fred—how had he gotten over there? Charlie wondered—and with a series of moves she could barely follow disarmed the man, ejected the gun's shells, and returned the gun to Fred before he could do more than squawk. "Wha—?"

"I'm Father Dan Allgood." Dan extended his hand. "I'm

sorry I had to rough you up a bit, but shotguns are touchy and I didn't want that one to go off, especially not with my friend Charlie close enough to absorb a lot of shot."

Fred gobbled, his face reddening, and looked from Dan to Charlie. Dan's calm finally seemed to work on the man, and his color subsided. He shook Dan's still-extended hand reluctantly. "Since when are Catholic priests looters? Not in my day." He shook his head sadly at the decline of the church's standards.

"I'm Episcopalian."

"Oh, well, then."

Charlie choked on a laugh at Fred's easy acceptance of an Episcopalian as a criminal. She pulled out her wallet. "Look, here's two hundred dollars. That should more than cover the food we ate and repairs to the door."

Fred took the bills and hurried to the front door. "You're vandals, too?"

"I'm sorry we had to damage the door to get in," Dan said. "You wouldn't have wanted us to freeze to death, though."

Fred didn't look like he was quite as convinced of that as Dan, but he nodded. "I suppose I can see why you thought it was necessary to vandalize and loot my store, under the circumstances."

Charlie and Dan listened for a few minutes as Fred told them how he'd come to own the store and how lousy business had been recently. When Fred quit talking to wipe his nose again, Dan said, "Did you say something about a snowmobile?"

"Sure did."

"I don't suppose you've got another one?"

"Sure do. The missus and me like to take 'em up to Winter Park and let 'er rip. There's a lot of squawking from environmentalists these days about snowmobiles 'negatively impacting the wildlife' and what have you, but I say it's still a free country—barely—and I have a God-given right to ride my snowmobile when and where I please."

His whiskery jaw jutted out, and he looked as determined as any Minuteman defending the Boston common. Charlie couldn't remember which article of the Constitution protected the right to ride treaded vehicles, but she didn't want to put Fred's back up by mentioning it.

"Any chance you could help us get to a town?" Dan asked. "We'd pay you."

Fred's eyes lit up. "Sure can. Long's you don't mind riding pillion."

Twenty minutes later, Charlie found herself clutching Dan's middle, both of them layered in cold weather gear supplied by the now-helpful Fred and his wife, Aileen, rocketing across the snow-covered countryside on what was possibly the loudest form of transportation ever invented. They followed Fred and Aileen; she would ride their snowmobile back. The storm seemed to have moved east, so the wind had diminished, but it was bitterly cold, and Charlie was grateful for the face mask, goggles, hat, and gloves that Aileen had loaned her. The jouncing of the snowmobile jarred every bone and muscle in her body, including her ass, and she was grateful when they reached a smooth stretch of snow she suspected was I-25. Dan pointed to the right, and she made out a snow-covered lump that might have been his truck. Nodding against his back to let him know she'd seen it, she pressed herself more tightly against him and hoped the motel wasn't too far away and that it would have rooms available. She'd pay half a month's salary for a hot shower.

Almost on the thought, she spotted lights. They cast a warm yellow glow across the snowy landscape, and she was relieved to find they belonged to a small motel with VACAN Y blinking redly from a sign near the office. After securing the last two rooms, Charlie and Dan thanked the store owner and his wife and shucked off the gear the couple had loaned them, packing it into a garbage bag supplied by the motel clerk for Fred and Aileen to carry back with them. They waved good-bye as the old couple fired up the snowmobiles with big grins on their faces and pointed the machines north.

Feeling utterly exhausted, even though it wasn't much past seven, Charlie fed quarters into a vending machine to get "dinner" in the form of snack crackers and peanuts and took them to her room after bidding Dan good night. He had enveloped her in a bear hug that did more to warm her than any number of showers or hot cocoas would and told her to sleep tight. The dialogue from a cop show on the next room's TV seeped through the thin walls, and Charlie wondered how many of the motel's guests were stranded travelers. Not giving it much thought, she stripped and headed straight for the shower. Fifteen minutes later, the water turned tepid and she stepped out, wishing she had clean clothes to put on.

The roads would be plowed by the morning, she told herself, and they could return to Dan's truck and finish their journey. Wrapped in a towel, she fished her cell phone out of her purse and called Gigi, wanting to know what her partner had discovered about Wilfred Cheney's disability and Patrick Dreiser. Just when Charlie was about to hang up, Gigi answered, sounding flustered.

"Charlie! I tried to call you twice. Are you home?"

"Stranded in Mead. The trip was a bust. Neither the sheriff nor the Eustis family could positively ID Heather-Anne as Amanda. What did you learn from Cheney?"

Gigi lowered her voice. "Ot-nay ow-nay. Es-lay ere-hay."

"No pig Latin, Gigi," Charlie growled. "We've been over this." Her mind translated. "Wait—did you say Les is there?"

"Es-yay."

Charlie heard shuffling sounds that seemed to indicate Gigi was moving; then a door closed.

"Okay," Gigi whispered. "I'm in the bathroom. By myself. I can talk now."

"What happened? Why is Les there? What does he have to say about Heather-Anne?"

Gigi explained about finding Les in the basement. "I smacked him good with the Ping-Pong paddle," she said with evident satisfaction.

"Too bad it wasn't a cast-iron poker."

"Charlie! Anyway, he said he didn't kill Heather-Anne—"

"He *would* say that."

"—and that someone is after him."

"Did he say who?"

"He said he doesn't know, but I think he might be lying."

Duh. Charlie thought for a moment. "Have you called the cops?"

"Why?"

"The man broke into your house. He's a wanted criminal!"

"Oh."

Charlie could almost hear Gigi thinking and knew that turning Les in had never crossed her mind. She let almost a minute pass before saying, "Gigi?"

"I don't think I can do that, Charlie. Not hand him over to the police. I mean, it was awful of him to run off with Heather-Anne, and of course I understand that the embezzling was criminal, but it seems so *mean* to call the cops on him."

"You need to be meaner."

"I know." Gigi said it sadly, as if meaner were an unobtainable goal.

"Well, if you're not prepared to hand him over to the police, at least make sure he sticks around long enough so I can talk to him. He's got to know why Heather-Anne was killed, and maybe who did it."

"I'll try. He's not going anywhere tonight—he's drunk enough Scotch to put a sow to sleep. When do you think you'll be back?"

"Noon tomorrow," Charlie said optimistically. Assuming the plows cleared the highway overnight, they found someone to drive them back to Dan's truck, they were able to dig it out and get it back on the road, it wasn't damaged, and no more snow fell. *Piece of cake,* she thought, hanging up.

32

A snowplow's growling woke me the next morning. I snuggled my face into my pillow, trying to ignore the sound, but eventually I sat up. Sunlight streamed through the window, and last night's storm was a thing of the past, except for the foot or so of snow covering the neighbors' roofs and lawns. The night's events came back to me, and I remembered Les was in the basement. After he'd stumbled down the stairs, too drunk to make a move on me, I'd locked the door. He could still get out the window, I supposed, if he wanted to leave, but he hadn't seemed in any shape to go crawling through windows. I wondered vaguely how he'd gotten here.

A faint pounding and Les's voice calling "Gigi!" got me scrambling out of bed and into my clothes. By the time I'd brushed my teeth and put on just a dab of makeup, it was only fifteen minutes later, but Les acted like I'd left him stranded on a desert island for a week and a half when I unlocked the basement door.

"For God's sake, Gigi! I've been pounding on the door for half an hour. What? You were so busy putting your face on you couldn't come down and let me out? You didn't have to lock the door in the first place." He stomped to the fridge, smelling like stale alcohol. He jerked the door open so hard the condiment bottles clinked. "There's no orange juice!"

Hangovers made Les surly.

"I suppose there's no paper today, either," he said, peering out the window at the snowy driveway. "Lazy buggers. Any excuse not to deliver the paper. If you're making eggs, I'll have mine over easy."

Crossing my arms over my chest, I glared at him and decided to practice being meaner. "Charlie thinks I should call the police on you."

That got his attention. He whirled and tried out a smile. "Gigi. Hon. That's not necessary. I'm sorry if I sounded a bit . . . testy. It's just that I'm worried. Look, I'll scramble us both some eggs, okay?"

"I want cereal." I crossed to the pantry for the Honey Bunches of Oats, poured some into a bowl, and added milk. After a moment, Les did likewise. We sat at the kitchen table, eating in silence. "Heather-Anne told Charlie you guys had a fight and that you left," I said finally, stirring the leftover milk in the bottom of my bowl.

Les burped. "I need some coffee." He got up and began to make a pot, complaining that I didn't have his favorite brand anymore. Finally, with the coffee brewing, he came back to the table. "We did. That newspaper clipping arrived and I lost it. Heather-Anne and I had been reasonably honest with each other about our pasts. She knew that my business dealings weren't always on the up-and-up, and I knew she'd made a habit of . . . of separating men from their money. I knew she'd been married before and that she'd walked away from those marriages with a lot of cash."

"Marriages? How many?"

"Two that I knew about. A guy named Cheney in Tennessee and another guy in Oklahoma when she was younger.

Parnell Parkin, his name was. Three," he added reluctantly, "if it turns out she was the wife referred to in the Wyoming clipping. She had a rough childhood. Her dad left when she was only three or four, and her mom found herself a succession of sugar daddies who often didn't want Heather-Anne or her brother around. He was younger and sick. They were always trying to scrape together money to pay for doctors or get him medicine. Anyway, her mom pretty much brought her up to think that the best way to make a buck was to use her assets to con some poor schmuck out of it."

I was thinking "poor thing" when images from Reba's video of "Fancy" started playing in my brain and I wondered if Heather-Anne hadn't made the whole story up after hearing that song. She probably didn't even have a brother, sick or otherwise. Les got up to fill his coffee cup and actually brought me one.

"Thanks." I took a sip, wondering how Charlie could possibly prefer a cold Pepsi to coffee. "So you got mad when you read the clipping and . . . ?"

"We fought. Argued. I accused her of lying. She slammed out of the house and I drank. You know how I get sometimes." He looked a little sheepish. "I guess I fell asleep."

Or passed out.

"When I woke up it was the next morning and she was gone. Gone gone, not 'out walking the beach in a snit' gone. I couldn't think of where she might have gone except here, so I got a ticket to Denver and followed her."

"Heather-Anne told Charlie that you left first and *she* followed *you*."

He flapped a hand. "No, it was the other way around."

231

"Why were you in Aspen?"

"I've kept in touch with Cherry and Moss. I knew they were out of the country. I needed to keep a low profile because of the arrest warrant, and I missed skiing, and I thought Aspen would be a romantic place for me and Heather-Anne to make up when . . ." He trailed off, looking sad.

I didn't know what to believe. Staring at his profile as he sipped his coffee, I realized something. "You really loved her, didn't you?" I felt like someone had squeezed my rib cage too tight. "You wouldn't have risked coming back to the States if you didn't."

Les's expression told me all I needed to know. Before he could say anything, though, the front door creaked open and Dexter called, "Mom, I'm home. James's family took off for a day on the slopes, so they dropped me. Mom?"

Les and I exchanged panicked looks. Well, mine was panicked. Les's was more resigned.

Dexter appeared in the kitchen, snow clods falling off his boots. The cold had reddened his handsome face, and his blond bangs half-hid his eyes. "I thought I'd—" He caught sight of his dad and stopped.

"Hi, son—" Les started.

"It's not what it looks like," I said. I didn't know what Dexter thought it looked like, but whatever it looked like, that's not what it was.

Dexter turned on his heel and marched away, leaving a trail of snow melting on the floor.

I started out of my chair. "Honey—"

Les grabbed my arm. "Let him go."

A door slammed upstairs. I pulled away from Les and trotted up the stairs. Knocking on Dexter's door, I tried the knob. It was locked. "Dexter, your dad didn't have anyplace to stay last night, so I let him stay in the basement. It's not . . . we're not . . ."

No response. I tried explaining again but got only silence. "Your dad will be gone soon, okay?" I waited a few more minutes, hoping he would say something, but he didn't. Trudging back down the stairs, I heaved a sigh. Parenting was a lot easier when the kids were in elementary school. Now that they were in high school . . .

The kitchen was empty when I returned to it, the mugs still on the table. Had Les gone down for a shower? Before I could even move the mugs to the sink, the doorbell rang. I hurried to open it and found four burly police officers on the porch, patrol cars behind them striping the snow with red and blue. My mouth fell open.

"Mrs. Goldman? We've had a report of a wanted felon in the area. Is Lester Goldman inside?"

"Uh . . ."

"May we come in?"

I nodded, and they stamped their feet on the mat before stepping into the foyer. I wished I could train the kids to do that.

"Do you feel threatened? Are you under duress, ma'am?" the policeman with three chevrons on his jacket asked, his narrowed eyes taking in the living room, the staircase, and the opening leading to the kitchen and the study.

"Um, no, I'm fine." How did they know Les was here? A

slight noise made me look up, and I saw Dexter looking down at us from the landing, cell phone in hand, triumphant smile tightening his lips. Oh.

"Where can we find Mr. Goldman?"

Even if I'd wanted to protect Les—and I wasn't sure at that moment if I did or not—there was no point in lying with Dexter standing right there ready to paint a bull's-eye on his father's back. "I think he's in the basement."

"Where's that?"

I pointed to the door.

"Is he armed?"

The question startled me. "No! I mean, I don't think so."

They headed for the basement door, saying, "Wait here. You, too." They beckoned to Dexter, who slouched down the stairs and propped himself against the wall, texting furiously. The tall cop with ears that stuck out stayed in the front hall with us while two others started down the basement stairs and the last one slipped out the front door and around toward the garage, drawing his gun.

"They won't shoot Les, will they?"

The young policeman's eyes slid to me and then went back to tracking his partner outside. I could tell he wished he was chasing Les rather than babysitting me and Dexter. "Probably not."

He sounded sorry about it. Before I could respond, one of the cops called from the basement, "All clear. There's no one down here."

"Hey, Sarge, I found footprints out back." The outside cop's voice came over the radio.

I scurried across the living room and looked down into

the backyard. Dexter and the jug-eared cop followed me as the other policemen pounded up the basement stairs. Pretty soon, we were all craning our necks to look down. Sure enough, a set of footprints, big dents in the drifted snow, led away from the house and across the Klamerers' backyard. Les must have seen or heard the police pull up, I guessed, and taken off. Dexter snapped photos with his cell phone.

One pair of cops started following the footprints, and the sergeant came inside, talking into the radio clipped near his shoulder. Pulling out a notebook, he asked me, "What was Goldman wearing?"

"Would you like some coffee? I'm sure you must be frozen, after—"

"Just answer my question, please, Mrs. Goldman."

I was only trying to be thoughtful; he didn't have to get all huffy. "Um, jeans," I said, "and a cerise-colored sweatshirt."

"Say what?" The sergeant twisted one brow inward and looked up from his notebook.

"Red," the tall young cop said.

The sergeant and Dexter eyed him suspiciously, and he blushed. "My sister's an artist," he mumbled.

The questioning continued for ten minutes until the pair of cops chasing Les radioed in to say they'd lost his trail. I wasn't sure if I was glad or sad. The cops left soon after that, the sergeant getting all stern and telling me to call immediately if Les turned up again. "Harboring a wanted man is a crime," he warned. "You can be charged as an accessory."

When they had driven off and I had closed the door behind them, I turned to have it out with Dexter. "Did you call the police on your father because he wrecked your car?" I asked, hands on my hips.

He gave me an incredulous look through the bangs draped over his eyes. "You just don't get it, do you, Mom?"

Before I could ask what he meant, because I had no idea, he was halfway up the stairs. I called his name, but he kept going, waving the cell phone over his head. "Gotta put these on Facebook."

When I was growing up in Georgia, having a daddy in prison, like some of my classmates did, was something to be ashamed of. In fourth grade, the Farrell twins went around saying their dad was working in a car factory up north, and it wasn't until I heard a couple of women whispering in the frozen food section at the Piggly Wiggly that I learned Mr. Farrell was really in jail for robbing a Smyrna bank. Now, the police tracking your dad through the snow gave you bragging rights on Facebook.

I called Charlie to tell her what Les had said about Heather-Anne's earlier husbands and how he followed her to Colorado Springs, and that he was gone again. She answered the phone sounding out of breath.

"Digging out Dan's truck," she said. "What's up?"

When I told her Les had run off, she asked, "Did he leave anything?"

"I don't know. I'll check the basement and call you back." Hanging up, I hurried downstairs, happy to have something to do that didn't involve trying to talk to my son about why he sicced the cops on his father. The basement felt colder than usual, and I found the open window Les must have gone out of. If it wasn't just like him to leave it open so the heater was warming the whole backyard! *He wouldn't have done that if he were still paying the utility bill,* I thought, trying to close the window. It wouldn't latch, and I realized Les had broken it climbing through. Putting a throw pillow against the half-inch gap to keep all the hot air from leaking out, I crept back to the guest bedroom, sneaking along as if Les might still be there. He wasn't.

The bed was unmade, the coverlet tossed on the floor, and the room smelled a bit sour. I wrinkled my nose. Stripping the bed, I looked around but didn't see anything that might belong to Les. In the bathroom, I found a minitube of toothpaste, a wet washcloth on the floor, and a pocket-sized spiral notebook on the toilet tank. Excited, I seized it and riffled through the pages. Nothing. Not one single solitary phone number or list or note. Tiny bits of paper caught in the spiral wire showed where pages had been torn out.

Disappointed, I shoved it in my pocket and headed back upstairs. I didn't have the faintest clue who to call about fixing the window. That made me reflect that one of the hard things about being a divorced single mom, which I'd never thought about before I was one, was not being able to fix a broken window or blow out the sprinkler system for winter, or know how to find someone to do it for you who wouldn't cheat you. I sighed heavily, closed the basement door, and got myself the last slice of lemon cake and the Yellow Pages.

33

Charlie and Dan were back on the road again by nine o'clock, but it was too late for Dan to comfort the dying woman; her family had called to say she'd passed on early that morning. Charlie felt guiltier than ever for having dragged Dan to Wyoming, but he swept aside her apology.

"Jean Warren and I had many conversations about this life and the next over the past couple of months. She was a woman of faith and had come to terms with dying," he said. Charlie wondered what Dan would have to say about the next life, one she wasn't sure she believed in, but a fellow guest offered to drive them back to Dan's truck, and she didn't pursue it.

Once they dug the truck out of the snow and got it back on the road, the rest was easy since plows had cleared I-25 while they slept and the state police had reopened the highway. Twenty minutes saw them in Denver, where billboards advertising the stock show gave Charlie an idea.

"Is it okay if we make a half hour detour?" she asked Dan, pulling out her cell phone.

"You want to talk to Eustis, don't you?" Amused resignation sounded in his voice, though he kept his eyes on the road and the lighter than usual traffic.

She smiled at his acuity and nodded.

"I've got to see what I can do for the Warrens and talk to

Joseph about funeral arrangements, but I don't suppose an hour one way or the other will matter greatly."

With that tacit agreement, Charlie called Sheriff Huff, who called Tansy Eustis and got her husband's cell phone number.

"Do you know something I don't?" the sheriff asked Charlie when he called back to give her the cell number.

"Undoubtedly," she said, "but not necessarily about the Eustis case. I'll keep you posted."

Huff laughed and rang off. Charlie dialed Eustis's number and explained who she was and why she wanted to talk to him.

"Hell, yeah, I'll talk to you if you think you've got a lead on that bitch who killed my father," he said in a cigarette-roughened voice. The sound of a bad PA system echoed in the background, and Charlie had to put a finger in one ear to hear his directions to a meeting place. Dan was taking the I-70 exit toward the stock show grounds even as she hung up. Ten minutes later they pulled off the highway and parked in a dirt lot packed with pickups and livestock trailers. A rancher was leading a bison on a line, and the animal lowered his shaggy head to stare at Charlie and Dan as they got out of the truck. Snow had turned the dirt underfoot to a mire, and an overzealous plow operator had gouged furrows into the lot, making walking hazardous. Piles of dirt-blackened snow edged the lot. By the time they made it to the exhibition building where Eustis had said he'd meet them, Charlie's jeans were spattered with what she hoped was only mud from ankle to knee, and her boots weighed an extra two pounds each from all the muck caked on them.

Charlie and Dan stamped their feet vigorously on the concrete pad outside the warehouselike building and stepped into an atmosphere humid with moisture from damp coats, mud, and, it seemed, a few thousand rabbits. Charlie sneezed.

Hutches lined several aisles, and crowds of people ambled past, admiring the gray, white, brown, black, or speckled inhabitants. Some of the bunnies were the size of cocker spaniels, while others would have fit easily in Charlie's hand. If they hadn't been making her eyes itch and her nose run, she might have enjoyed looking at them. As it was, she glanced around for Eustis and saw a man in a gray cowboy hat waving at them from tables clustered near a hot dog stand. She and Dan wormed through the crowd to Eustis and introduced themselves. Not wanting to distract Eustis by mentioning Dan's title, she introduced him merely as "an associate."

Eustis was in his early forties, Charlie guessed, but looked older. He was a lean man in well-used jeans and a pearl-snapped shirt under a worn leather jacket. He pushed his hat back on his brow as he shook their hands, and Charlie eyed it, almost certain she'd seen it and him leaving Heather-Anne Pawlusik's hotel room at the Embassy Suites a few days before the woman was strangled.

"Sorry about this," he said by way of greeting, his voice gravelly, "but the rabbit judging is happening now, and my youngest has several rabbits entered." He gestured vaguely toward the hutches and, Charlie assumed, his kid. "M'other boys raised Simmental calves and made themselves a bundle on the sales, but, no, Eric's got to raise goddamn rabbits. Still, he's won a few ribbons." Distaste for the rabbits warred with pride in his voice. He sank into a metal folding chair and pulled a pack of cigarettes out of his jacket pocket. Sliding one out, he fingered it but didn't light up. "Can't smoke in here," he complained.

"We won't take much of your time," Charlie promised as she and Dan also sat.

"Tansy said you were out at the Triple E yesterday, that you showed her a photo of a woman that might be Amanda?"

Charlie unfolded the photo and pushed it across the table to him. It stuck on the tacky surface, and Eustis reached for it. "Could be her," he said. He gazed at it a moment longer, covering Heather-Anne's hair with his thumb. "I think it might be her. Where did you get this?" The page trembled.

"She lived in Colorado Springs for a while," Charlie said, "and recently moved to Costa Rica. Do you know anyone named Les Goldman?"

Eustis's brow crinkled. "Doesn't ring any bells."

"He's not someone you or your dad did business with?"

"Not me. Dad had deals going I wasn't in on, though. Why?" He tapped an impatient foot on the dirt floor.

Without answering, Charlie asked, "What do you remember about your father's death?"

Eustis put the cigarette in his mouth and let it hang there. Like a pacifier, Charlie thought. "Dad met her here." Eustis flung a hand wide to encompass the entire stock show. "They were married within two months. Indecent. My mother was barely cold in her grave."

"Some people are more comfortable married," Dan put in. "They need companionship, someone to do for, or to do for them."

Eustis slanted him a look that didn't agree or disagree.

"You wanted to know about his murder," he said to Charlie. "I found him." His lips worked at the cigarette. "Dead. Stone cold. Alone. She poisoned him with brake fluid in his Long Island iced tea, ransacked the bank accounts, and lit out. The sheriff never found a trace of her."

Charlie got the impression Eustis wasn't going to be voting for Sheriff Huff in the next election. "You weren't worried that the murderer had killed or kidnapped her?"

Snorting, Eustis pulled the cigarette from his mouth and began to shred it in his fingers. Bits of tobacco drifted to the floor. "Nope. She did it. His drink was poisoned, for chrissake. Who else could have done it?"

"Your wife mentioned that you inherited the Triple E, and rumor had it that your dad was firing you. You threatened to kill him."

The words hung between them for a moment as the PA system named the best of breed for something called a Champagne d'Argent. It sounded like a bottle of bubbly, Charlie thought, rather than a rabbit.

As Charlie's words sank in, Eustis leaped to his feet, overturning the metal chair. Several people turned to look as it clanged to the floor. "I did not kill my dad! That woman did. Amanda or Heather-Anne or whatever she calls herself."

Charlie and Dan exchanged a look. "We didn't mention she was calling herself Heather-Anne," Dan said, rising slowly to his feet. "Why don't you sit down again, Mr. Eustis?"

Charlie remained seated, thinking that Dan's six-foot-five presence came in handy. If she had to have a partner, she thought as Eustis righted his chair and sat again, why couldn't she have one who intimidated clients and witnesses, instead of Gigi who wouldn't intimidate a . . . a bunny.

She leaned forward, deciding to go with her instincts. "I saw you come out of Heather-Anne's room at the Embassy Suites," she said, startling both Eustis and Dan.

"I wasn't— You're making this up! I don't have to—" Eustis looked around, as if seeking an escape route. He jerked the Marlboros from his pocket, stuck one in his mouth, and lit it with a disposable lighter.

"I'm sure the police will be able to spot you on the surveillance videos," Charlie said. "It was Wednesday afternoon, late."

Slumping forward, Eustis drew hard on the cigarette, then expelled a stream of smoke. A woman at the next table ostentatiously fanned the air and shot him a disapproving look.

"How did you know she was there?"

Eustis looked up from under his brows. "I got a phone call. Last Tuesday. A man's voice said Amanda was in room 115 at the Embassy Suites in Colorado Springs. Before I could ask anything, he hung up."

"Why didn't you tell Sheriff Huff?"

That earned her a "you've got to be kidding" look. "I didn't even tell Tansy. I thought it was a crackpot, a troublemaker. I decided to check it out for myself before I got the law all spun up about it. I was headed to Denver the next day anyway, so I dropped Eric at the hotel here, told him I had business to take care of, and drove on down to Colorado Springs."

"What did she say?"

Eustis's eyes widened. "I never saw her. You've got to

believe me. I showed up at the Embassy Suites on Wednesday and knocked on her door. I don't know what I'd've said if she'd answered. I probably would have left and called the police."

Riiight, Charlie thought. She drummed her fingers on the table.

"When no one came to the door, I walked around for a bit. I saw a maintenance man go in and waited in the hall until he came out. Holding my credit card like it was a key card, I acted like it was my room and caught the door before it closed. I don't know what I expected to find, but there was nothing useful. No photos, nothing about my dad or anything that tied the room's occupant to Amanda. I decided that the caller was playing me for a chump, so I left. I drove back here, and I've been here ever since. End of story."

"Really?" Charlie let her skepticism show. "You didn't stake the place out to get a glimpse of whoever was in the room, didn't confront her about your father's death, didn't strangle her with her own scarf?"

"No!" Eustis was beginning to look like a hunted rabbit. Charlie searched for another image, wishing her brain would let go of the rabbit comparisons. She sneezed. He looked like a man with a secret, she decided. A scared man with a secret.

"So your son will say you've been with him the whole time—"

"Leave my son out of this!"

"—and the videotapes won't show your truck in the Embassy Suites parking lot or you walking through the lobby. Come on, Mr. Eustis. It's only natural that you would want to catch up with the woman who probably killed your father.

No one's going to blame you for wanting to know if it was her."

"Sir, you can't smoke in here." An officious-looking woman stood at Eustis's shoulder.

With something like a growl, he threw the butt to the dirt floor and ground it out savagely with his booted foot. The officious woman looked like she was going to say something, thought better of it in the face of Eustis's glare, and walked off.

"All right," Eustis spat. "I went back. On Saturday. I stewed about it for a couple of days and decided I couldn't live with myself if there was any possibility Amanda was in Colorado Springs and I didn't find out for sure. She put Dad in his grave, and it wasn't right that she was running around free, spending his money on nice hotels and who knows what else. So I went back. This time, I didn't even have to go into the hotel. I saw her in the parking lot. It took me a few minutes to be sure—she'd lost a lot of weight and dyed her hair—but when I saw her walk I was sure."

"What did you say?"

"I didn't talk to her." Responding to Charlie's look, he insisted, "I didn't. She was with a man. It looked like they were arguing. In a way, I was glad, because I was afraid of what I might do if I met up with her face-to-face." His hands balled into fists. "It scared me—the way I felt. I drove off. I was shaking so bad I pulled over at the next exit and just sat for about twenty minutes. Then I came back here, to the motel. I was going to call Sheriff Huff, sic him on her, but then I heard on the news the next morning that she was dead and I, well, I was afraid to say anything, afraid that the police would jump to the wrong conclusion if I called and told them who she really was." He gave Charlie and Dan a baleful look. "Like you two did."

Charlie didn't refute him. "What did the man look like, the one you saw arguing with Heather-Anne?" She wasn't sure she believed him, but she readied her notebook anyway.

Eustis shrugged. "Average. I didn't see him up close. There were cars passing between us, and he was facing away from me. I was more focused on Amanda."

"White, black, old, young?"

Squinting as if trying to recall, Eustis said, "White, I think. He wore a black baseball cap, and I couldn't see his hair. I suppose he could've been bald. Taller than Amanda by a few inches, so he was maybe six feet or six foot one? Held himself like a young guy; you know—shoulders back, not all stooped over or anything."

Charlie looked up from her notebook and said, "You have to tell the police."

Before Eustis could respond, a lanky boy of maybe fourteen came toward them, a grin on his thin face, holding a champagne-colored muff in the crook of one arm and a ruffled blue ribbon aloft in the other hand. "Hermione won, Dad," he said, coming to a stop beside their table. He looked curiously from Charlie to Dan.

Charlie sneezed and realized that the "muff" was a rabbit, apparently named Hermione. Her pink nose twitched, and her thick fur looked as soft as dandelion fluff. Eustis's look pleaded with them not to say anything in front of his son. "That's great, Eric."

"Can I pet her?" Dan asked. Charlie gave him a surprised look and then suppressed a smile at his kindness.

"Sure," the boy agreed, thrusting the rabbit toward him. Unable to resist the soft-looking pelt, Charlie stroked Hermione's fur, too, and thought a rabbit would be a good pet if it *did* anything.

"She's beautiful," Dan said. "Congratulations."

The boy beamed, and Eustis rose to put his arm around his son's shoulders. "Don't want to miss the Simmental judging," he said, drawing the teen away. "Great seeing you again," he called over his shoulder to Dan and Charlie. His movements were jerky and hurried, betraying his tension.

Charlie didn't try to call him back as they walked away, much the same height, the boy chattering excitedly as they turned down a row of hutches that hid them from view. She sighed and sneezed.

"Let's get you out of here," Dan said, taking her elbow and pulling her toward the entrance.

"Did you believe him?" she asked Dan as they retraced their steps across the parking lot. The cold air biting at her face felt good after the stuffy interior of the livestock barn.

Dan thought, a certain tightness around his eyes revealing his concentration. "In part," he said. "I believed him about being scared by his reaction to seeing Heather-Anne and the urge to violence he must have felt."

"The question is: Did he act on it, or did he drive off like he said?"

"That's a question for the police," Dan said, closing the truck door when Charlie got in. "You're going to tell them?"

"Absolutely. Eustis might have killed Heather-Anne. Equally, he might have seen the man who did. Either way, the police need to know. They can question Eustis further, look at the surveillance tapes."

"Assuming he was telling the truth, who called him and put him onto Heather-Anne at the Embassy Suites?"

Charlie puzzled over that question for a moment. "Maybe Les?" she finally suggested. "He had the newspaper clipping about Eustis Senior's death. Maybe he wanted to see how Heather-Anne would react if Eustis Junior confronted her."

"Possible." Dan put the car in gear and pointed it toward Colorado Springs.

Inside Swift Investigations after Dan dropped her off, Charlie beelined for the minifridge and liberated a Pepsi. After a couple of long swallows, she called Gigi and learned that Les had left nothing of interest during his brief stay. Then, after a moment's thought, she dialed the police department and asked for Detective Lorrimore. When the woman came on the line, Charlie filled her in on everything they'd learned about Heather-Anne's past, including the possibility that she was both Lucinda Cheney and Amanda Eustis. She detailed her conversation with Robert Eustis Junior and gave Lorrimore both Sheriff Huff's and Eustis's contact information. The detective listened well, asking a question now and then.

When Charlie finished, Lorrimore said, "There's a lot of guesswork in your theory. We have no proof that Heather-Anne Pawlusik was Amanda Eustis, much less that she was Lucinda Cheney."

"Granted. You could get something from the Eustises or Cheney that might yield fingerprint matches, though, or DNA."

"There's not enough for a warrant."

"My money says you won't need one. The Eustis family, at least, is royally ticked. If they thought that giving you something to get fingerprints off of would help you catch up with Amanda, they'd cart a hairbrush down to the local police department without passing Go or collecting two hundred dollars. Cheney probably feels the same."

"I'll give it a try," Lorrimore said, sounding a shade warmer than when she got on the phone. "Thanks for the tip. Even if we get a match, though, it doesn't get me much closer to finding the murderer. In fact," she continued, a hint of asperity creeping into her voice, "it widens the field if I have to consider that the men she swindled, and/or their families and heirs, might have wanted revenge. I'll call this Sheriff Huff, and we'll bring Eustis in for questioning today."

"Do you have anything more implicating or clearing Dexter Goldman?" Charlie asked.

Lorrimore hesitated, then said, "Nothing new has turned up. He's still a person of interest in this investigation."

"The person you ought to be interested in is Les Goldman."

"Oh, we are. Given his connection with the deceased and the way he vanished this morning, we're very, very interested in Lester Goldman."

Charlie hung up and drummed her fingers on the desk. She had actual paying cases she should be working on, but she wanted to clear Dexter's name and find Les Goldman, not only because it would make Gigi feel better, but because it was a hell of a lot more interesting than investigating possible insurance fraud or doing background checks on potential employees for Danner and Lansky. After a moment's thought, she decided to try to get hold of Parnell Parkin or his family. She didn't have much hope that talking to them would yield much, but the leads were drying up, and she didn't want to leave any stone unturned. After talking to Parkin, she'd drive out to Gigi's. Maybe Gigi had missed something; at the very least, they could put their heads together and brainstorm places to look for Les. First, though, she needed a long soak in the hot tub and a change of clothes. Locking up the office, she headed down to Albertine's to bum a ride home.

34

By midafternoon, Kendall was home and sulky about having to do her algebra homework. Dexter was still locked in his room refusing to talk to me, and Nolan was insisting he needed a walk, even though the snow was still a foot deep on most of the sidewalks. I thought guiltily of the snow shovel in the garage, and city laws that required homeowners to clear the sidewalks, but I just didn't have the energy. Maybe a little exercise would get Dexter out of the mopes. I knocked on his door and said, "Dexter, the sidewalks need shoveling."

To my surprise, he unlocked the door and headed downstairs without a word to me. Shrugging into a fleece jacket, he disappeared into the garage. Moments later the overhead door rumbled up. I went downstairs myself and, looking out the narrow windows beside the front door, saw Dexter trudging through the snow, shovel in hand. He dug the shovel down, roughly where the sidewalk would be, and flung the snow toward the lawn. I opened the door a crack and called, "Gloves, honey. It's cold."

He ignored me and kept shoveling. Nolan did his little potty dance at my ankles, and I opened the door wider. There were leash laws in Colorado Springs, but who was going to be out to complain on a day like this? I watched Nolan do his duty and then make his way toward Dexter, almost disappearing into the snowdrifts that came over his shaggy black-and-white head. Stooping, Dexter made a snowball and tossed it into the air for Nolan. I smiled. My son could be very sweet. Nolan leaped for the ball and then looked around, confused, when it splatted onto a bare patch of sidewalk and disintegrated. He barked, and Dexter made another snowball, tossing it toward the lawn.

A funny *bump* caught my attention. It seemed to have come from the basement. If Kendall had snuck down there to play Wii instead of finishing her homework . . . I hurried to the basement door. "Kendall?" I called down. The lights were off, but daylight coming through the garden-level windows made it light enough to see pretty well. I didn't hear the Wii. Then Kendall said, "What, Mom?" Her voice came from upstairs.

I stared down into the basement. If Kendall was upstairs and Dexter and Nolan were out front, what made the noise in the basement? The answer came to me in a flash. Les! Les had come back. He'd seen the police leave, waited a while, and snuck back into the basement. I stomped down the stairs, furious. He had messed up our lives one too many times. I wasn't putting up with it any longer.

"Les, if you think I'm going to let you spend the night here again, you've got another think coming. I don't care if it's ten degrees below zero out there. You're not—"

I came around the corner and stopped. Wind swished in through the now wide-open window, and I shivered. It wasn't the cold making me shiver, though. It was Patrick Dreiser standing near the big-screen TV, a long and nasty-looking knife in his hand.

Snow was melting off his boots onto the shag carpet, and I said, "Why can't anyone wipe their boots before coming into this house? Is that too much to ask?"

He looked taken aback but then raised the knife menacingly. "I knew you knew where Goldman was. The more I thought about that whole scene at the gas station, the more I knew you two were trying to scam me again. Well, that's not going to happen. Where is he?" Dreiser jumped forward and looked behind the couch. He looked disappointed not to find Les crouched there.

"I don't know!" I said. "He's not here."

"Right. That's why you came down the stairs talking to him." Dreiser swiped the hand with the knife across his mouth, wiping away spittle. "Come out, Goldman," he yelled, "or it's not going to be pretty for your pretty wife!"

He thought I was pretty? That lit a tiny bulb inside me that went out when he lunged forward with the knife. I backed up and found myself against the Ping-Pong table again. I reached for a paddle but had barely gotten hold of it before Dreiser knocked it out of my hand. "Down the hall," he ordered.

Maybe if I showed him Les wasn't here, he'd leave. "Fine," I said. I marched down the hall and shoved the bathroom door open. "No one here," I said, turning on the light. Pushing aside the shower curtain, I stood aside so he could see the empty tub. "No Les."

Wearing an unconvinced sneer, he backed away from the door so I could return to the hall. I strode past him, trying to ignore the knife, and flicked on the lights in the bedroom. I slid open the closet door—that's where my red Vera Wang dress got to!—and floofed the bedskirt onto the mattress. Nothing but dust bunnies. It probably hadn't been vacuumed since I had to let the maid service go. "No one," I sneezed.

For the first time, Dreiser looked uncertain. "How about in there?" he asked, pointing to the utility room, where the hot water heater and furnace were. "Open it."

I did. An unpleasant musty odor drifted out, and a scuttling sound made me jump back so I bumped into Dreiser. He shoved me away.

"You've got mice," he announced with satisfaction.

Yuck. "I'm not going in there." I don't like rodents. Their long, whiskery snouts make my skin crawl. I'd never let Dexter have the rat he wanted, even though Les was okay with it. I knew who would end up cleaning the rat cage, and I knew Dexter and his friends would let the rat loose accidentally-on-purpose to scare Kendall and her friends. It was one of the few times I put my foot down.

With a put-upon sigh, Dreiser shouldered past me, banged around in the utility room for a moment, and came back looking frustrated. "He's not in there."

"Told you."

"He must be upstairs."

"He's not! He's not anywhere. Not in this house, anyway." I did not want Dreiser anywhere near Dexter and Kendall with his knife and his bad attitude. I tried to think of a way to keep him down here, or better yet, get him to leave. There was a phone in the bedroom, on the far side of the bed. If I rolled across the bed . . . No, I couldn't grab it and dial 911 before he stopped me. I'd noticed the back brush hanging from the showerhead, but it was plastic, and it would probably only make him mad if I swatted him with it. A Gorman statue of a firefighter stood on a pedestal beside a bookcase in the rec room just to the right of the hall opening. I didn't know what it was made of, but if I could get Dreiser to go ahead of me, I could pick it up—I hoped—and dent his skull with it. The thought made me feel sick, but it was the only plan I could come up with.

I half-jogged toward the end of the hall.

"Hey! Where are you going? Stop." Dreiser snagged the back of my sweater and pulled me back. I gagged and coughed but felt a flicker of triumph when he said, "I'll go first."

He stepped from the hall into the rec room, and something hurtled into him, knocking him sideways. I gasped and froze. Curses and the sounds of a struggle pulled me forward. I came out of the hall to see Les atop Dreiser, trying to mash his face into the carpet while keeping him from wriggling away. Dreiser was trying unsuccessfully to buck Les off his back. He was having trouble shifting Les's weight. Good thing he hadn't lost his paunch.

"Knife," Les wheezed when he saw me.

I looked around and spotted it under the Ping-Pong table. Skirting the struggling men, I ducked down and reached for it. That didn't work, so I had to crawl under the table. My sweater snagged on one of the metal supports, but I pulled it loose and kept going. "Got it!" I yelled.

Neither man answered. I backed out and saw that they were tangled together like Adam Bomb and Moondog Manson from the WWE. "I'll call the police." I started toward the phone.

"No!" both men gasped.

I chewed my thumb cuticle.

"Mom? What's going on down there? Sounds like an elephant stampede." Kendall's voice came from the top of the stairs.

Both men stilled, and their eyes swiveled to me. "Uh, just moving some furniture around," I called up to her. "You know I never liked the poppy couch in the middle of the room."

"Oh." Kendall lost interest. She didn't offer to help, I noticed, grateful for her self-absorption for the first time. We watched the ceiling, following her footsteps with our eyes. Les took advantage of Dreiser's distraction to wrench his arms behind his back.

"Give me the knife and get the duct tape, Gigi," he said. He was sweating, and his breath came in little puffs, but he looked determined.

Staying out of Dreiser's reach, I gingerly handed the knife to Les and found the roll of bright pink duct tape Kendall had used to decorate her T-shirt for the first dance of the school year. I peeled up the edge with my fingernail, pulled a length free, and bit it off with my teeth. I handed it to Les. "Here."

He shook his head. "I'll hold the knife on him, you tape his hands."

"But—"

"This is kidnapping!" Dreiser objected loudly.

"Ssh," Les and I said together.

Reluctantly, I stepped behind Dreiser and began to wrap the tape around his wrists. It kept getting tangled and stuck on itself, and I had to use half the roll, but I finally got it done. I pffed hair off my forehead. "Now what?"

"Yeah, now what, Goldman?" Dreiser asked in a hateful tone. He'd wiggled into a sitting position with his back against the wall. Rug burn left a red smear on his cheek, and his dark hair stuck out wildly, as if Les had pulled it.

Les flapped his hand. "I'm thinking."

I watched him anxiously. "How did you know he was here? I was never so glad to see you before in my life."

"Thanks."

Dreiser barked out a laugh.

I looked from one to the other, confused. "Were you already down here?"

"No," Les said. "I was hiding in the shed. After you called the cops on me, which I never thought you'd be vindictive enough to do—" He glared.

"I didn't! It was Dexter."

"Dexter? Why would he do that?" He paused, but then

continued, "Anyway, I hid in the Klamerers' hot tub—pretty smart, right?" He puffed his chest out.

I eyed him. He didn't look wet.

"It's been empty for two years," he reminded me. "Remember it sprang that leak during their Fourth of July party and the water drained out and we were all sitting there naked?"

Did I ever. I'd never been so embarrassed. I blushed at the memory.

"That Janet!" Les shook his head admiringly. "Anyway, Albert's too cheap to fix it."

"This is all very entertaining," Dreiser said sarcastically, "but can I leave now? I've got to take a leak."

Les ignored him. "So after the police left, I came back here and hid in the shed, planning to sneak out tonight and borrow the Hummer. I saw this dickhead jimmy the window and creep in. I was worried about you, so I followed him."

"Oh, Les." I felt quite warmly toward him since he'd saved my life. Of course, I realized a second later, my life wouldn't have been in danger if Les hadn't ripped off Patrick Dreiser. "What are we going to do with"—I lowered my voice—"im-hay?"

"Stop with the pig Latin," Les said, exasperated. "I can't stand it when you do that."

"I'm right here," Dreiser said. He rolled his eyes. "I can hear every word. Even the pig Latin ones. I'll tell you what you'd better do with me, and that's turn me loose right now. Otherwise, I'll slap a lawsuit on you so fast your grandchildren will be eighty-five by the time you're out from under it."

"You broke into our—my—house!" I told him. "You can't sue me."

"Wanna bet?" A wide, oily smile cracked his face and made me wonder if he was right. Hadn't I read somewhere about a burglar suing the people whose stuff he was stealing when he broke a leg on their stairs or something?

"I'll disappear. You call the cops," Les said to me. "Tell them Dreiser broke in and you caught him."

Dreiser laughed again. "Oh, right. Like any cop's gonna believe Mrs. Pink Marshmallow here overpowered me."

I was starting to dislike this guy—again—even though he'd said I was pretty. I turned my back on him and told Les, "He'll tell the police you were here. In fact, I've got to tell them you were here or they'll arrest me for harboring a fugitive. I can't go to prison, Les; I've got the kids to think about."

"Okay, then," Les said decisively. "We'll lock him in the storage room. Just until I can get away. Then you can take him to the police and it won't matter what he tells them."

"There are mice in there."

"All the better."

Dreiser looked slightly nervous for the first time. "Hey, I wouldn't really have hurt her. The knife was just for show. C'mon, Les, we were partners for a long time. You can't turn on me like this."

"It'll only be for a few hours, Patrick," Les said. "Until I can get some papers together and disappear. I've got contacts here, people that can get me ID. I can't leave until I've got them."

"You mean like a new identity?" I stared at him. Charlie

and I had worked a case not long ago that involved a ring of identity thieves who created new identities for criminals.

Les continued as if I hadn't spoken. "As soon as I'm on my way out of the country, Gigi will take you to the police, or let you go, or whatever she wants. For now, get up." He gestured with the knife. Les wasn't very good with knives. The way he hacked the turkey up on Thanksgiving was a neighborhood joke.

"No." Dreiser thrust his chin forward mulishly.

"Then we'll drag you. Gigi, take a foot."

I was too tired and confused to argue. I grabbed Dreiser's left foot, and Les put the knife through a belt loop—making him look like a middle-aged, paunchy pirate—and grabbed the other one. We yanked. Dreiser slid down the wall and his head banged onto the floor. "Ow," he complained.

"You had your chance," Les said. We dragged him down the hall. It was harder than I'd have guessed, especially since Dreiser was kicking. It was tough maintaining a grip on his leg, and one of my fingernails broke when it snagged on his bootlace. That pissed me off. Manicures weren't free.

"We need to tape his ankles, too," Les grunted. He dropped the foot he was holding, headed into the rec room, and returned seconds later with the duct tape. He wrapped it several times around Dreiser's ankles and then kicked open the door to the storage room.

I stopped him. "Can't we at least put him in the guest room?" I couldn't stand the thought of making anyone sit in the storage area with the mice.

"Oh, all right, if you want to be a bleeding heart about it."

Together we rolled Dreiser into the guest room and then sat back on our haunches, panting. Securing a prisoner was hard work. "We need to tape his mouth." Les returned to the hallway for the duct tape, and Dreiser immediately started in on me.

"You don't want to do this, Gigi. Kidnapping is a federal crime, a felony! It won't be Les the cops nab, because he'll be in Guadalumbia or some place. It'll be you. If you let me go right now—"

"Shut it," Les said, coming in in time to hear the last bit. He slapped tape over Dreiser's mouth. "There. The cops won't be arresting anyone except you, Dreiser, when Gigi calls them and tells them you broke in and threatened her with a knife. Come on, Gigi." He pulled me out of the room while Dreiser mumbled angrily behind the tape.

"He can breathe, can't he?" I asked, giving a worried glance over my shoulder as Les shut the door.

"Of course he can."

I felt a hot flash coming on and flapped the hem of my sweater. I'd have pulled it off except I knew Les would misinterpret.

Kendall's voice floated down the stairway again. "Mom, did you die down there?" She sounded irritated at the idea. "You didn't, like, have a heart attack or anything, did you?"

"Coming, sweetheart," I called back. I gave Les a flustered look. "You can't come up," I said. "I don't think the kids should be involved." Could minors be charged with harboring a fugitive? I didn't want to find out.

"I've got to meet someone," Les said. "A guy who can help me. Get me the Hummer keys, will you?"

"Dexter's shoveling the driveway."

"I'm not going now! I'll watch TV or something until it's dark."

Biting my lip with indecision, not quite sure how I ended up with my fugitive ex-husband and a prisoner in my basement, I slowly climbed the stairs.

35

Refreshed by another shower and a change of clothes, Charlie climbed into her Subaru to return to the office. It was good to have the steering wheel beneath her hands again; being driven around by Dan or Albertine made her feel like an invalid, and she wasn't one. Not anymore. A strong sun was melting the last of the slush in the roads, and by tomorrow you wouldn't be able to tell there'd been a snowstorm. That was one of the pluses of living in Colorado Springs, she thought, getting out of the car: It might get cold or snowy for a day or two, but you could always count on the sun shining before too long. No seasonal affective disorder for folks living in Colorado Springs.

Two Motrin swallowed with a gulp of Pepsi had dulled the ache in her ass, and she was able to ignore it as she used a database to find a phone number for Parnell Parkin in Oklahoma. There was no Parnell listed, but there was a P. Parkin in Enid and another one in Stillwater. Dialing the first number,

Charlie reached a Pamela Parkin and apologized for disturbing her. A man answered at the other number.

"Parnell Parkin?" Charlie asked.

"Yes. If you're selling—"

She explained who she was before he could assume she was hawking time-shares and hang up.

"A private investigator? That's cool."

Too young, Charlie thought. Maybe she had the wrong number. As succinctly as possible, she told him about her search for Heather-Anne's real identity and the woman's habit of marrying men, bilking them of their money, and possibly killing them or trying to kill them. "I understand that at one point she was married to a Parnell Parkin of Oklahoma," Charlie finished. "I don't suppose that's you?"

"You want my pop," the young man said, his voice much cooler. "But you can't talk to him. He's been in a coma for twelve years, ever since the accident."

Charlie sat up straighter, her spidey senses tingling. "Was he married to someone like the woman I've described?"

"Oh, yeah. Look, can we Skype or something? I'd rather do this face-to-face."

Charlie had never Skyped, but she didn't want to miss the opportunity of finally learning something about the real Heather-Anne before she became Heather-Anne, so she followed young Parnell's instructions and soon found herself looking at a college-aged man with a Justin Bieber haircut sitting in a room plastered with OSU pennants, baseball trophies, and what looked like newspaper clippings on the walls. An unmade bed sat under a window through which Charlie could see a backyard and a swing set.

"OSU fan, huh?"

"Starting shortstop," Parkin said with a strained smile.

Charlie wondered if he lived at home instead of in a dorm because of his dad's situation. "Can you tell me how your dad met . . . what was Heather-Anne calling herself then?"

"Annie Bart. I don't think she was 'calling herself' that. It was her real name. The Barts lived next door to us for years."

Finally! Charlie felt a surge of triumph. She had worked her way back to the real Heather-Anne. "What happened between Annie and your dad?"

"My mom ran off when I was only five and my brother was three. My dad raised us alone. I saw Annie around—she lived next door, after all—but she was ten years older than me, and I never took much notice of her until she started coming over to hang out with my dad on the porch after dinner. I remember thinking she was really pretty, with blondy-brown hair that hung to her waist, and green eyes that were . . . well, really green."

Charlie thought she could safely assume young Parnell was not working on a degree in advertising or creative writing.

"She made my dad laugh. I don't ever remember him laughing so much." Parnell sounded wistful.

"Where were her parents during this courtship? Were they happy to see their daughter hook up with a man so much older?"

"It was just her mom. I don't remember ever meeting her dad. Folks said her mom . . . well, rumor had it that one of the doctors in town bought the house for Annie's mom as a . . . well . . . Anyway, she'd gone off with some man a few months before Annie started hanging out with Pop."

"So they got married."

Parnell nodded. "I was best man, even though I was only nine."

"Which would have made Annie about nineteen," Charlie mused.

"Right. She was nice enough to me and Tim, and we liked her, even though it was hard to think of her as our stepmom. She just wasn't mommish, you know? Anyway, you've got to remember I was only ten or eleven, so I'm sure I missed a lot of the 'relationship dynamics' "—Parnell put air quotes around the words he'd probably picked up in Intro to Psychology—"but I think Annie got tired of living with my dad, maybe because he was so much older, maybe because she'd felt like there was more to life for a woman as beautiful as she was. By the time he had his accident, she was really beautiful—Megan Fox beautiful."

Charlie thought Megan Fox was more trashy than beautiful, but she wasn't a twentysomething man. "Can you tell me about your dad's accident? What happened?"

"No one knows for sure. He was up on a ladder, cleaning out the gutters, and he must have fallen, because when we came home he was on the ground, unconscious." Strain tightened Parnell's voice. "We called 911, and they came quickly, but the doctor said he must have hit his head on an exposed root from the old oak tree, because there was a dent in his skull. Subdural hematoma, bleeding into the brain . . . He's never woken up."

Parnell turned away to look out the window for a moment, and Charlie thought he was hiding tears. "I'm sorry," she said.

"I won't deny it's been hard," Parnell said. "Annie didn't help at all. She was gone the next morning. Disappeared during the night and just left me and Tim there alone. We woke up and went looking for her, but she was gone: suitcases, clothes, everything. We didn't know what to do, so we fixed ourselves some Lucky Charms and waited. You've got to remember we were only eleven and a half and nine. I guess it was almost noon before we called my best friend and his folks came to pick us up."

"What did you do?" Charlie asked, knowing it had no bearing on her investigation, but caught up in the young boys' plight.

"Moved in with our aunt and uncle. Mom's sister and her husband."

Charlie could relate to that, having lived with her Aunt Pam and Uncle Dennis for several years while her parents missionaried around the globe. "Was there . . . was there any hint that Annie could have been implicated in the accident?"

Parnell shook his head definitively. "No way. She was with us, me and Tim. She had taken us to the zoo in Oke City for the day. Pop stayed home to do some chores around the house. He said if you'd seen one giraffe you'd seen them all." He smiled faintly at the memory.

Charlie rocked back in her chair. *Well, there goes that theory,* she thought, momentarily stumped. She'd been so sure Annie had engineered Parnell Senior's accident. Maybe, she thought slowly, his accident really *was* an accident, but it gave Annie the idea for getting rid of future husbands.

"When she left," Parnell volunteered, "she cleared out the bank accounts and took Pop's car. All we had left was the house. My aunt and uncle moved in here with us because it was bigger than their place and they didn't want to take us away from our home since we'd already lost our mom and pop."

"They sound like nice people."

"They are."

They seemed to have covered everything, but Charlie felt vaguely dissatisfied, like she was missing something important. She couldn't come up with a question that would get at it, so she was on the verge of thanking Parnell and saying good-bye when he said, "I'd say the only good thing about Annie leaving was that apparently Adam went with her. At least, he disappeared at the same time. She was nice in her own way, but he always gave me the creeps."

Straightening, Charlie leaned forward. "Adam?" She tried to keep her voice neutral to keep from startling Parnell.

"Annie's brother."

Jackpot! Charlie barely refrained from pumping her fist. "Tell me about Adam."

By the time she said good-bye to Parnell twenty minutes later, she felt like she was finally on the right track. Adam and Annie, she surmised, better known to her as Heather-Anne Pawlusik and Alan Brodnax, were a team. They used Heather-Anne's beauty to trap vulnerable men and then, when they'd gotten their hands on enough of the men's money, they—or more likely Adam—killed them. Or tried to kill them, Charlie thought, thinking of the alive-but-crippled Wilfred Cheney who swore there'd been another vehicle involved in his accident. Adam had been driving it, Charlie bet. Adam was a researcher, he'd said. He probably dug up information on the men, their likes and dislikes, and helped Annie mold herself into the kind of woman each man would be attracted to. Tansy Eustis had mentioned that Amanda Two bore some interesting resemblances to Amanda One. Right down to the name.

Adam, Charlie decided, had sent the newspaper clipping to Les in Costa Rica. Who else would have known about Eustis's death and known that Eustis's widow was in South America with Les Goldman? Why had he warned Les, though? Had Adam grown a conscience? Was he worried that his sister would siphon off Les's money and find a way to drown him in the ocean surf or feed him to the sharks? Charlie popped open a Pepsi, propped her feet on her desk with the chair balanced on two legs, and thought. Dusk crept in the window, but she was barely aware of it. Various bits and pieces of the puzzle drifted around her brain, glancing off each other, refusing to form a coherent picture.

No! She brought the chair back to the ground with a clang. No, just the opposite. Adam was afraid that Heather-Anne was getting cold feet about the murders, or that she was genu- inely in love with Les. Charlie found that latter thought almost incomprehensible—how could the gorgeous Heather-Anne be attracted to dumpy Les Goldman?—but accepted it for the sake of her theory. Adam feared that Heather-Anne and Les would ride off into the Costa Rican sunset, enjoying their ill-gotten millions, while he—Adam/Alan—was left in the Colorado Springs rental house, sans money, sans job, sans sister. Charlie wondered about the relationship between the brother and sister but decided it didn't matter whether they'd fought, or whether Heather-Anne felt threatened by her brother, or whether she'd simply fallen in love with Les and decided to leave the family business of seducing, bilking, and killing.

There was little doubt in Charlie's mind that Adam had killed Annie. Charlie couldn't hazard a guess about the siblings' conversation in the Embassy Suites room, but she was convinced Adam had lost it, grabbed the nearest weapon— the scarf—and strangled Heather-Anne to death. Had he been sorry after the fact? It didn't matter, but Charlie thought so. At the very least, she thought, he'd have been upset at the loss of his cash cow, the beautiful bait that attracted the rich men to his snare.

Without trying to work out more of the details, Charlie called Detective Lorrimore back. She was gone for the day, the officer who answered the phone reported, but he could transfer Charlie to her voice mail. "Unless it's an emergency, and then I could phone her and have her call you back."

Not quite ready to insist the desk officer connect her with Lorrimore's cell phone if the woman was off duty, Charlie asked to be put through to voice mail. She had no reason to think Adam Bart was likely to make any moves that night; chances were he'd already left Colorado Springs. With his sister dead, there was nothing for him in Colorado.

She left a long message for the detective before locking up and deciding to take Albertine up on her offer of a beer before hitting the road for Gigi's.

36

Dexter had finished shoveling the driveway and sidewalks by the time I came upstairs and had, according to Kendall, walked over to his friend Milo's house to work on a biology project.

"Not that I think they'll be doing any homework," Kendall said, tossing her hair. "They'll just play that stupid Grand Theft Auto."

She was probably right, but I didn't say so.

"Do you think Dexter will really go to jail?" she asked. She was fixing herself a peanut butter and banana sandwich and kept her eyes on the knife as she swiped Jif on the bread. Her blond head was bent so her ponytail almost swished in the peanut butter.

"Of course not!" I said, crossing my fingers. "He didn't do anything wrong." I thought about that for a moment and hastily added, "You know your brother would never kill anyone."

"I suppose not." She sounded unconvinced.

I crossed to the counter and gave her shoulders a squeeze. "You don't need to worry about him, Kendall. He's got a good lawyer, and Charlie's working hard to figure out who really killed Heather-Anne."

"Oh, I'm not worried about him," Kendall said, clunking the knife into the sink. "I was just wondering if I could have his room if, you know, if he's not going to be living here. We need to leave now or I'm going to be late."

I noticed she was wearing her skating gear of pink sweatshirt over black leggings. Her skate bag sat near the garage door. "Oh, right. Let me grab the keys." While I had Kendall trapped in the Hummer, we were going to have a talk about her selfishness, I resolved. I was fed up with her me-me-me attitude. How could she even joke about taking Dexter's room if he ended up in jail? I decided against trying to sneak back into the basement to let Les know that we were leaving; if he wanted the Hummer before I got back, that was just too bad.

As I backed out of the garage, I said, "Kendall, honey, Dexter's the only brother you're ever going to have, so—"

"Thank God."

Our talk was not off to a good start.

By the time I got home, it was almost dark. I wished daylight savings time weren't still six weeks away. I was ready for warmth and sunshine. Lots of sunshine. Neiman Marcus and Spiegel spring catalogs had come in the mail today. They got me thinking about capris and wedge sandals, sundresses— Why don't they make sundresses with sleeves that cover the upper arm area?—and all the colorful spring clothes I hadn't worn in nine months. I could sort through them tonight after Les left . . . that would make me feel cheerier. Maybe it was also time to switch my nail polish color to my spring collection. I held my hands out, fingers fanned, and studied my garnet red nails, including the one Dreiser had broken. Coral would be more springy, or that mint-colored polish Kendall had bought. I'd never used green nail polish before, but I was in the mood to change things up, go out on a style limb.

I didn't know whether the thought of Les leaving, possibly forever, cheered me up or made me gloomier. Kendall had left the peanut butter and bread out, so I made myself a sandwich, using marshmallow fluff instead of banana, and wondered if I should take one to Les and Patrick. Before I could decide, the doorbell rang. Hastily swallowing the sticky lump of peanut butter and bread, I hurried to the front door. I peered through the side window, wondering who was out on a night like this. Probably not a high school band member selling candy or a Girl Scout with cookies. Maybe a neighbor needing to borrow a snow shovel or a couple of eggs.

A man stood there, backed a few feet away from the door like he didn't want to make the homeowner nervous. I appreciated that. I didn't know him, but he looked respectable in a Fair Isle sweater over dark blue slacks. He had longish dark hair slicked back from his face and a charming smile. "Mrs. Goldman?" he said when I opened the door. "My name's Andrew Brett. I'm an associate of your husband's. May I speak to him?"

"Um . . ." I crinkled my brow, not sure what to make of Andrew Brett. I'd never heard Les talk about him. "He's my ex-husband. He doesn't live here anymore." I didn't see any need to mention that he was camped out in the basement waiting for dark to fall so he could skulk out and meet some criminal.

"Oh." Andrew Brett raised his dark brows and looked puzzled. "I was sure he told me to meet him here. We have a business matter to discuss."

The light dawned, and I smiled with relief. This must be the man who was going to supply Les with whatever documents he needed to get out of the country. He looked much more respectable than I'd anticipated—not scuzzy at all. Les had undoubtedly come up to get the Hummer while I was taking Kendall to the Ice Hall. When he found us and the car gone, he'd called Andrew Brett and changed their plans. "Of course," I said, opening the door wider. "He mentioned you."

"He did?" A frown twitched the man's brows but then smoothed away. He stamped his feet outside, eased himself into the foyer, and wiped his feet on the rug again. I liked him.

"Let me just get Les for you," I said. "Please sit down." I gestured toward the living room and went to the basement door. "Les," I called. "Mr. Brett is here to talk to you."

Les yelled back something I didn't understand and then appeared at the foot of the stairs. "Why don't you tell the whole world I'm here, Gigi," he complained, clomping upward. "You're the one who didn't want the kids to know."

"They're gone," I said. "Mr. Brett is here. I suppose he's the one who's going to make you a new passport or something." A thought popped into my head. "Have you picked out a new name?"

"It doesn't work like that, Gigi," Les said irritably. He paused, halfway up the stairs. "I don't know any Brett, and I already told you: I'm meeting my contact later. I wouldn't let somebody like that come to the house. Jesus! What kind of lowlife do you think I am?"

My brow wrinkled. "Then who—?" Ooh, I got a bad feeling. Maybe it was from what felt like a gun barrel poking into the base of my spine. I slowly turned my head to see Andrew Brett standing behind me, grim smile on his lips, big gun in his hand.

He beckoned with his other hand. "Get up here." When Les hesitated, Brett's voice got harsher. "*Now,* Goldman. I've had this house staked out for days now, waiting for you to turn up, and I'm about out of patience. I almost caught up with you when you came by here in the Beemer with your kid—I followed you for twelve fucking hours. I wanted to get at you at the truck stop, but those damn truckers never went to sleep. There was always someone coming or going."

"You slept in the car?" I asked. *Brrrr.* No wonder he'd broken into the basement.

The men ignored her as Brett continued, "I thought I had you at the movie theater, but you got away. You're a slippery bastard."

Les climbed the stairs heavily, confusion twisting his face. "That was you? I don't know you, do I? What do you want with me and Gigi?"

"I don't want her," Brett said, herding us into the living room with the gun. "I want you. More precisely, I want my money, my three-point-eight million dollars that you stole."

Les breathed out heavily. "Look, Brett, or whatever your name is, I've never done business with you. I don't have any of your money."

I'd been studying Andrew Brett while he threatened Les, and now it came to me. It was in the shape of his brow and jaw, the way his ears lay close to his head, the identical nose. "You're related to Heather-Anne, aren't you?" I blurted.

He swiveled his head and stared at me. "You're not half as stupid as Annie made out. You're probably a lot smarter than this guy." He waved the gun casually at Les.

"She called me stupid?" I was incensed. That was the out-side of enough! "Well, she was a home-wrecking, husband-stealing, trashy tramp who had less style than a Barbie doll, and—"

"Gigi, you don't want to annoy the man with the gun," Les said, putting a calming hand on my arm and giving Brett a nervous look. Indeed, the other man's face had dark-ened.

"She was my sister," he bit out.

"Ooh, I'm sorry for your loss."

I couldn't read the look Brett gave me. "Sit down," he said finally.

"I've got to be somewhere—" Les started.

Brett stiff-armed him with a hand to his chest, and Les plopped down into the recliner behind him. "You're not go-ing anywhere until I get my money. You, too." He pointed to me. "Sit."

I perched on the edge of the blue leather sofa. "This must all be a big mistake," I said. "If Les had your money, he'd give it back. Right, Les?" I tried not to think about Dreiser in the basement, still trying to get his money back from my ex-husband.

Sweat beaded Les's forehead and ran down his temples,

even though it wasn't that hot. "I don't know what you're talking about," he said. I could tell he was lying.

Apparently, so could Brett. "You're lying." He pressed the gun barrel against Les's knee. Les tried to squirm away, but Brett leaned into him. "Maybe a bullet in your knee will help your memory. Do you know what a .38 slug would do to your knee? Let's just say I don't think you'd be playing racquetball at the Y anymore. And from the look on your wife's—"

"Ex-wife!" I said.

"—face, I don't think she'll be lining up to push your wheelchair. So tell me where the money is, and I'll disappear as soon as we've transferred it from whatever offshore account you've got it in to my account. You'll never see me again." He dug his free hand in his pocket and pulled out a slip of paper, smoothing it onto the end table. "Here's the account number."

"I don't understand . . . How did Les get your money if you've never met?" I looked from Andrew Brett to Les. His eyes shifted away from mine.

"He stole it from my sister."

"From Heather-Anne? She had almost four million dollars?" Here I'd always thought she hooked up with Les for his money; now I wasn't sure. This was too confusing.

"Let me tell you a story," Brett said. He looked relaxed, like an invited dinner guest, not at all sweaty and nervous like Les. Maybe being the one with the gun made it easier to relax. I always felt keyed up when I held my gun, even at the shooting range, but it might be different for men.

"Once upon a time there was a brother and a sister. She was beautiful, and he was very, very smart, and not unhandsome himself." His lips twisted. "They had a shitty upbringing with

275

a shitty mother, but we won't go into that. Suffice it to say that one day, the mother took off, leaving them to fend for themselves. Which they were perfectly capable of doing."

"Where did they live?"

"Oklahoma."

"Tornadoes." I'd never been to Oklahoma, but I knew about the tornadoes.

"Not in this story. Anyway"—Brett spoke more forcefully, as if to keep me from interrupting again—"a man came along who wanted to marry the sister even though she was only eighteen and he was in his fifties. Perv. We agreed that it was the smart thing to do because the man had money and we didn't. After they'd been married a couple of years, though, Annie started feeling her oats. She was twenty by then and drop-dead gorgeous in an innocent sort of way that made men want to protect her, take care of her. Right, Goldman?" He prodded Les's knee with the gun, and Les jerked, refusing to answer.

I thought Heather-Anne needed about as much protection as a scorpion, but I kept my mouth zipped.

"We decided that it was time to move on."

"So she left her husband?"

"He had an accident." Brett's lashes shadowed his eyes, but I didn't like what I saw there. "It was fortuitous because it made it possible for Annie to withdraw everything from his bank accounts, cash in some investments, and disappear."

"Was the husband okay?"

Brett shrugged. "Who knows? The point is, we were able to start over someplace where people didn't know us or our mom, didn't look down on us. We went to Atlanta. But then the money started running out. I discovered I had quite a flair for computers and research, and we turned that to good account. We'd identify a possible mark, and I'd learn everything about him, down to the kind of underwear he preferred and what he ate for breakfast, what was important to him and the kind of women that appealed to him. Annie was quite the actress, and she'd remake herself in the image of what the mark preferred. It worked more often than not. Sometimes she married the mark, sometimes we turned a profit another way. If the mark started getting suspicious, or if someone in his family started looking into Annie's background too hard, we cut our losses and moved on."

"How many?" Les asked. "How many husbands?"

He looked like the answer mattered to him, and I felt sorry for him.

Brett shrugged. "Six? Seven?"

Les sagged back against the recliner cushions. "She lied to me."

"Well, you stole her money, so I'd say you were even," Brett said nastily.

"Only after she lied to me. I got that clipping in the mail . . . Why'd you send it? It was you, right?"

Brett nodded. "Things started going wrong as soon as we got to Colorado Springs. Annie started talking about how she was getting older, about wanting to settle down. She got her own apartment for a while but then moved into the house with me. She even mentioned children once." He barked a harsh laugh. "Can you imagine her as a mother?"

"We talked about it," Les said.

My mouth fell open, and I stared at him. "You did? About having more children? With Heather-Anne?"

Les's chin sank down. He didn't meet my eyes.

"When Annie ran off with you to Costa Rica, I was as surprised as the business partners you embezzled from," Brett said. "She didn't tell me that she was leaving. If she'd left me my share of the money, I might have let her go. But no. She took it all. Cleaned out our account and transferred it somewhere. Must have been your influence." He glared at Les. "I tried calling her, sending e-mails. She wouldn't reply. I didn't understand. Not after all that we'd been through together!"

"She wanted her own life, you jerk," Les said. "She was tired of being your puppet."

Brett smacked Les's face with the hand holding the gun, and Les yelped. "So I sent you the clipping about Eustis. I thought it might make you ask some questions. If you showed it to her, she'd know I'd sent it. She'd have to respond. She did." Smiling with satisfaction, he said, "She came straight back here to me."

As if he couldn't stand to be still anymore, Brett stood and began pacing, his words coming faster. "She contacted me. We met. She was difficult. So I told her I'd called Eustis's son, that he was on his way down from Wyoming to confront her, to accuse her of murdering his father. She'd end up in jail, I told her, if she wasn't gone before he arrived. I didn't know if he'd show up or not, but it scared her. She agreed to give me my share of the money. While I stood over her, she logged on to her computer—she was going to transfer the money from her account to mine. When she told me there was no money in her account, that it was gone, I thought she was lying. I—" He broke off and wiped a hand down his face.

It took me only a moment to realize what he'd almost said. He'd killed Heather-Anne. Strangled her. My breaths started coming faster, and I felt light-headed.

"It was your fault." Brett whirled to face Les and spoke between gritted teeth. "I figured that out when it was too late. You stole that money from my sister, just like you stole everything from your business partners and your wife here."

"Ex-wife," I choked out.

"That's why Annie hired her"—he nodded toward Gigi— "to find you. She knew you'd stolen our money. She wouldn't tell me that because she knew what I'd do to you. I figured it out too late," he said again. His eyes narrowed to slits. "You've got a nasty habit of cheating the people who trust you, don't you, Goldman?"

"I thought she'd left me. I didn't know," Les gobbled. "When I woke up after our fight and she was gone—no note, no explanation—I . . . I'd found her bank account data months earlier. Habit. When I realized she was gone, I transferred the money out of hurt and anger. I was going to give it back!"

"It's too late for Annie," Brett said coldly. "And if you don't transfer exactly three-point-eight million to my account within the next ten minutes, it'll be too late for Gigi, too." He swung the gun toward me. My eyes widened as I looked down the long, dark barrel, a tunnel leading nowhere good.

37

Charlie Swift pulled into Gigi's cul-de-sac near the Broad-moor Hotel shortly before seven thirty. The sun was long gone, but a half-moon reflected off the snow to give the city a dim late-dusk glow. Her headlights raked a black car parked on the far side of the circle. As she beeped the Subaru locked, she gave the black car another look. Something about it . . . It was a Saab. The witness outside the movie theater had said a black sports car ran Les's BMW off the road, and there'd been a black Saab in "Alan Brodnax's" garage. Adam Bart was here. The knowledge froze Charlie momentarily. She cursed herself for not having insisted the desk officer have Detective Lorrimore call her. There was no telling when she'd get Charlie's voice mail about Adam Bart.

Keeping low, she crunched across the melted and refrozen snow to Gigi's front door. The blinds were drawn, and she could see nothing through the narrow leaded windows on either side of the double doors. The snow was still deep against the house, drifted in places, but she plunged in and slogged around to the back, wishing she had her H&K with her. If Bart was in there, Gigi was in trouble. Whatever he wanted from her, he was unlikely to leave her alive after he got it. Not with a track record that included a half-dozen deaths or accidents across several states and his own sister's strangulation.

Reaching the rear of the house, she climbed stairs leading to a deck that looked like it opened off the kitchen and living room. Snow slicked the steps, and she clung to the rail, her ungloved hands burning with the cold. She bumped a chair protected by a canvas cover, and it moved with a faint metallic scrape. Charlie stilled, listening for any indication Bart had heard the noise. After thirty seconds, when no one emerged on the deck, she crept closer to the French doors. Gauzy curtains obscured her view somewhat, but she could clearly see a woman who had to be Gigi seated on the sofa, with Les in a recliner catty-corner to Gigi. A second man stood with his back to the window, facing Gigi and Les, and his long dark hair convinced Charlie it was Adam Bart, alias Alan Brodnax and probably a dozen other names. She couldn't see a gun, but she knew from the way he stood that he had one.

A moment's contemplation told her that trying to break through the French doors and tackle him from behind was a losing proposition. He'd have time to shoot Gigi and Les and probably compose a sonata before she'd be able to batter the doors in, sprint the fifteen or twenty feet from the doors to the seating area, and tackle him. There had to be another way in.

Edging back down the stairs, Charlie pulled out her cell phone as she scanned the windows on the lower level. Reaching the same desk sergeant at the police department, she told him she now had an emergency with an armed man holding two people hostage at Gigi's address. He promised to send a patrol car immediately and relay the message to Detective Lorrimore.

"Don't let the patrol car come screaming up with lights and sirens blazing," Charlie cautioned. "This guy's got nothing to lose, and if he thinks he's going down, he's the type to take the hostages with him." When the officer asked for more details, Charlie hung up, having spotted an open window that apparently led to the basement. *Gigi should be more careful about locking up,* she thought, dropping to her stomach and sliding feet first through the opening.

She landed with a barely audible thump, took off her boots, and looked around. A news show played quietly on a huge-screen TV. Comfy seating surrounded the television, which was mounted midway down the room's longest wall. A Ping-Pong table sat nearest the window, and past the TV area, Charlie could see a pool table positioned crosswise. Passing the Ping-Pong table and TV, she ignored the hall leading off to her right. It was unlikely she'd find a weapon in what were probably only guest bedrooms. Instead, she pulled a pool cue from the rack on the wall behind the table. Not exactly the weapon she'd choose for going up against a gun, but better than her bare hands.

Easing up the carpeted stairs, she considered her strategy. She'd only been in Gigi's house a couple of times and wasn't that familiar with the layout, but she thought the basement steps emerged into the kitchen. The kitchen, she was pretty sure, opened to a dining room on one side and the foyer and living room on the other. Did the dining room connect to the living room? Almost undoubtedly. Reaching the top step, Charlie found the door open and nudged it a touch wider. She couldn't see Gigi and Les and Bart, but she could hear the rumble of voices. Peering cautiously around the door, Charlie discovered there was no line of sight from the basement door to the living room.

Relieved, she made herself as skinny as possible and edged through the door, immediately taking three steps deeper into the kitchen. It smelled faintly of bacon. Passing the acres of granite counters and top-of-the-line appliances worth enough to put a dent in the national debt, Charlie padded in her stocking feet into the dining room. She could suddenly make out words as Bart said something about it being too late for Annie.

Placing her feet lightly and holding the pool cue upright so it wouldn't bang against anything, she edged along the wall until she could peer around it into the living room. She hoped Bart was still facing Les and Gigi. He was. She saw his back, rigid with tension, and saw Les sweating in the recliner. He looked awful, his face a clammy gray, his right arm rubbing his left shoulder. His pained expression could have been because Bart was aiming his gun steadily at Gigi. Gigi's eyes slid sideways, as if she were desperately seeking a way out of the situation, and she spotted Charlie. Her eyes widened. Charlie hastily put a finger to her lips and was relieved when Gigi blinked twice and refocused on Bart.

"Time's running out, Goldman," Bart said. "Tick-tock, tick-tock."

"My computer's in the basement," Les said. "I need to get it to make the transfer."

"Bullshit! I saw you dive through the basement window. You weren't carrying a computer."

"I left it here yesterday," Les said.

"He did," Gigi seconded.

Charlie wondered if Les was telling the truth or if he was planning to escape out the basement window if Bart let him go downstairs. She wouldn't put it past him. Apparently, Bart had the same read on Les.

"We'll all go down to the basement and get your computer. If it's not there, if you're lying to me . . ." He waved the gun menacingly. "Get up."

"I'm not sure I can," Les said, his voice weaker. Sweat poured off him, and Charlie thought she saw panic in his eyes. "I think I'm having a heart attack."

He was telling the truth, Charlie realized, and she could see that both Gigi and Bart realized it as well.

"Then the sooner we get the transfer done, the sooner you can get to a hospital," Bart said coldly. He reached his left hand down to pull Les out of the recliner. Either by accident or on purpose, Les pushed the chair into its recline position and the footrest popped out, smacking Bart in the shins. He staggered and his finger tightened on the gun's trigger, sending a bullet into the ceiling. Gigi jumped at the noise but then, taking advantage of Bart's distraction, put her feet against the coffee table's edge, braced herself on the sofa, and slammed it toward him.

"Charlie, help!"

Charlie was already moving when the heavy table cracked into Bart's legs and set him teetering. Holding the cue like a baseball bat, she swung the fat end at his head. He had half turned at Gigi's words, though, and she caught him on the arm as he raised the gun to fire at her, his lips drawn away from his teeth in pain and fury. The cue impacted with a crack that sent a jolt up Charlie's arms. Bart cried out and lost his grip on the gun. He snagged the trigger as it spun out of his hand. A window shattered. Charlie ducked instinctively—*like evasive maneuvers helped me dodge a bullet in my last gun battle,* she thought—then lunged toward Bart, raising the cue over her head. She shouted, "Gigi, the gun!"

Bart flung himself full-length at the gun before Gigi could get there, and she dropped on top of him with the full weight of her forty-too-many pounds. Bart let out an "Oof!" but managed to get his hand on the gun. Before he could bring it into firing position, Charlie drove the cue down onto his hand. The sound of bones snapping was almost drowned out by the doorbell.

All four of them looked toward the door. Charlie took the opportunity to kick the gun away from Bart, even though his hand was clearly broken and she didn't think he could pick it up or fire it. It skittered under the couch. Les lay gasping like a landed fish on the recliner.

"Should we answer it?" Gigi asked. Her beigey-blond hair draped over one eye, the neckline of her sweater was pulled halfway off one shoulder, and her ample bosom heaved. She struggled into a sitting position so she straddled Bart and leaned forward to pin his shoulders to the ground. He bucked, and Charlie raised the cue threateningly.

"Police!" came the muffled shout through the door.

At the word, Bart went limp beneath Gigi. Seeing the fight drain out of him, Charlie hurried to the door and opened it. She knew she looked disreputable, her dark hair disheveled, her face flushed, breathing heavily. Before she could say anything, the female officer, a woman about Charlie's height but half again as broad, said, "We received a phone call from a man saying he was being kept prisoner in your basement. May we come in?" Her tone was polite, and she seemed skeptical of the prisoner-in-the-basement story, but her eyes took in every detail of Charlie's appearance, and she held herself as if poised for action.

"Absolutely." Charlie backed away to let them in. "We need an ambulance," Charlie said. "A man's having a heart attack."

The cops took one look at Les, and the rangy male cop radioed for an ambulance while the female officer, whose name tag read PADGETT, asked, "Is he the one that was imprisoned in the basement?"

"No one was locked in the basement," Charlie said impatiently, wondering if maybe Dexter Goldman or one of his buddies had called the cops as a prank.

"Actually . . ." Gigi said, a guilty look on her face.

At the sound of her voice, the officer walked toward the living room and looked over the sofa to see her sitting atop Bart on the floor.

"Actually," Charlie said, "that man"—she pointed to Bart—"was holding the Goldmans hostage. I phoned it in ten minutes ago. We disarmed him—his weapon's under the couch—"

At the word "weapon," the cops drew their guns and backed away, looking much grimmer. Through the open door, Charlie saw two more squad cars skid into the cul-de-sac with the big black SWAT van trundling behind. *Ah, the response to my call about the hostage situation,* she thought, beginning to see some humor in the situation. An ambulance, siren screaming, pulled up seconds later. Neighbors cracked their doors or opened their blinds, and chaos reigned as the EMTs raced into the house while cops in full protective gear jumped out of the SWAT van and fanned out.

All we need now is a news crew or two, Charlie thought. She groaned as the Channel Five van passed the crowded cul-de-sac and parked half a block away.

The EMTs prepared to cart Les off to the hospital, hooked up to an IV and a heart monitor, and Gigi clambered off Bart to go with her ex-husband in the ambulance. "He's got to have someone," she said to Charlie, giving her a beseeching look. "I'm sorry to leave you with this . . . this . . ."

"Go," Charlie said. She noticed Adam Bart crawling toward the deck on his knees and one hand and trotted over to head him off, holding the pool cue like a spear.

She convinced Officer Padgett to cuff Bart by pointing out that the gun recovered from beneath the couch was his and by suggesting that Detective Lorrimore would want to interrogate him about Heather-Anne's death. Bart shot Charlie a venomous look but refused to say anything at all as Officer Padgett dragged him to his feet. He bit out a curse when she pulled on his injured hand to cuff him, and she had him loaded into a separate ambulance with a policeman to accompany him to the hospital.

A thumping sound came from the direction of the basement stairs, and Charlie spun around. So did half a dozen cops, guns leveled. They stared in astonishment as a man, feet bound with hot pink duct tape, hopped into the kitchen. With his hands bound behind him, he stumbled but managed to stay upright. A piece of duct tape dangled from his face where he'd managed to mostly scrape it off his mouth. "I've really gotta take a piss," he announced.

38

For most of a week, I thought I was going to jail again, but then Charlie looked at that little notebook I found in the bedroom after Les ran off the second time, and she rubbed a pencil lightly over the top page. Turns out, Les had used it to write down the number of his offshore bank account. Charlie talked me out of turning it over to the police right away and went to visit Dreiser. I'm not sure exactly what she said to him, but I know she offered to repay him the money Les had stolen from him, plus interest. I think she pointed out it might be months, or even never, before he got his money back if he waited for the police to sort through everything and decide who got how much from the account. Dreiser dropped the kidnapping charges. Thank goodness!

So now the police have the notebook, and they're trying to figure out what money belongs to the investors Les embezzled from and what belongs to the people swindled by Adam Bart and Heather-Anne. (I just can't call her Annie because that name makes me think of the musical and that darling curly-headed orphan who would not have grown up to be anything like Heather-Anne.) Her brother's in jail, awaiting trial for her murder (among other things), and the district attorney told me I'll have to testify. The thought makes me nervous—I never want to see that man again!—but I can do it if I have to. I'm thinking about wearing the blue Chanel suit, the one with the bouclé jacket, but only if the trial comes up in the winter. I'd need a new cami to wear under it, though, and maybe a brooch big enough to make a statement . . .

Kendall's been to see Les in jail a couple of times, but Dexter won't go. They're both mad at me for not transferring the money from Les's offshore account to our account.

"It's not our money," I told them again and again. "It belongs to the investors your dad cheated and the men or their families who Heather-Anne and her brother cheated."

"Some of it's got to be ours," Kendall said, "since Dad took all of our money, too."

"Probably. The police will sort it out and . . . and be fair."

"But that won't be in time for you to buy me a car for my sixteenth birthday," Kendall objected.

"You're not even old enough for a permit yet," Dexter said.

Kendall stamped off, muttering about vile, loathsome brothers and the selfishness of insensitive parents. I sighed.

"Don't worry about her, Mom," Dexter said. "Now that I've got the Beemer back, I can drive her where she needs to go."

I looked at him, surprised. "Oh, Dexter, honey, thank you. That's very thoughtful."

Silence fell between us as we split a cinnamon roll at the kitchen table. We both shifted in our seats, and finally Dexter said, "You know, I called the cops on Dad because I couldn't stand the thought that you might take him back after he treated you the way he did." He kept his eyes on his plate, where he was crumbling a bit of cinnamon bun into sandy grains. His hair hung down over his eyes. "You wouldn't have, would you?"

My mind darted back a couple of days to when I'd last visited Les in his hospital room. He'd still been hooked up to all sorts of beeping machines, but his color was much better than on the day he had his attack, and he was sitting up in bed eating a Fudgsicle when I came in. Little bits of chocolate clung to his mustache. It scraggled down over his lips since no one had trimmed it. That nice Officer Padgett had been on guard duty outside his door, and she'd said they'd be moving him to the jail the next day.

"I hear you're moving," I said, sitting in the chair beside his bed.

"Oh, Gigi," he said, giving me a tired smile, "everything's gone wrong since I left you." He reached for my hand.

I let him hold it for a moment. My heart didn't go pitty-pat like it used to when he was affectionate with me.

"I made a horrible mistake when I left you."

"Yes."

"What?"

"Yes, you made a big mistake," I said. "In fact, you made lots of them."

"That's all water under the bridge," he said, clinging to my hand when I tried to pull it back. "It's not too late. We can start again."

"No and yes."

"What?"

"No, we can't start again, and yes, it's too late." I smiled a huge, relieved smile. I didn't want Les back. My life might not be perfect now, and I might spend lots of time worried about money and how to handle the kids, but I liked being a private investigator, and I liked being friends with women like Charlie and Albertine. I even kind of liked driving that awful Hummer, although if I could afford it, a Miata convertible might be more fun. "I'm sorry you're going to prison, Les, and I'll come visit you now and then, but I'm over you."

"What!"

He sounded so disbelieving that I giggled. I felt like someone had blown up a big balloon inside me, so light that I could float away. I stood up. "Buh-bye, Les."

I walked toward the door.

"But, Gigi, I need you. You don't want to walk away—"

Officer Padgett gave me a thumbs-up as I came through the door, and I was momentarily embarrassed since she'd clearly heard every word. "Way to go, Gigi. Ma'am," she said. "Hey, I like that nail polish. What's it called?"

"Mischievous Mint."

I ducked my head now so I could see up into Dexter's face. "No, I wouldn't get back together with your dad. I've moved on."

Dexter nodded, and I could see his shoulders relax. "Good." He scraped back his chair and stood up. "You deserve someone nicer."

I blinked back tears, knowing my son would get grossed out if I started crying. "Thanks," I said, my voice all squeaky. He shrugged one shoulder and slammed through the garage door. My son thought I deserved someone nice. That must mean he thought I was nice. The thought warmed me until I remembered I had resolved to practice being meaner. Tomorrow. There was always time for meaner tomorrow.